LG '4-

for a Short time

by

Lori Lapekes

Heres a little stress relief, Suzanne!

Lori Lapekes

LBF Books

www.lbfbooks.com

Published Internationally by LBF Books,
Imprint of Lachesis Publishing, Inc.
2221 Millar Road West, RR 4,
Spencerville, Ontario K0E E0

A catalogue record for the print format of this title is available from the National Library of Canada.

ISBN 13: 978-1-897562-49-9

A catalogue record for the Ebook is available from the National Library of Canada.
Multiple Ebook formats are available from
www.lbfbooks.com

ISBN 13: 978-1-897562-50-5

"It can't be over between us, all the signs were there for you to finally be the right one for me," Keri insisted.

"What signs?" Keith asked.

Keri stared into his shadowy face. Clinging tatters of mist drifted across it, obliterating his eyes for one moment, his mouth the next moment. The fog was cool and clammy to the skin in the dismal mist.

"The signs," said Keri. "You know, the *signs*." But, suddenly, she couldn't think of a one.

He turned his back on her, and began to fade away into the mist.

"Keith, come back!" Keri said. "I'll remember them, I know I will. It'll make a difference!"

But Keith continued to shrink into the fog. Soon he was only a dark patch in the distance, then that was swept away by the wisps of lonely swirling mist.

Keri was left in silence. A silent world of emptiness and chill.

"Keith…" she whimpered, "come back, I need you…." Only silence.

Keri heard her heart beating against her chest.

"Keith." she whispered, tears trailing down her cheeks. Her knees went weak, and she sunk into the ground. "Don't leave me, I need you, don't leave me."

"Straighten up, Keri," came a voice behind her.

"What—who?" Keri asked, and slowly turned around. It was clearer where he stood, almost as though the sun was ready to break through the mist that was strangely falling away from him.

Jeremy.

"Please, stand up," Jeremy said again. Something about the tone of his voice, oddly authoritative yet gentle at the same time, made Keri gather her strength and stand.

"Come here," Jeremy said, and held out his hand.

Keith left me," Keri sobbed, but found herself

drawing nearer to Jeremy. He seemed spectral as she stared at his hand, his comforting hand, and it drew her closer. When she reached him, she took his hand, and he pulled her close.

A jolt of something indescribable, joy mixed with peace and an incredible calmness pulsed through her at Jeremy's touch. He held her hand tighter, pulled her closer, and Keri began to quiver as she found herself face to face with Jeremy, gazing into wonderful eyes radiating a calm assurance and wisdom she had never before encountered. Heat raced through her and her legs became weak.

Jeremy's eyes glimmered. It paralyzed her to stare into them. Those eyes seemed to search into hers, gently probing, as though trying to connect with her soul. Keri became lightheaded, intoxicated, the poison of Keith's rejection now drained away.

You're going to be all right now," Jeremy said, and his voice seemed to roll like thunder and yet felt a breathy whisper at the same time. It echoed as he continued, and suddenly the fog parted and a warming blaze of sun fell across them.

"I'll stay with you," said Jeremy. "You don't have to be afraid anymore. You can finally be yourself."

Those words flowed through Keri in cascades of relief. Finally, finally she felt it. She couldn't quite grasp what it all meant, but a weight had lifted.

"Thank you, thank you, Jeremy," Keri said, gulping in great breaths of air. "What would I do without you? You're the one I need, you're the one I was meant for all along."

At those words, Jeremy smiled. Keri's eyes strayed toward his lips, and lingered there. His mouth smiled, his eyes smiled, and Keri was sure his heart smiled, too.

And so did she. Keri let go of his hand, and slowly wrapped her arms around his neck. He put his arms

around her shoulders and drew her tighter to him. When they fully connected, the warmth of their touch was explosive, and Keri could scarcely control herself. She closed her eyes and suddenly, tantalizingly, his lips were pressed against hers. She gasped inwardly as the warmth and movement of his kiss sent shivers down her spine and into her toes. At first Jeremy's kiss was sweet and gentle, but as it became more urgent, its
passion leached all of the strength from Keri's limbs until she was practically hanging limp in his embrace.

All she could think was—*how did he learn to kiss like this?* Was it the way it was supposed to be when two people were genuinely… in love?

No—it couldn't be! Jeremy was just her dear friend, like a brother, really.

Yet…

"Aunt Keri, get up!" said a wee voice far, far away. "You promised to play opera lady with me this morning."

"What?" Keri moaned.

There was a soft shaking on her shoulders. "Aunt Keri, Keri, get up, sleepyhead! Take the pillow off your face."

Reality crawled back to Keri in a lazy wave. Jeremy's embrace vanished, and the scene dissipated into fragments as Keri awoke, reluctantly pulling herself from the dream. Only a dream.

"Jutht a minute, Kate," Keri mumbled. "Have thum patienth."

"What?" Katie asked. "You sound weird."

"It'th the pirrow on ma face," Keri said, rising slowly as she removed the pillow. "I like ta thleep like dat."

Keri noticed the oddity just as Katie's eyes bulged at her.

"What's wrong with your face?" Katie cried.

Keri's hand flew to the right side of her face, which felt heavy and numb. It seemed dragged down, contorted. She could barely see out of her right eye.

"There's drool coming out of your mouth, just like Rover's," said Katie. "I think your pillow got too heavy! It melted your face!"

Keri tried to gasp, but her mouth would not work correctly. It seemed weights were pulling her lip down on the right side, making it lopsided.

Dear Lord... *had she had a stroke?*

She flung off her blankets, twisted to the side of her bed, and sat up. It seemed her right arm worked fine, as well as her leg. And she could think clearly. But the horrified look on her niece's face confirmed the frightening fact that something was drastically wrong.

"I'm going to get Mom," said Katie as Keri pulled herself off the bed and rose, testing her legs.

"Mom!" Katie bellowed.

She ignored her niece and, after finding her legs quite sturdy, raced into the bathroom. Her heart pounded as she flicked on the light and looked into the mirror.

Her hands rose to her face in horror.

The mirror was warped, it had to be! Or water was on it, or something, anything!

She did not look like a monster!

Acknowledgements

Thanks to Ruth Harper—you have read nearly everything I've ever written, from days and years long past, even when it was worthless drivel—and you reassured me that it wouldn't always be worthless drivel! Also thanks to Laura Givens (who helped me find this wonderful publisher); my daughter, Shaunna Lawrence; my sisters, Lorraine Lapekes and Lisa Johnson; Laura Hogg (my typesetter and awesome web designer); Cindy Hogg (my proofreader); Khela Vanderleest (my invaluable query assistant); Brenda Harvey, my dear friend of so many years, and all those in my writer's group who felt I had the knack...particularly T.J. Cruzan, John Warnock, Roger Meyer, David Landrum and even the un-anti-Steve...you know who you are. Thanks also to everyone I have forgotten to list. You are no less important.

Dedication

This book is dedicated to those who have supported me in my many, often humbling, often frustrating, attempts at this roller coaster ride into publishing!

for a Short time

Chapter 1

Kelly grimaced, put her hands over her ears, and stomped her foot three times. "I'm trying to work up here!" she called downstairs. "Can't you go outside to teach my daughter how to screech, Keri?"

"She's just singing," came a reassuring voice. Kelly turned around to see her husband, Andy, grinning mischievously in the doorway. Her shoulders sagged.

"Can't you hear her, Andy? My screwball sister thinks she's teaching Katie how to sing opera, but her voice reminds me of how it sounds when a fork gets caught in the garbage disposal."

Andy raised his eyebrows, then scratched his sandy-colored hair. "And you want her to take to the great outdoors with that voice? Do you want to bring an airplane down on our house?"

Kelly snorted. "Never thought of that."

Andy strolled over and wrapped his muscular arms around his wife's ever growing stomach. His mustache tickled her cheek. "You need to relax. We have a new family member to think about. Do you think Keri will still be living in the basement when baby Quentin is born?"

"You mean baby Kyle, don't you?"

"No…I mean Quentin. I want to upset your mother as much as possible by not naming the kid with another K-name."

"Let's not go there," Kelly sighed.

"I'm sorry, couldn't help myself."

"Unfortunately, I think she'll be here a while," Kelly finally replied. "You know, it's so weird. Keri has lived all over the country like some big shot, and she's barely thirty years old. Now she has an identity crisis and wants to come back here to live on the little family farm. Maybe she'll finally settle down this time, but somehow I doubt it."

Another belt of the 'opera-lady' voice shrieked up through the register.

Andy pulled his arms away from Kelly and put them over his ears. "Man, do any of her friends know she acts like this?"

"Friends?" Kelly asked. "What friends? Most of them were too hoity-toity for Keri to be herself around. I think she only lets her guard down around us."

Andy rolled his eyes. "Aren't we fortunate. Do you think she acts this way around Glenn?"

Kelly snorted again. "Hardly. She's dated him for months already, you know. She's getting too close to screwing up and acting like herself. She'll probably send him back like a rented tuxedo any time now. Especially if she knew I spotted him looking at diamonds at the mall the other day."

"Oh man," Andy groaned. "Bad move."

"I know," Kelly sighed. "Poor guy. Maybe it's good she'll never stick with him long enough for him to get to know the true 'Scary Keri.'"

Andy shrugged. "At least you don't call her what those guys in high school called her...Keri Ferrita, the 'Man-Eat-a'."

"Well, you should know. She dumped you, too."

"I was only sixteen."

"You still picked *her* first."

"But you're the real pick of the litter."

"You calling us dogs?"

Andy crossed his arms. "Far from it. You're both beautiful women, just peculiar in your own ways."

Kelly sighed. She knew Andy meant 'peculiar' as a compliment, he was a bit eccentric himself. At thirty-two, he still insisted on getting toys for Christmas; not guy toys like power tools or computer games, but real toys, like pogo-sticks, Rock 'em, Sock 'em Robots, and Legos. His child-like sense of fun was something he shared more with Keri than with her, but as Kelly knew, it would never have worked out between Keri and Andy. It would have been like the 'Two Stooges' if they had stayed together, they would have driven each other crazy. Maybe even actually poked one of the other's eyes out.

Kelly winced at her gory thought, and laughed out loud.

Another belt of the supposed opera voice rang up from below, something completely incomprehensible.

Andy looked at Kelly, eyes wide, and clasped his hands on her shoulders. "She's not normal."

"I know."

"And she's got our three-year old daughter down there...*training* her."

"I know!"

"Maybe she won't want to stay here too long," Andy said. "You realize that the longer she stays, the more she'll break Katie's heart when she leaves. And she *will* leave. Not just the area, but the state. Maybe even the country."

Kelly sighed, knowing it was true, and walked toward the window of her small home office. She stared solemnly out at the snow-blanketed fields and outbuildings of their ten-acre 'gentleman's farm.' She watched their shaggy brown horse, Bennie, trudging through the snow rather aimlessly, as though looking for something to do. She could sense his impatience with this day, with winter in general. They ought to get another horse, she thought. Give the poor raggedy pony some company besides a few chickens, barn cats, and their ancient outdoor mutt, Rover. She ran her hands over her belly, and a tickle-like kick of the baby in her womb reached her fingers. At least Katie would be having company in the future, a little brother or sister to focus on after her fickle Aunt Keri hit the road to distant adventures again.

"Maybe she won't dump Glenn," Andy said all of a sudden. "Maybe, just maybe she'll stick with him and put down some roots here. Stranger things have happened."

Kelly laughed at that. "Stick with him? Put down roots? That's not possible, Andy. You don't know her like I do, you just think you do." She strode over to a wall filled with built-in cabinets and drawers.

"Do you remember how she asked us to store some things for her after mom sold the big house and moved to the cottage? Well, here are some of those things. I don't understand why she keeps it all." Kelly opened one of the larger cabinet doors. A six-foot stuffed snake uncoiled from the clutter and sprang out at her. She jumped back as it landed on the floor, followed by the toppling of several other stuffed animals, bottles of perfume, boxes of jewelry, ceramic figurines, and even a set of big red wax lips.

"What is all that stuff?" Andy asked, stepping back.

"Years and years of accumulated gifts from Keri's admirers," Kelly said as Andy bent down to pick up the wax lips. He stared at them, puzzled.

"Frederick Shindigger—sixth grade," Kelly said. "Gave them to her as a Halloween present."

"And the snake?"

"Probably a prize someone won for her at the fair."

Andy blinked as he gazed into the cabinet, which

was still crammed with darkened images hard to identify. "I had no idea all this stuff was in here," he said. "Maybe I should explore your office a little more often." Suddenly he leaned in and began sorting through the objects, as if looking for something.

"Did you give her something, too?" Kelly inquired, raising her eyebrows.

He nodded as he shuffled through the junk. "A pearl necklace. Well, not real pearls. Wonder if she kept them."

Kelly groaned, grabbed her husband by the arm, and pulled him away from his task. She shut the door and leaned against it. "Andrew Wood—get over it! You're my husband now, remember?"

"I was just curious."

"Still!"

He shook his head. "I can't believe she has so much stuff. It's weird, even for the Man-Eat-a. You're right, you know. How could anyone who's had so many admirers really settle down? I'm not sure I could have…" he paused as Kelly glowered at him. "Well, I suppose I could settle down because obviously I *did* settle down after I met you. But it is kind of sad, in a way. If Glenn tries to give Keri a diamond, and she does take it, it could end up here—in this crazy little closet of discarded loves." He turned his head to look fully at his wife, and then froze, a gasp of disbelief on his lips.

Keri was standing in the doorway.

"Glenn is going to give me a diamond?" Keri asked, her face ashen.

Kelly whirled to face…what was once her sister. Keri was dressed in a bright, oversized gown stuffed to make her appear busty and fat. Her short, chestnut-colored hair stuck out from the side of her head in tiny braids like handles, and a stirring bowl rested upside down on her head. Next to her stood Katie, her tiny hand clasped firmly in Keri's. At least Keri hadn't dressed her daughter up like an overdone opera singer.

"Glenn got me a diamond?" Keri asked again, her voice frantic. "How do you know?"

The skin prickled on the back of Kelly's neck. *Rats!* Now what was she supposed to do? Lie? Keri would never believe it, would never forgive her if she did lie and Glenn tried to give her a diamond anyway. She glanced helplessly at Andy, who shrugged.

"Don't look at me…this news is all second-hand," he said.

Kelly's shoulders slumped. Her eyes strayed involuntarily to a cobweb in the corner of the ceiling as she explained. "I saw him pick up a diamond at the jewelry store in the mall yesterday. He didn't see me."

Keri's pixie-like features contorted in a look of horror.

"But we've only been dating for a few months!"

Kelly's voice took on a defensive tone. "What do you want me to say? I saw what I saw."

"What did you see, mommy?" Katie asked, dropping Keri's hand and running over to hug her mother's legs. "A diamond? Like the one on your ring?"

"Yes, honey," Kelly said. "They have lots of them in the store."

Andy sank down and grasped his daughter's shoulders. "Hey, I've got an idea. Why don't you and I go outside and ride Bennie? I think he's kind of bored. How's that sound?"

"Yeah!" Katie squealed.

"Chicken!" Kelly called as he glanced back, smiled, then ushered Katie out the door fast as he could.

"I'm not getting involved in this," he called back, and then he was gone, leaving Kelly and Keri staring wordlessly at each other. Keri's eyes lowered to the cabinet's contents spread across the floor.

"I'd never put something like a diamond in the closet," Keri muttered, walking over to scoop up the items. She began to pick up the smallest treasures, collecting them in one hand, then pulled the bowl off of her head and dropped them in. As she bent over, a few tufts of toilet paper dropped out of her dress. She caught them with the bowl and continued.

"Glenn really is a nice guy," Kelly finally said, folding her arms.

"I know," Keri said. "Real nice."

Just then Katie came running back in, her coat halfway buttoned, and scurried over to Keri. She was wearing the wax lips.

"Daddy said to give you these," she said, handing them to Keri. She giggled, and then quickly ran out of the room again.

Keri stood and stared at the bowl of abandoned gifts in one hand, and the wax lips in the other.

"You look a bit ridiculous," Kelly said.

There was a prickly silence.

"At least I'm not *dull*," Keri finally mumbled, resuming her task. When she filled the bowl she opened the cabinet door and put the items in, arranging them carefully so nothing would tumble out again. As she started to pick up the snake and the other stuffed animals, Kelly's normally well-contained temper broke.

"So—I'm dull," she said. "Just flat-out boring because I'm a chubby brunette living in the Midwest with her husband and one kid, and another on the way. I work part-time at a dull little newspaper in a dull little town no one's ever heard of and live on a dull little farm. My life is so *dull* compared to yours that—"

"I didn't mean that," Keri interrupted, shutting the cabinet door.

"What did you mean?"

"I don't know."

"Listen," Kelly sighed, shifting a little uncomfortably. "I'm concerned. You're such a mess. Have you ever really been happy?"

"What is that supposed to mean?"

"It means I wish you would settle down one day, wherever it is, look around you and be thankful for what's there. Running to Texas and California and even France might have been fun for a while, but it's taking its toll on you. Did any of those people you ran with ever see the real you—like now—someone who thinks nothing of putting on a big fat dress with stuffing coming out of the boobs and their hair sticking out sideways?" She paused as Keri turned sharply back to the cabinet, re-opened it, and began to rearrange things again. "Now take Glenn," Kelly continued, drawing closer to her sister. "He's a great guy, and you two have a lot in common. He's a mortgage broker, you're a realtor. He's traveled a lot, you've traveled a lot. He likes Mexican food, you like Mexican food. There are all sorts of similarities, plus he's tall and handsome and owns his own home. He treats you like a queen, too. So, what's wrong with him?"

"And all that means we should get engaged after only a few months?" Keri mumbled, her face in the closet, "Is that what you think should happen to make me happy?"

"I'm not sure, but at least give the guy half a chance—unlike all of those fallen boyfriends who've packed that closet for you."

Keri spun around, her cheeks blazing. "What do you care, anyway? Are you sick of me staying here every once in a while, because if you are—I'll leave and sleep on the couch at mom's cottage if I have to. But I'm afraid then you'll be out of your live-in babysitter and housekeeper. Is that what you want?"

"I don't let you stay here just to watch Katie or to

do the dishes!" Kelly cried. "You're my sister. As flighty as you are, I just want you to be happy and you never seem to be. I've watched you for years! You're a fidgety wreck and it's time you relax and get a grip on things."

"Is that your professional assessment," Keri said, "or are you just jealous? I think that you are. Why don't you put *that* in the diary you're always writing in. You've never been to Europe, or hobnobbed with stars, or even driven a corvette. You settled down right out of high school with a guy who used to be *my* boyfriend and…"

Kelly's jaw dropped in astonishment. Tears sprang to her eyes as she fled the room, leaving Keri alone with her strange, sad cabinet of discarded love.

A pall of silence hung over the room.

Slowly, Keri turned back to stare into the closet. Her eyes began to sting, her former treasures becoming wavy and surreal.

Was Kelly right?

She always tried to be happy, enjoying life to its utmost. But how many of her friends *really* knew her? How many knew she grew up a country girl who raised rabbits as a kid, chased fireflies at night and caught frogs in the creek? Most friends she grew up with who had known, were now long gone, had drifted away. Or, had she drifted from them? She had a few friends left here, acquaintances really, that she'd worked with at one time or another as a teenager. But that was all. Now maybe it was only her sister who really knew her, only her sister with whom she could truly be herself.

Sensing movement, Keri glanced out the window to see Andy and Katie trudging along a snowy path towards the barn, hand in hand. There was a splat of snow on the back of Andy's brown coat. Apparently they'd had some kind of snowball fight. She watched them laughing. As they approached the barn, Bennie whinnied and trotted to meet them at the gate. It was all so sweet, so normal. An unusual sorrow swelled inside of Keri as she turned away from the scene to find herself once again facing the cabinet, the open door and its contents appeared to gape at her like creatures hidden in a cave. She backed away, turned from its accusing mouth and headed toward the door in a trancelike state, suddenly just wanting to get out of there. The cabinet seemed to pull her back, but she forced herself forward.

What did all of this mean? She hated the closet for the things it implied about her.

Shallow. Vain.

It wasn't true, of course, but how do you fight a cabinet?

She'd get over this as she'd always done. By fleeing the sinister room she'd be fine again in a little while, but her heart was pounding and a cool sweat broke out across her forehead as she reached the door and grasped the knob.

Freak! The cabinet-mouth seemed to call from behind her. She twisted the doorknob and bolted from the room.

Chapter 2

Glenn whistled lightly to himself as he drove, unconcerned by the swirls of snow that made it nearly impossible to see the road. Keri sat silently in the seat next to him, hugging her arms around her abdomen.

"Are you cold?" Glenn asked. "I can turn the heater up a little."

She shook her head, lost in thought.

"Are you feeling sick?" he asked more cautiously. "You haven't spoken much all night."

"No—I'm fine."

There was an extended silence, unusual for the couple. Eventually Glenn began to whistle softly to himself again, but it sounded uneasy this time.

Keri sighed and tried to relax, but it felt as though tiny insects were crawling across her skin. She studied Glenn from the corner of her eye; calm as a cucumber he was, intelligent, chatty, and confident. Thick, sandy blonde hair, nicely styled of course. Slim moustache, aquiline nose, John Lennon-style glasses. He was pleasant, capable, and dependable. All wonderful things.

But all Keri could do was sit in icy terror, wondering when he was going to try to give her the diamond. *What was wrong with her?* They'd arranged this Valentine's Day date two weeks in advance; it would have been impossible to break it. Keri was a horrible liar. She couldn't say she was sick when she wasn't, couldn't even fake it—although she'd thought about it, thought about it hard.

She was certainly feeling sick now.

They'd gone to a movie first, a typical date with no real chance for him to ask her to marry him. She hadn't been concerned about that there. It was the dinner afterwards that frightened her...reservations at Manciano's, an elegant Italian restaurant notoriously difficult to get into on weekends. It would be the perfect spot for him to give her the ring, especially being Valentine's Day. She'd pictured it ahead of time, had even figured out how she'd handle it if he asked...

They'd finish dinner, small talk prevailing as they sipped wine. The atmosphere would be quiet, with a dreamy ambience filling the room. As conversation waned, Glenn would look deeply into her eyes and take her hands in his. Candlelight flickering across his features, he would lean closer and say something sweet and romantic like, "The only regret I have about meeting you is that it didn't happen sooner. I know we've only been dating a short time, but I knew from the moment I met you that we were destined to be together..."

At that point, if Keri hadn't passed out from dread, Glenn would release one of her hands, reach into a pocket and bring out the ring. Or, maybe he'd be a little creative and have it delivered by the waiter on a dessert tray or even hide it at the bottom of her wine glass. Whatever. But, after he'd shown her the glamorous ring, probably a huge one as Glenn was a generous person, Keri would have to do the unthinkable...

...she'd feign delight. She'd swoon in ecstasy as people at other tables caught on to their little drama and watched with great expectation—maybe even sighing and clapping as she accepted.

And she'd *have* to accept, at least temporarily.

Keri had turned a proposal down once before. Paul Meyer. Poor Paul Meyer. It'd been at a huge New Year's

Eve Party in Houston. His proposal had come out of the blue. At the strike of midnight they'd kissed, then Paul had gotten down on one knee, held out a box with the ring, and the first few moments of the New Year stood still. There was immediate silence; the only sound was the silent screaming of Keri's mortified heart as he asked her to marry him. Her world became a woozy, gelatinous haze, like trying to breathe underwater.

She'd adored Paul, she'd dreamt about him. One of *those* dreams, dreams she'd learned to love at first, then dread later. Those fairy tale dreams that snatched a man and held him on some superhuman pedestal that no one in the waking world could possibly equal—ever. Pure fantasy. Pure fairy tale.

The first kiss would be silky and smooth and have that magical, melt-away bliss she'd dreamed of. At least, *almost* like she'd dreamed of. As days passed and reality shoved in, the kisses would be cooler, a little dull. At last, they'd become emotionless, as though she were kissing a statue, and then, she'd have to run.

When Paul had asked her to marry him the roar of blood rushed in her ears and her head began to spin and in front of one hundred and fifty guests, she'd grunted– "I don't think so."

Paul's eyes had widened. He froze. Everyone froze. No one spoke, no one dared. It was the hush of horror.

At last, Paul came back to life. The first sound was of the box snapping back shut, then Paul silently turned away and threaded out of sight through the dismayed crowd. Everyone felt his humiliation. Everyone. He'd never forget it, neither would his friends. It was awful. Painful. Almost sickening in its sadness.

Keri could never do that to a man again. So, no matter how Glenn asked her to marry him, she would say yes, and he would save face.

Later, she'd find a way to tell him the truth.

Yet dinner hadn't gone as she'd imagined, and now they were back in the car, listening to the soft hum of the heater. With the windshield wipers slapping at the snow, she couldn't believe her plan had been ruined. She'd been so determined, so set on things working out as she'd hoped.

But he hadn't asked her yet. Just when she felt he was about to at the restaurant, just when she'd taken a deep breath and steadied her nerves, there was a murmur of soft oohs and aahs at the tables around them. Both she and Glenn looked to their right, three tables ahead, to see a young, redheaded man with a goatee bending down on one knee in front of a starry eyed brunette. He held a velvety box with a diamond sparkling inside in a trembling hand, the brunette agreed to his proposal, and there were teary hugs and polite applause all about.

The red-haired man had stolen Glenn's thunder.

Now what would Keri do?

Presently they were on their way to Glenn's house for a nightcap. He'd probably ask her there—in private. That *should* be a good thing, but she hadn't prepared to tell him the truth tonight, she'd prepared to make him happy, not miserable. If she accepted now, she couldn't tell him later that she just hadn't wanted to embarrass him in front of people.

What was with some guys, anyway? Why ask a girl to marry him publicly if he wasn't rip-roaring absolutely sure she wanted to marry him? How could Glenn be that certain? Or, was he that naïve?

If he was so certain, well, how pompous of him!

"What are you thinking?" Glenn's voice came suddenly, snapping Keri back to her senses. "You have a strange look on your face—like you're angry. Did I do something wrong?"

Keri looked at him and smiled limply. "No, everything's fine. I was just thinking about a little argument I had with my sister the other day."

Glenn's smile flashed in the shadows. She knew he was relieved, but should he be smiling about the fact that she and her sister had a fight? Even if the fight had been about something similar to the situation now.

"That's good," he said, "I mean, good that you're not mad at me."

There was silence. Glenn didn't ask her if she wanted to talk about the spat. He was only thinking of himself.

Why am I picking him apart? Keri's mind screamed.

"You know—I really don't feel so good," she said finally, "and the storm is getting worse. Maybe you should just take me back to Kelly's."

"My house is much closer," said Glenn. "You're welcome to stay the night. I'd be happy to wait on you if you get sick; I'm actually a pretty good 'nurse' when I have to be. I grew up taking care of a little brother and sister, so nothing phases me. I've seen it all."

"I'm not sure I want you to see my *all*," Keri replied, as her stomach began to roll and coil for real.

"Don't worry, you'll be fine with me. I'd look forward to taking care of you."

"No—no. Thanks, but take me home."

"Really, it's no problem! I *want* to take care of you."

Keri's nerves began to jump. Her throat constricted. "Just take me home!"

"You have nothing to worry about with me…"

"Turn around!" Keri screeched.

At that, Glenn hit the brakes, the car spun in a dizzying circle through sheaths of snow and wound up facing the opposite direction. A car that had been following skidded around them, missing them by inches, then was lost in the blizzard.

Both Keri and Glenn's hearts pounded. He finally caught his breath, glanced around for more traffic, then gingerly pulled the car in the appropriate lane and began to drive. He said nothing, his mouth a grim line.

"Boy, when I say turn around—you *turn around*," Keri said, attempting to break the silence.

Glenn remained solemn, from anger or embarrassment, Keri wasn't sure. She was aware, however, of just how strange her outburst had been. Maybe Glenn would think she was too unstable for him now, which wouldn't be a bad thing in this situation. Still, she didn't actually *enjoy* anyone thinking she was a crackpot. She tried to make idle conversation as her stomach and nerves began to settle.

"I'll bet it's the fettuccine that's not sitting well, especially after the spin," she began. "It was a great dinner, though, thank you for taking me. I don't want to seem ungrateful just because I'm nauseated. That's not your fault." She paused, then, "Sorry I bellowed at you. It's been a long day, and I'm tired."

It worked. She could see Glenn relax, and eventually smile.

"It has been a long day," he admitted, "and this snow isn't helping any. I'm a little uptight myself, but it shouldn't ruin our evening. After all… it is Valentine's Day."

A chill slithered down Keri's spine.

Glenn continued to talk about Valentine's Day, how much it meant to him, how most men thought it was just an excuse for card companies and jewelry stores to make a little extra money. This was an old holiday, he explained, not a newly manufactured one, and it was meant to be special.

Keri's stomach churned. He was leading up to the ring; he had to be. Soon she couldn't hear him talking with so much white noise filling her ears. It became dark and smothery in the car; suddenly the freezing, whitewashed world of snow outside seemed inviting.

She tried to force herself to calm down and not to get too excited again. They were so close to home now—the gravel road leading to Kelly's house was barely a mile ahead. She could hold on, she could! *Surely* Glenn wouldn't try to give her the ring now, but wait for another day. When there wasn't a blizzard, a near car wreck, or a stomachache in the vehicle.

Suddenly, Glenn was pulling the car over, way over. They were on the corner of Kelly's road. Snow shot past the window as Keri turned to Glenn in astonishment.

"What are you doing? Is this safe?"

"Nobody will hit us here, we're too far off of the road," he said, smiling as he turned off the ignition and leaned toward her. "I meant to give you this in the restaurant," he added, pulling something out of his overcoat. "But I guess it's best to do this in a private, memorable place like this."

Keri's heart slammed against her chest. *Memorable place like this?*

"This is something to show how much I care for you."

She backed closer to the window, and he pressed closer, showing her a small, velvety box. She stared at it like it was a dead frog.

"Glenn—please, don't," she said.

"Go ahead. Take it. It won't bite."

"I need air—I feel really sick," Keri said. She reached behind her and fumbled for the door handle with one hand as Glenn took her other hand in his. He rested the box in it, unaware of what she was about to do. "Take it, open it," he said.

But it was the door handle Keri grasped and pulled. Her fingers closed in on the box as an impulse, then she twisted in her seat, away from Glenn, as the wind caught the door and yanked it out of her grasp. An icy blast of air punched her face and hands; whirls of snow blew in the car. Keri found herself scrambling outside, stumbling in the snow, gasping for breath.

"Keri! What are you doing?" Glenn called. His eyes looked as big as plates as Keri backed farther away, her feet and ankles burning with cold in the snow.

"I need air—I'm walking home!" she yelled above the storm. She shoved the box into her coat pocket, hiked her scarf up around her head and began to crunch down the road. The wind bit into her face and froze her nostrils as she stumbled on, heading into the storm. Kelly's house was only half a mile ahead. She'd be fine, even in the dark with snow blinding her and freezing her eyelashes.

Just then a hand grabbed her arm from behind, pulling her to a stop.

"This is madness!" Glenn cried. "Get in the car with me. I'll drive you home!"

Keri jerked out of his grasp. "You don't understand, I need air. I need to be by myself! I'll call you tomorrow."

"Come with me!" he shouted above the roar of the wind. The snow streaked across his face, creating tan and white ribbons of color. Already, his glasses were caked in snow and his hair frosted white. His slacks slapped around his ankles in the wind. Keri knew Glenn was right, it was madness, but she could not go with him. He tried to grasp her again, but she pulled out of his grip.

"I'm serious!" she shouted. "Leave me alone!"

He stared at her, his mouth hanging open as if on a hinge. Keri whirled back around and began to forge ahead again, knowing she was hurting him, knowing he couldn't possibly understand her, knowing she'd never quite understood herself. She glanced back once, and could vaguely see his shadowy, fragmented form heading back to the car. Soon both he and the car were lost behind curtains of snow.

A few moments later, however, she heard the sound of his engine and could see yellow cones of headlights piercing the snow. But instead of turning away or passing on, the headlights turned in her direction.

"Crap!" Keri said to herself. Her heart raced—she couldn't take another confrontation. She glanced around desperately, wondering what to do, how to get out of this. Suddenly she found herself stomping into the ditch at the side of the road, wading through snow up to her knees. Hoping Glenn couldn't see her tracks in the blizzard, she plowed on. Heedless of the needles of pain in her legs and feet, she scurried behind a thick tree on the edge of the woods and ducked out of sight just as the car lumbered by like a beast on the scent of prey.

A wee thought skirted the edge of Keri's mind; the thought that Glenn was doing everything right, and she was the odd one, doing wrong things, crazy things, and he just wanted to help her. He was a good man, a wonderful man. But she stayed in place as the car moved out of sight.

She kicked her feet together. Her dress shoes were ruined, her feet feeling like blocks of ice. She'd been wearing slacks, thank goodness, but they did little to shield her legs from a foot of snow. They were already soaked through and clinging in hardening creases to her numbing legs. She had to move on.

Keri wedged frozen hands into her coat pockets and trudged back up the ditch to the road. She pressed toward home, squinting as the snow stung her face. She decided if Glenn had turned around to come look for her, she'd veer off into the woods again. She'd keep doing it until he gave up. She imagined Glenn would probably pull into Kelly's driveway and wait for her to show up, or worse, tell Kelly and Andy what she'd done so they'd *all* come looking for her.

Let them come. This was Glenn's fault! Why buy her a ring now? She curled her stiff fingers around the box and grimaced… most girls would be thrilled with a diamond. Why was she so different from everyone else?

By the time Keri could see the faint lights of Kelly's house through the snow she could no longer feel her face. As she drew closer, her heart dropped—Glenn's car was parked in the driveway, and she still wasn't ready to explain things. Once again she took to the ditch and hopped through the snow, across the yard, then angled down to the barn. She waded through snow above her knees before reaching the gate, unlatching it, and stepping into the pasture. There was a light outside the barn; if anyone was looking out the house window they might see her shadowy form through the blizzard, so she ducked through the barn door, dodged a pile of horse doo, then leaned against the wall in relief. The wind whistled around the barn as she inhaled the sweet, strange scent of hay, straw, and horse. She closed her eyes. Bennie neighed quietly and stuck his head over a stall near her, gazing at her with soft curious eyes.

"I'm fine, Bennie," Keri murmured. "Just got myself into a little predicament is all. I'll have to go up to the house eventually though, or they'll have the whole county looking for me."

At last she opened her eyes and the interior of the barn took shape in the gloom. It was a cozy place for a horse and a few barn cats. There was no sign of the dog, though. On nights like this, Kelly and Andy quite often let Rover sleep inside the house. Rover was a huge, furry old beast, part Saint Bernard and part mystery. Keri would have been glad for his company right then, but Bennie was a good listener, too. Keri reached out to stroke his muzzle, then pulled the box out of her coat pocket and held it with stiff fingers.

"Look at what he got me," she said to the horse. "After only a few months. What was he thinking? So what if it is Valentine's Day…a box of chocolates would have done just fine. If he really knew me, a big jar of Polish dill pickles would have been a more exciting gift." She turned the velvety box over in her fingers, barely able to feel it.

"Should I peek at it, Bennie? Just once before I give it back to him? Maybe I'll even try it on, just for the heck of it. See if he guessed my ring size."

Keri grinned as Bennie shook his head and nudged her. "Okay…here goes."

She took a deep breath, then glanced around cautiously as though someone might be spying on her. She caught the glint of a barn-cat's eyes in the rafters, but nothing moved. The air was still and expectant.

Slowly, Keri fumbled with the lid. As it opened, she closed her eyes for a second, as if willing the contents to disappear. Finally, she opened them, and stared down. Her eyebrows shot up in disbelief. "What?"

Instead of one big shiny diamond, there were *two* diamonds.

Two. *Earrings.*

"I'm going to strangle Kelly!" Keri muttered, staring into space.

She closed her eyes, and then looked in the box again. Earrings. Still there. A smile flickered at the corner of her mouth; eventually, it turned into a grin. All at once, she was laughing.

"I'm safe," she said, snapping the lid shut. "I'm safe!"

Now she could go up to the house. She'd tell everyone just how sick she'd been, but she felt a lot better now, she'd admit; the cold air had cleansed her.

Keri sighed, and relaxed her shoulders. All was well, sort of. She'd still have to find a way to say goodbye to Glenn. This had been too nerve-wracking even for her.

Chapter 3

It's May 17th, and Katie is four years old today! And in a few more weeks, she'll have a new little brother or sister to play with. I'm blessed, I know. I hope I don't jinx myself by writing that. I hope Katie doesn't pick up Keri's wishy-washiness and will one day find someone she can really love and settle down with. What am I thinking? That's years away from now.

I can't wait to have this baby. My poor ankles look like basketballs. Thank goodness everyone is helping out with Katie's party today, I could never do it alone.... I think Jeremy will deliver the baby's new bed today, too. What a masterpiece! It transforms from a crib, to a daybed, to a full size bed as the child grows. I wish I could have known about Jeremy Quinn when Katie was born so she could have a bed like that. But I think Katie will love this birthday present even better. We got her another pony, and he looks just like the pony Keri and I had when we were kids. It's going to be such a great day! The sun is shining, the birds are singing, and Andy is in the kitchen making Belgian waffles. Can it get any better?

Keri blew up a final long pink balloon, and stuck it in the neck of her clown suit. Pink balloons now ringed her neck, gently rubbing against her pasty white face with its silly grease-paint clown grin and giant red nose.

Katie squealed with glee, but Kelly rolled her eyes at her sister.

"Honestly, Keri, it looks as though your neck has sprung hemorrhoids," she said, squeezing the last of the frosting onto Katie's birthday cake.

"Mommy—what's a ham-rod?" Katie asked.

Keri looked at Kelly with enormous arched clown eyebrows. "Explain that one, sis," she said.

"Oh honey, that just means big rosy fingers," came the voice of the two sisters' mother, Katherine. "Come here, baby, let's have another look at that pretty new dress!"

Katie laughed, running to the table and heaving herself into Katherine's strong arms. "Is it really pretty, Grandma?"

"It sure is, honey, wish I had one just like it."

"But you never wear dresses."

"I would if I had one that pretty," the wiry, flaxen-haired woman replied. "I didn't always drive trucks, little one. And I won't ever again, I'm going to spend the rest of my days sitting at my little cottage and fishing every day."

"Can I go with you?"

"Sure! Pretty soon the bluegill will be in their beds. We can catch some and have a fish fry."

"And I'll catch a clownfish with big feet and a red ball on its nose!" Keri said, stomping over to her little niece like a clown on attack.

"Don't scare her, some kids are afraid of clowns," Kelly said as Keri reached down to tickle her little niece's ribs.

But Katie just laughed, her light brown curls bouncing against her cheeks and her amber eyes sparkling. She really was a little doll, thought Keri. Maybe she'd have a kid herself one day, as ridiculous as that seemed with her crazy lifestyle. She'd already broken up with another man since Glenn. This one she'd met briefly at an open house. She hadn't thought much of Michael Ford at the first introduction, but a few nights later she'd had one of her dreams. One of *those* dreams again. Michael appeared in it like some modern-day Prince Charming, speeding up on his motorcycle to save her from a mugging. She'd jumped on the back of his Harley, wrapped her arms around his chest and off they cruised into the sunset. Later Keri was rather shocked to find out that Michael didn't actually own a Harley. The closest he'd gotten to it was a dirt bike when he was twelve.

Still, as usual, their first kiss was a dream, lingering and magical. The second was less so; she'd gotten to know Michael a little better by then. Then Keri's friend Darci commented about the hideous shoes he wore. He was becoming much too common, Kelly later warned Keri in her sarcastic voice. It wouldn't last, and, it hadn't. There'd been no third kiss, and Keri had sworn off men for good.

"Aunt Keri would never scare you, would she?" Keri heard Katherine ask while lifting Katie off her lap. "But your daddy just might, with all those goofy toys of his. He might just build a spaceship and fly you away!"

"Mom," Kelly warned. "Andy's not *that* goofy."

"Where in the heck is he, anyway? All the kids will be here in half an hour," said Keri.

"He's… out," Kelly said mysteriously, jerking her head toward the barn while Katie wasn't looking. "He'll be here in a little while."

"Oh, I see," said Keri, she and her mom looking knowingly at each other as Katie scampered away. He was "installing" the new horse.

Then came a knock on the door.

"Oh no, someone's early and the decorations aren't all up yet," Kelly moaned. "I was afraid this would happen!"

"Relax, sis! Don't have a cow—or a baby," said Keri. "I'll get it."

"Well, don't scare the kid when you let him in, you do look a little absurd."

"What's new," Keri shrugged.

Keri tucked a few balloons in tighter around her neck, and went to the door. She opened it, stunned to find two young men standing there, no children in sight. One man was tall, blonde and movie star handsome. The other guy was cute, with a mop of brown curly hair and impossibly blue eyes. Too bad he was rather short. He grinned at her, and looked impish—like an elf.

"We're here to deliver a bed to…to Kelly Wood?" he said as more of a question, staring past Keri at all the party arrangements. "Did we barge in on something?"

Kelly broke away from her cake decorating and came to Keri's rescue. "It's my daughter's birthday," she said. "Thanks for coming, guys!"

The tall blonde glanced at Kelly's well-rounded stomach. "You're sure today's the day?" he asked.

"No, not this one's birthday," she replied, patting her belly. "That's my four-year-old daughter, but the bed *is* for the one on the way. The room's all set up, go ahead and bring it in."

The two men nodded and turned away, both giving Keri a bemused last glance.

"I have that effect on men," Keri said, winking at her sister.

"That's Jeremy Quinn and his cousin Keith," said Kelly. "I heard of them through a friend at church. Jeremy is a master woodworker, he can make anything. He's got his own shop in Rockport. This bed is his own design."

A few moments later, Keri watched as the men carried in a gleaming, honey-oak crib. It was somewhat longer than a normal crib, allowing for its sides to transform into different kinds of beds. At the top of one of the rails a lovely K-W was carved. Kelly and Andy didn't know if they were having a boy or a girl, but, in an attempt to keep the all-important family "K" tradition, they had tentatively chosen K-names for the baby—Kenny if it was a boy, and Karen if it was a girl. Anything to keep her mother happy. The men followed Kelly into the baby's room just as Katie ran out of her own room and followed them in.

Keri and her mother sat at the table, waiting. Katherine gave Keri the creepy, 'I can tell what you're thinking' eye.

"I saw how you looked at that big guy, Keri," she warned. "I suddenly think you haven't totally sworn off men anymore."

"Oh stop it, mom. He's probably married, anyway."

"I didn't see a ring."

"Why were *you* looking?"

"Your father has been gone for years. I can look all I want."

"I think both guys might be a bit too young for you, mom."

"Maybe twenty years younger, big deal. Tell you what, I'll go for the tall one. You can have the short one, he's more your size. And he's adorable."

"Mom, stop it. I'm not interested in either of them. Leave it alone."

"I know my daughter—and I *did* see a glint in your eye."

"Like he'd really be interested. Look at me," Keri said, pinching her clown nose and clapping her big clown feet together. "I'm a clown!"

"Well, he'd find that out for himself, eventually."

Keri shook her head and tugged one of the pink balloons away from her face.

Moments later, the conversation in the bedroom moved into the hallway and everyone came into the kitchen. "Have a seat, guys, and I'll find my checkbook," said Kelly. "I love the bed! Andy is going to freak when he sees it!"

The two men pulled chairs away from the table and sat across from Keri and Katherine. The short one was about to say something when Katie walked over to him, looked straight into his eyes, and then shifted her glance to Keri.

"My aunt Keri," she began seriously, "has ham-rods on her neck."

Keri's eyes rounded. There was a silence, and then everyone broke into laughter. Katie laughed too, although she looked rather confused about it.

Keri couldn't help noticing how perfect the tall man's teeth were when he laughed. That was Jeremy, she presumed. She then found herself looking discreetly down at his shoes. Tan docksides. Her friend Darci would approve.

When the laughter calmed down, the short guy looked Katie straight in the eye. "Your aunt may have ham-rods," he said, "but *I* have the fearless floating arm."

With that, he leaned on the table with his chin in his hand, and his other arm slowly, slowly lifted up as if of its own accord. When it got too high, he quickly adjusted his position and gently pulled the arm down to his lap with the other hand.

Katie's eyes bulged.

After he let go of the arm, it slowly began to lift once again, but he quickly caught it and pulled it down. "Don't want it to float away," he said, "it might take all of me with it."

"And it could, too," his handsome cousin said. "Unfortunately, there isn't a whole lot of him to lift."

A sudden uncomfortable silence filled the room, but the short man, presumably Keith, didn't seem to mind.

"I've got a floating arm, too," said Keri. "But sometimes it's stronger than me and I can't stop it." With that, she lifted her right arm slowly into the air, and then pulled it down with her other arm as Keith had done. Katie moved over to watch her aunt in awe.

"Oh no, what's scary Keri going to do now?" Katherine whispered.

Again, Keri's arm lifted, again she pulled it down. But the third time it rose, she could not lower it with her other hand. It seemed stiff.

"It's stuck!" said Katie.

"It is!" said Keri. She got to her feet and began to push down harder on the arm, but to no avail. Then, suddenly, the arm seemed to come to life. The hand formed a claw, and thrust itself at the balloons around her neck.

"Oh no…it's pulling out my ham-rods!" Keri wailed as Katie watched, spellbound. "I have to stop it, I have to stop it!" Everyone laughed as Keri struggled to keep her wild hand from pulling out all of the balloons. Finally, she got a grip on her hand and flung it to the table.

Keri handed Katie one of the balloons. "Hurry! Clobber it before it wakes up!"

With that, the hand began to twitch, then rise. Keri took another balloon and began to whack at it, and Katie squealed with glee, whacking at it, too. The hand twisted and turned, then flopped like a fish at the onslaught. Finally, its futile convulsions slowed to a complete stop.

Katie stared breathlessly at the forlorn-looking appendage lying pitifully across the table. "I think we killed it!" she cried.

"What is that nutty aunt of yours doing now?" came Kelly's voice as she walked back into the kitchen.

"I believe I started all this," Keith admitted, twisting in his chair to face her.

"We're always getting into some kind of trouble together," Jeremy laughed. "But it usually comes to no harm. I'm not sure about that poor clown's hand, though," he added, winking at Keri.

Keri felt her cheeks warm beneath the pancake makeup. "Oh, it's fine now, back to normal!" she announced, lifting it and petting it like a kitten. Suddenly, however, she looked at Jeremy's beaming, handsome face, and a stab of fear coursed through her; all at once she felt intimidated, ridiculous in her outfit.

How could she have acted like this in front of him?

"I think I'll go run some water over my hand, just to make sure it's all right," she said, hurrying from the room. Her heart pounded as she shut herself in the bathroom. She couldn't come out until the Quinn cousins left and the birthday party began.

Chapter 4

"I can't stand it, Darci," Keri lamented. "All day long I was driving around with the Freemans, showing them houses and trying to act interested, but all I could think of was Jeremy Quinn."

Darci nodded, and took a sip of her drink. She seemed as oblivious to the men staring at them as Keri. She spoke low, just above the murmurings of voices and the clicking of glassware in the lounge around them. "You're obsessed, Keri."

Keri agreed. "I know. And all he did was wink at me."

"That's so unlike you. Usually guys follow you around, and this one didn't even ask for your phone number."

Keri leaned forward and stared into her friend's big green eyes. "I was dressed up like a clown, Darci! I had balloons sticking out of my neck and tons of pancake makeup on. He probably thought I was a kook, the way I was goofing around."

"Not if he winked at you."

"I think it was a pity wink. You know, the kind guys give old ladies."

"Oh, I don't know. I'm sure he could tell how gorgeous you were beneath all that stuff. By the way," Darci added, leaning closer. "What kind of shoes did he wear?"

"Decent ones," said Keri. "I can't believe I even

looked."

"It is important, you know. Shoes tell a lot about a man."

"I liked his smile," said Keri. "It was perfect. Great teeth."

"What about his eyes—nice eyes?"

"Yeah, eyes that wink."

"And…his tush?"

"Cute. Small."

"Good girl."

"I liked everything about him. I only met him for a total of maybe ten minutes, but it took over the whole day. I haven't gotten him out of my mind all week. Maybe I'm changing, Darci. I liked this guy almost instantly and I didn't even have a dream about him first. Too bad his name doesn't start with a K, though. You know how important that kind of thing is in my family. Kelly already messed that up by marrying an *Andy*."

Darci sighed and leaned back in her chair. She flipped her long, cinnamon-colored hair over a shoulder pretending she didn't notice a particularly obvious young man at the bar eyeing her. Darci was in love, again, with a distinguished, divorced lawyer named Steven. When she was in a relationship, she tuned out the world until the relationship soured, as it always did, but she wasn't in the 'souring' stage in this relationship, yet. As a realtor, she'd just sold Steven a half-million dollar house. It might be quite a while before the souring stage set in this time.

"And what did you say he does for a living?" she asked Keri. "Some kind of furniture business?"

"I think he designs furniture. He made a crib for my sister's baby," said Keri.

"You mean—he makes just one design, or does he design for a company?"

"I'm not sure. I didn't ask Kelly a lot of questions. I

didn't want to be too obvious; she already thinks I'm as drifty as they come. I didn't want a lecture this time. She's due any day and she's getting cranky."

Darci nodded. "I can believe that. I remember those days. They were the pits. You feel like a whale and ache everywhere, and you're always so hot. I'll never do that again."

"Never say never," said Keri, thinking of Darci's six year-old son, Nathan. He was often completely unmanageable. Maybe Darci *should* never 'do that' again.

Keri sighed and rested her forehead in her hands. "What am I going to do? How do I get this guy out of my mind? He's driving me crazy and I don't even really know him. I freeze up just thinking about him. It's like I'm under a spell."

Suddenly Darci's eyes widened. "You have to see him again, somehow. Make an excuse." She paused, then, "If he designs furniture, go to him and pretend you're interested in him making something for you. You know, a business relationship front. See what happens."

Keri's eyes brightened. "Hey, that's good. No, that's a great idea!" As she contemplated the situation, her mind began to whirl for a plan.

Of course she could, she should see him again. The ball was in her court. Could this be fate—at last? The cosmos making *her* go out of her way for someone? Something like this hadn't happened in years. Or, had it ever happened?

"So, tell me more about what he's like," said Darci, clasping her hands eagerly in front of her. "Everything you can remember."

Keri's eyebrows lifted. It was surprising Darci was so interested. She usually had a rather annoying habit of diverting most conversations back to herself, but she seemed genuinely curious this time.

It must be a sign. Another sign!

"When they came to the door, his cousin, Keith spoke first so I didn't focus on Jeremy right away," said Keri.

"Wait, wait, wait," said Darci. "*They* come to the door? His *cousin*? I may be dating someone, but I'm still a single girl. What was the cousin like?"

Keri cocked her head in thought. "Cute. He had thick, curly brown hair that went to his shoulders and baby blue eyes. Friendly eyes." She paused. "But you wouldn't be interested in him, Darci. I guarantee it."

"Why—is he an axe murderer or something? Drug addict? Cyclops?"

"No. Worse. At least to you."

Darci gave Keri a puzzled look.

"He's *short*. About as tall as me."

"Oh no," Darci giggled. "I'm five-ten! He'd be five inches shorter than me. Poor guy. He must have a rough time of it."

"Think so?"

"Keri! That short? Think of it! No girl likes a short guy, it's just the way it is. So, how tall is Jeremy?"

"At least six-one, I'd say. Keith looked like a leprechaun next to him."

"The proverbial flunky sidekick," Darci said. "Anyway, back to Jeremy. Sorry for the distraction."

Keri looked at her friend oddly, feeling vaguely uncomfortable about something. Something about Darci's words about Keith bothered her, but she wasn't quite sure why. She shook her head and pulled herself together, then continued to tell Darci everything she could remember about that special day, one week before.

Chapter 5

This was it. Keri smoothed her eyebrows, straightened her finely tapered red blouse, and pulled into the driveway of the brick bungalow. The home was cute; red brick, green shutters, bay windows. It had lots of what realtors called "curb appeal," although it was half-hidden from the road, nestled in a forest of well-tended trees and shrubs. The home sat on a rolling, wooded area outside of town, on possibly five to ten acres. Keri's realtor's mind snapped to business… how much was it worth? What was the condition of the well, or the septic system? She had to shake her head to scatter these thoughts and focus on her objective….

To ask Jeremy Quinn to build her a bookcase.

Keri took a deep breath and wiggled her shoulders, trying to loosen up. Being this nervous about talking to a man was new to her. She stared at the house again. There was no sign of movement, everything was still and quiet. The home puzzled her; she'd expected to find Jeremy lived in something newer, more polished. Something to match the person—or what she perceived the person to be. This country home seemed more the destination of Little Red Riding Hood. Maybe Jeremy wasn't as much of a hotshot as his appearance suggested. Just because he was tall and handsome didn't mean he was confident and distinguished, like Darci's boyfriends always were. After all, this man was a craftsman, a creative sort. He might be confident, but distinguished in a more unique way.

Artistic. Eccentric.

She could live with that.

She'd find out soon. All she had to do was crack open the car door, get out, and follow the little cobblestone path to a front door festooned in hanging flowers.

Flowers?

That was kind of a 'girl' thing. Keri stiffened. Maybe he lived with a woman. A girlfriend. Or, even worse, a mother!

Or, a sister, said a little voice in her mind.

But she was here, and there was only one way to find out.

Keri popped open the door and scurried out of the car before her thoughts paralyzed her into inaction. She really *could* use a bookshelf. Maybe she hadn't a place to put it just yet, but someday she might. She readjusted her blouse again, and stretched long legs covered in snug black jeans. Spunky, heeled sandals completed her outfit. With a little extra makeup and gold-studded earrings, Keri knew she looked good. It was time to gather her normal confidence and get the job done. Or, begun. As she headed down the path, Keri felt unusually stiff and uncomfortable. By the time she reached the door, her heart was beating fast and her palms were sweating. What was wrong with her, anyway? She reached the door and pressed the doorbell before frazzled nerves forced her to turn around and run for her car.

As she waited, she studied a beautiful wooden plaque with the house number and the name "Quinn" carved into it. Had Jeremy made this? Probably. It was beautiful work, custom-made. Not something you could pick up at the local lumberyard.

Time passed. Maybe he wasn't home, after all, there hadn't been a vehicle in the driveway. She turned her head and craned her neck to get a better view of where the drive led. Not to a garage, but around the rear of the house. Maybe that's where the garage was—a house *had* to have a garage, after all. It was only civilized.

Keri's skin jumped at the sound of the door cracking open.

And there he was. Tall. Handsome. Tanner than she'd previously noticed, and his hair was so blonde it was practically white. He must have bleached it, she thought.

"May I help you?" he asked.

"Don't worry, I'm not selling anything," were the first words out of her mouth. "But I was hoping you were," she added. Keri froze as she said that. How stupid did that come out?

Jeremy cocked his head oddly at her.

Keri hastened to explain. "I'm here on business. I need to have a bookshelf custom-built," she said. "I was there when you delivered a crib to my sister, and was impressed by your work. You probably don't recognize me since I had a clown outfit on at the time. I helped your cousin entertain my niece with the silly 'floating arm' trick," Keri chuckled. "But, as you can see, I'm actually a grown-up."

Keri felt the blood rush from her face. *Why had she said that?*

Suddenly Jeremy's face brightened. "Oh—I remember!" he said, smiling. His teeth glowed within the new tan. "Yeah, I was there, but I think you have me mixed up with my cousin, Jeremy. He's the woodworker."

Keri's jaw dropped. "You're not Jeremy?"

"No, I'm Keith. Jeremy's parents are my aunt and uncle. I'm just visiting, and helping him out when I can."

Keri shook her head, looked at the ground, then at the ceiling, and finally back to… Keith.

"Are you okay?" Keith asked.

"I just feel…backward," Keri said. "All this time, I just *assumed* you were Jeremy."

"Nope. I'm Keith."

Keri just stared at him. *Keith.* Not Jeremy. He wasn't the craftsman, he was just a visiting relative. No wonder this home didn't seem like him! The disparity hadn't been real; if Jeremy was the short, humble one, then this house fit him perfectly.

But, *this* guy was Keith.

Keith. Starts with a K, she suddenly thought. Just like all her family's first names did. Was it… *could it be another sign?*

"Jeremy is out back stomping around in the woods looking for sticks," said Keith. He paused, eyeing her in the way she was used to being eyed. "I'd be glad to show you his shop, maybe get you started with ideas from photographs of his work. His pieces are all one of a kind, so he doesn't keep much around, but you could get a better feel for what he could do for you."

"Yes, that'd be fine," Keri said.

"We'll walk around to the rear of the house," Keith said, coming out of the door. "It's this way—follow me. We'll take a shortcut."

Keri found herself following Keith around the west side of the home. She dodged overhanging branches and flowering shrubs as he led her through a wooden gate encrusted with leaves, and suddenly, she was in a cave-like tunnel with sheathes of vines arching overhead. Sunlight streamed through and dappled the ground below her. The earthy, woodsy scent was fabulous.

"This is *fantastic*," said Keri.

"It is kind of neat," Keith agreed. "Jeremy's parents used to own this place, and he bought it from them a few years ago when they retired and moved to Georgia. He couldn't stand to see it go to anyone else."

"I can understand that," said Keri. She turned around, noting that the arbor led to the back door of the house. She turned again to see the tunnel leading to a quaint, barn-like structure. The shop, she assumed. It was all so romantic, so 'secret-gardeny.'

Keith stopped as he reached the door and looked at her. "It's not modern," he said, "and can be a little bit of a mess, but it's Jeremy's world." With that, he opened the door and they both stepped inside.

He was right. The shop had a cement floor, but cracks of light peered in between the wide, craggy boards on the walls. Dozens of tools, chisels, and saws were everywhere, either hanging on pegs on the walls, or scattered over enormous workbenches. Lathes and drill presses and other forms of equipment Keri didn't even know the names of rested against a far wall below a dusty, six-paned window. The place smelled aged, of wood and sawdust. She saw the dark forms of lumber in what probably used to be a stall, and then something else took form in the din.

"What in the world," Keri mumbled, heading toward it.

"Isn't it something?" Keith said, coming alongside her. "He's been working on this for months for some rich lady out East. It's finally done."

"I never heard of such a thing, let alone *seen* such a thing," said Keri. "A crib—with a canopy!"

Keith nodded. "I know. What the rich can conjure up."

Keri stood dumbfounded. Even in subdued light, the crib glistened with a warm, reddish hue. In the front, dozens of beautifully carved scrolls and stars gathered around a crescent moon. The foot of the bed featured a carved sunrise, with glorious rays streaming out to the corners of the bed. Clusters of carved daisies, tulips and wildflowers covered the arched, wooden canopy. The piece was a marvel.

"A hundred years from now, it'll be worth a fortune," said Keith. "It's a rare wood, Cuban mahogany. It's illegal to harvest it now, but Jeremy's dad had it sent up after a hurricane damaged some trees down south. Jeremy says the contrast between that stuff and regular hardwood is like the difference between burlap and satin. Let me find his scrapbook—show you some of his work. I'm sure there's a bookcase or two in it."

"Yes, let's see," said Keri, readjusting her mind to the mission at hand.

As Keith searched the workbenches for the scrapbook, Keri struck up a more personal conversation.

"So… how long have you been visiting?"

"A few months," he replied, "I'm sort of between jobs, taking it easy for a while."

"That's a coincidence, so am I," said Keri. "I'm just visiting, too. Staying with my sister a while, but I grew up in the area. You?"

Keith stopped searching, turned and leaned casually against a workbench. His piercing blue eyes seemed to stab at her, making her catch her breath in a giddy way.

"Actually, I grew up in the Midwest. But I live and work in L.A."

"Really?" Keri said. "I've lived there, sold real estate for a few years. What did you do?"

Keith tipped his head. "Ever see the cable show 'Prehistoric Story?'"

Keri thought hard… she hadn't. It sounded familiar, though. Her expression gave her away.

Keith chuckled. "I thought not. It's okay, though. The show only lasted about a year. I played Anton, the cocky warrior prince of the ancient city of Zendor."

"You're an actor!"

"That's right. Cable shows, a soap opera here and there, and lots of commercials."

"That's intriguing," said Keri. "What do you plan to do, return one day and keep acting?"

Keith paused, and looked away as if the decision was difficult for him in some way. "I'll probably return some day," he said. "My agent thinks he can get me more exposure soon, but I needed this break. It can be a real rat-race out there, but part of me loves it."

Keri agreed. "It *is* a rat race. It can be fun, too. I once sold a house to Tom Bannon, and he invited me to a housewarming party. People got wild, and I watched Penny Cartwell get so drunk she waded into the pool with all her clothes on…"

"And then threw up in it!" Keith said.

Keri's eyes bulged. "You were there?"

Keith nodded. "What a coincidence! Yeah—I was there. It was one of the craziest parties I've ever been to."

"Wow," said Keri, "small world, isn't it?" An unbelievable, ironic, *wonderful* small world!

Keri and Keith stared at each other in wonder before Keith finally broke the spell. "Well, enough of that. Back to business, right?"

"Right," Keri said softly.

"I can't seem to find Jeremy's scrapbook," Keith continued, looking around. "He may have it in the house somewhere. I have no idea when he'll return from his romp, so maybe if you just leave your name and phone number I can have him contact you."

"Right—sure," Keri nodded, feeling even giddier inside.

How convenient…leaving her phone number. How beautifully it was all fitting together. Finally! And Keith was an actor. Just wait until Darci heard about that.

She'd never even known an actor, let alone potentially dated one. She'd be green with envy….

Keri's thoughts were interrupted as Keith handed her a piece of paper and a pen he'd found on the workbench. When Keri bent over to write her name, Keith made a strange whistling sound. She looked at him curiously.

"Another coincidence," he said.

She raised her eyebrows. "What?"

"We're both lefties."

Keri straightened. "Really? I've been bugged about it all my life. People always acted like I was from outer space or something."

"I know. There aren't that many of us."

"Hmmm." Keri finished writing her phone number, glowing inside. Another sign! Then she wrote down her address as well—just in case he couldn't remember where Kelly lived. After all, he'd had no reason to remember the address. Keri had just been a silly clown at a birthday party when they'd first met.

Not some sweet, sophisticated babe, said the little voice in her mind.

She handed him the paper. "Well, that's it, I guess. Have Jeremy give me a call, and we'll talk. Or I can come back and get a look at those photographs."

"I'll do that," said Keith.

They left the shop and headed back to the front of the house. There Keith said goodbye, and offered her his hand. When they shook hands she was somewhat disappointed that the contact didn't create the electric-shock sensation she'd expected. It was cool and dry, nothing more. But after they released hands, Keith winked at her. That wink again!

She smiled briefly, turned away, and walked weak-kneed to her car.

What was it with that wink?

She watched Keith fold his arms together as she got in the car. Flustered, she rummaged for her keys. When she finally found them, she shot him a simple wave, started the vehicle and backed out. She felt almost relieved when she was out of his sight. She loved his company, but why was it so nerve-wracking? Was it because he was an actor? She'd been around actors before. Maybe not big, big names, but it wasn't that new to her.

No, it was something else.

Love? Love, or infatuation? She'd had dozens of infatuations; her life had teemed with infatuations. But, never love. She felt she'd know the difference. She *should* know, anyway. Was *this* the difference?

A warm feeling of delight filled Keri as she accelerated down the country road. She felt light. What did they call it? Floating on air? The sun seemed brighter, the air more sweet. A sudden 'blot' in the road ahead snapped Keri back to Earth. She swerved around the object, then, heart pounding, slowed and pulled over to the side of the road.

"I almost hit you!" she murmured, glancing in the rearview mirror. She stared back at a medium-sized painted turtle in the center of the asphalt. Far beyond, Keri could see a red truck approaching fast.

"Run, little one, run!" Keri said, but she knew better—turtles don't run. And the truck was growing nearer in the mirror.

"Oh, heck," Keri muttered, pushing open the door. She slammed it shut, then hurried down the road to the potential road-kill victim and scooped it up fearlessly in her hands. She edged to the side of the road just as the truck zipped by, a rush of wind in its wake. Keri lifted the turtle so they were eye to eye. Its head shrank back into its shell as she peered at its simple reptilian eyes.

"You could have been soup," she scolded quietly.

"What's so important on the other side of the road that you risked your life for it? She looked to the side of the road, past tall reedy grass and a ditch filled with weeds and burs. A swampy bog lay beyond. "Oh, I see," she said. "You need the water. Well, don't worry, little critter, I grew up around woods and ponds. I'll take you there myself so you don't get hurt."

Keri forgot all about Keith as she concentrated on her new mission. She'd always loved animals, and had never been afraid of handling them. From green-broke horses to garden snakes, she'd seen it all. At one point in her teenage years she'd toyed with the thought of becoming a veterinarian, until she found out how often sick animals had to be put down, and suddenly, she hadn't the heart for it. Real estate was much safer.

Keri picked her way through the brush and weeds toward the edge of the swamp. The ground became spongy as she neared the water, and she had to watch her steps carefully. The smell of mud and ooze drifted up to her as she moved on, cradling the turtle in one hand and holding the other out for balance. Her shoes were becoming caked with mud and began to stick, creating a suction sound as she pulled them in and out of the goo. Finally, she stopped.

She sighed heavily.

"This is it, Buddy. I can't go on."

Then, movement caught her eye. Another painted turtle was inching off a log into the water about eight feet away. "Hey!" Keri called to it, "Don't go, I've got your friend." She leaned forward and took another step to release her captive.

Mistake.

With the next step, her foot sank…and sank. Wild-eyed, Keri released the turtle. It sloshed happily away as she continued to sink, pin-wheeling her arms. Her foot didn't find solid ground until she was stuck in the sludge well above her knee and stooped in a precarious position.

"Rats!" she muttered, wrinkling her nose at the stench of the cold wet goop encompassing her leg. To make matters worse, her free leg began to sink, too.

More disgusted than afraid, Keri leaned back as far as she could on the good leg and pulled with all of her might on the buried leg. Slowly, slowly, it eased out of the suction, unfortunately taking her shoe along with it. A moment later, her leg was nearly home free.

The good leg sank faster as more of her weight and balance reverted to it. The leg folded, and Keri lost her balance. Down she went, front first into the slime.

Water and muck oozed up her shirtsleeves and down her top. Mud splattered her eyes as she sloshed around, pulling herself free at last. She stumbled, soaked, filthy and stinking, back to solid ground.

"What have I done?" Keri groaned, drawing her dripping hands to her face. Another mistake. Her mud-coated fingers slathered over her cheeks and hair. "I hope you're happy, Mr. Shellback!" she called to the swamp. She kicked and shook off as much mud as she could, but her clothes still clung in gooey wetness just as the mud in her eyes began to itch. With a disgusted sigh, Keri limped back through the brush toward her car, trying to let the vegetation scrape away as much mud as possible. She reached her vehicle as a dripping, forlorn mess, and stared at the car in dismay.

She'd just cleaned and vacuumed the cream-colored, velvety interior of the corvette. To drive this way would possibly stain the upholstery. Being a convertible, she could lower the top and possibly dry off as she drove...but her eyes were beginning to itch mercilessly now...and to sting. She'd never see well enough to make it home. Keri moaned, and looked toward Jeremy's house a quarter of a mile back. What if

Keith saw her like this—a muddy, stinking horror? But she had to go back there to clean up, what other option did she have?

Just then she saw a green SUV back out of the Quinn's driveway. Startled, she ducked behind her car. What if it was Keith? What if he drove by? Keri's heart pounded as the vehicle backed toward her, and then accelerated off in the other direction. A sigh of relief escaped her lips. *That was close.*

She'd remembered seeing a hose at the back of his house. Even if Jeremy was gone she'd be able to clean up somewhat. Stinging and cold, Keri slogged down the street, limping on her gimpy, shoeless foot. She passed one other house on the opposite side from the Quinns' home, but thankfully there was no sign of life from the older Cape Cod. When she reached Jeremy and Keith's driveway she hurried all the more, tripping across the cobblestone path to the rear of the home.

Suddenly, from behind a patch of shrubbery a huge, misshapen dog skidded to a stop in front of her and began to bark. Keri leapt back, then noted his bark seemed more excited than vicious. As she studied the poor canine, he had every reason to be vicious if he'd wanted to. The most obvious impediment was a frighteningly crooked front leg, and as her eyes wandered higher, she noted a missing left ear and an eye gnarled with scar tissue on an ancient-looking, square face. Seeing no reaction of panic from Keri, the dog calmed and drew closer, sniffing at the muck caked on her body.

"Scalawag, come!" a voice ordered.

Instantly the dog pulled away and ran in the direction of the voice. Keri turned toward the woods to see a curly-haired fellow in a green vest, jeans, and hiker's boots hurrying her way. He looked dumbfounded.

She recognized him instantly. Jeremy, the *real* Jeremy.

"Are you all right?" he asked.

Keri looked down at herself sheepishly, but not nearly as mortified as if it'd been Keith who'd discovered her. In fact, she felt quite calm. "I sort of fell in the swamp by the road," she said slowly, watching him eye her in concern. "I was moving a turtle off the road."

Jeremy's eyebrows rose. "Are you hurt?" he asked, looking her up and down.

She shrugged. "My eyes sting, and there are a few burs sticking to my legs, but that's about it. I came by earlier and talked to Keith about having you build a bookcase, but I didn't expect to become the Swamp Thing."

Jeremy grinned, his smile warm. "You should get cleaned up—get that stuff out of your eyes before we talk bookcases," he said.

Keri nodded. "I may look bad, but then I got a look at your dog." She glanced down at the dog that was sitting contentedly next to his master, a comical look on his lopsided face. "The name Scalawag suits him. What happened?"

Jeremy hooked his thumbs casually in his pockets. "I found him lying half dead in a field a few years ago. I think he was hit by some kind of farm equipment, but the farmer claimed he'd never seen him before. So, I took him home. He's been my faithful companion ever since."

Keri smiled. "That was nice of you, to take him in."

Jeremy shrugged, but was silent as he stared adoringly at his dog. "You should go in, use the shower," he said finally. "I can wash your clothes in the meantime. You can't keep those things on, who knows what kind of vermin are in that mud." He paused, and then continued, "I'm offering you my shower, and I don't even know your name, but your voice is familiar for some reason."

"Keri Ferrita," Keri said, extending her hand. She quickly withdrew it after noting the mud on her palm. "And we did meet, about a week ago. You were there when I showed my niece the floating arm trick."

Jeremy's face brightened. "You're the clown!"

"That's me. And not just when I'm suited up."

Jeremy gestured toward her. "That outfit is just about as interesting, minus one shoe."

"I lost that in the gook."

All at once it dawned on Keri—Jeremy had no idea what she really looked like. His only two glimpses of her were either as a clown with 'ham-rods' or as a Swamp Thing, and, if she took a shower here, she'd be scrub-faced and plain.

Oh well, no real problem. Jeremy wasn't Keith.

"Let's get inside, Keri, before some of that sludge morphs into you and you *do* become something out of a comic book," said Jeremy. "If you're not too appalled, you can wear a pair of my jeans and a sweatshirt until your stuff is clean. I think we're about the same size."

"Aw, come on, just jeans and a sweatshirt?" said Keri. "Don't you have a Spiderman outfit or a gorilla suit?"

"They're at the cleaners, along with my tutu," said Jeremy.

"Ah."

Jeremy led her to a back entrance bordered in rosebushes, then pushed open the door and invited her inside. "Ladies first, watch the bare foot."

Keri went inside, wondering why she had to be careful of having a bare foot. She found herself in an old-fashioned, low ceilinged kitchen with pine cabinetry and a large, antique stove; the quarry tile floor was worn and cracked in a few areas. Was that what he was worried about her stepping on?

Suddenly, a small gray blur sprang into the kitchen, followed by an orange blur. Startled, but only for a moment, Keri laughed as the two young kittens tackled each other. Scalawag cocked his head at them, as though wanting to play also, but appeared to sense he'd be out of line. The kittens paid the dog no mind whatsoever, and continued their play before darting out of the room again.

"That's Moe and Curly," said Jeremy. "Larry is around someplace."

"What, no Shemp?" asked Keri, laughing.

"He's the father."

"Oh. No girl kittens?"

"Curly is female. She routinely beats the other two up."

"Atta girl. What's the mother cat's name?"

Jeremy hesitated before answering, and then quietly said, "Hannah. But she ran away." He quickly changed the topic, which struck Keri as odd. "I'll show you to the bathroom. Just set your clothes outside the door, and I'll wash them."

"Okay," Keri said hesitantly. "Do you have a little plastic bag I could use?"

Jeremy looked at her curiously. "Sure, but for what?"

"Well…my underclothes. I can't have you *seeing* them, you know."

Keri watched in amazement as Jeremy's face transformed into a shade of red nearly matching the floor. He looked away, flustered. "I hadn't thought of that."

Keri laughed. "Relax, Jeremy, I don't think you're a pervert or anything, although I'm not sure about Scalawag."

Scalawag's ear perked up at the sound of his name. Jeremy led Keri through a cozy living room filled with older, traditional furniture, then down a hallway. He pushed open a door. "I hope it's clean," he said, eyeing the toilet bowl suspiciously. "Keith tends to be a little less than tidy."

"Sure—blame it on Keith," said Keri, warming at the sound of Keith's name. She stepped into the narrow room and tried to sound casual and indifferent. "Does he plan to stay here long?"

"It's hard to say with him, he's a bit eccentric," Jeremy replied.

"He seemed pretty normal to me."

"Oh, he is. I just know him a little deeper than a lot of people is all. Being eccentric can be good...*Swamp Thing*," he added playfully.

"I'm not eccentric, I'm just unique," Keri said, tilting her chin.

Jeremy laughed. "Clean towels are in the cabinet. Turn the water on carefully, it gets hot fast. Just set your clothes outside the door when you're ready, and I'll be sure to get to them before Scalawag or the kittens do. Wait just a minute, and I'll get you something else to wear."

As he walked away, Keri sighed. She turned in circles looking at the bathroom, the bathroom Keith used. It was a far cry from a movie star's getaway. A rosy pink tile decorated the walls behind a single, old-fashioned pedestal sink with rust stains. Flowered linoleum covered a floor with a slight warp. The tub was nice, deep and accommodating, and the shower looked new. If it were her choice, the shower curtain would have to go, though. An ocean scene—tacky. She wondered what Keith thought of it.

Suddenly Jeremy was in the doorway behind her, a pile of clothes in his arms. "Here's a few pairs of pants to try, and a sweatshirt," he said, as he dug something out of his pocket. "Oh—and here's your plastic bag."

"Thanks," said Keri, accepting them.

Jeremy smiled shyly and left, and Keri shut the door, suddenly aching to get in the shower. Her mud-caked clothes were getting crisp and burned against her skin, and her eyes smarted. She took a few steps back and glanced casually in a small mirror above the sink. "Oh my goodness!" she muttered at the shock of her reflection. Her face was grotesque with globs and streaks of mud caked on it. Even her hair had clumps of muck smeared into it, flattening it against the side of her head. Trails of mud drained down her neck into her… Keri looked down and pulled her shirt out. She groaned again, seeing the mess.

Suddenly she couldn't get out of her clothes fast enough. She wadded everything into a pile and scooted them out through a crack in the door. Then she practically lunged into the shower, shuddering as the mud and slime ran off in foul brown streams. She stood, rinsing and scouring, scrubbing and shaking, until the spray of water grew warm, then cool, and finally cold. At last, she felt cleansed.

She got out of the shower, dried off, and searched the bathroom for any signs of things a girl could use—skin lotion, hair gel, powder, anything, but she only found man-type shavers, shaving cream and soap. She supposed she'd have to leave the bathroom cleansed, but hampered with dried out, scaly skin.

Then there was the matter of clothes. Keri looked at the neatly folded bundle Jeremy had left her. *How odd this is!*

They did seem to be about the same size. She was skinny she knew, and had always had a somewhat boyish figure. To put on a stranger's clothes, minus her own underclothes, seemed kind of creepy, but she had no choice. Apparently Jeremy didn't have much use for things like robes.

She drew on the first pair of jeans, a loose-fitting painter pants style, and zipped them up. They were rather loose, the denim soft worn, and comfy. They were just the right length for her, too, adding to her suspicion that Jeremy was really close to her height. He seemed like such a nice person, she thought, pulling on a thick black sweatshirt. It was too bad he was so short. Maybe not shockingly short, but enough so to bother some women. Darci would be absolutely floored to know Keri fit into his clothes! She wasn't even sure she'd tell Darci about this little mishap with the swamp; she'd never let Keri live it down. She wasn't even sure she was going to tell Kelly.

Finally, Keri pulled on a pair of socks Jeremy had left her. She fluffed her fingers through her hair a few times, took a critical look at her freshly scrubbed, naked face, and felt ready to face the world again.

As long as Keith hadn't returned yet, that was. She heard no indications of voices or movement outside the bathroom door, though, so she slipped out as quietly as she could.

"Hello?" she asked softly, wondering where Jeremy was. The house was quiet and still as she tiptoed through it, wondering what to do next. "Jeremy—you there?"

She caught movement at the corner of her eye, and turned to see the dark shape of Scalawag hopping silently across the living room on his three legs. He disappeared into a half-opened door beyond.

"Scalawag—come!" Keri said in a muted, whisper-like call, wondering why she was being so quiet. She felt like she was being sneaky, but knew that was ridiculous. Jeremy had to be around someplace, maybe in the room the dog entered.

Keri padded across the room, ever watchful of the

zany kittens, but saw no sign of them. She reached the door and stood outside, unable to see much within.

"Jeremy, you in there?" she asked. There was no reply. "Jeremy? Scalawag?" Slowly, Keri pushed open the door and stepped inside. She found herself in a dark, richly paneled den with thick, sage-colored carpet. A large desk with a computer and stacks of papers resting on it sat against the wall. Opposite that was an easy chair with an antique floor lamp sitting nearby.

"What the…." Keri mumbled to herself, for there was no sign of the dog anywhere. She turned in circles, looking for a hiding spot, but saw no nooks or crannies for Scalawag to hide in.

She shook her head, bewildered, and stepped back out of the room. She was certain she'd seen the dog go in there! She felt uneasy, and the skin on the back of her neck began to prickle.

She glanced around to see if there was another room or hallway for the dog to have disappeared into, but there were only solid walls. "Maybe he's a ghost dog and he did die in that farm accident!" she whispered nervously to herself.

Suddenly she wanted out of the room, and willed her tense body to move. She hurried across the living room, through a dining room with a beautiful mahogany table and cabinet, and into the kitchen. There she found all three kittens curled on the floor in a sleeping wad of colorful fur. She slipped past them and went out the back door, hoping to find Jeremy in his shop. She needed noise, conversation, something in the *real* world to shake her out of this weird state. She wouldn't even mind if Keith saw her like this now.

As she picked her way across the arbor to the shop door, a voice suddenly called from behind. She turned to see Jeremy standing by the back door. There was a concerned, almost worried expression on his face. His hands were clasped behind his back.

"There you are!" said Keri. "I thought you were in the shop." She came toward him, and the expression on his face grew more concerned, almost frightened. His eyes were huge.

"Jeremy—what's wrong?" she asked, stopping in her tracks, wondering if he'd somehow seen his beloved dog disappear into thin air, too.

"I couldn't do it," he said.

Keri cocked her head. "What?"

"I couldn't do it."

"You couldn't do what?"

Jeremy's face flushed. "I couldn't wash your clothes."

Keri stood back, confused. "You couldn't wash my clothes?"

"You didn't use the plastic bag you'd asked for," he said.

The light bulb clicked on in Keri's mind. "Oh! I guess I didn't. I just felt so gross all of a sudden I stuck all my clothes in only one pile."

"Maybe you can wash them now," Jeremy offered. "Running the machine while you were in the shower would have ruined the water pressure anyway, right? And taken up too much hot water."

Keri looked at Jeremy intensely. He seemed so achingly sweet all of a sudden in this shy, flustered state, and all because he couldn't bring himself to look at her unmentionables.

"Right," she said, wanting to make him feel better. "True—and I needed all the hot water I could get!"

Jeremy relaxed visibly. "Good. I'll show you where I left your things when I realized… well, you know. The washer is in the basement."

"If you don't mind, I'd rather wash them at home, and return your clothes tomorrow," said Keri, glancing around. The episode with the dog had faded already, and seemed unreal. Now the worry that Keith might return and find her in this plain-scrubbed state came back full force, but she couldn't explain that to Jeremy.

"Would you mind?" she asked. "I promise I'll return the clothes. I'm tempted not to, they do fit nicely!" she added, grinning. "But I have things to take care of at home."

"Sure, keep them as long as you need," Jeremy said. "I'm glad I could help you."

With that, Jeremy led her back into the house. The kittens were still sleeping on the kitchen floor as they passed. One yawned and stretched, but did not waken. Keri kept a wary eye out for Scalawag, though, as Jeremy led her back into the hallway where the bathroom was and pointed out an old chair she hadn't paid attention to before. Her clothes rested on it, along with her lone shoe. A paper grocery bag sat on the floor, awaiting the clothes.

Keri bent down and put her grimy things in the sack.

"How far away is your car?" Jeremy asked.

"Just up the street, not far," said Keri.

"I can walk you there."

"No, don't worry. I'll be fine"

Jeremy looked at her feet and raised his eyebrows. "You want to borrow a pair of tennis shoes? I'm sure they'll be too big for you, but you'll need something."

Keri glanced down at her stocking feet and nodded. "Sure."

Jeremy smiled, and left almost as soundlessly as his dog had disappeared. She no longer felt uneasy in the house. She was certain now that she'd just imagined Scalawag going into the den.

But, where was he?

A moment later, Jeremy returned with a pair of

black sneakers, and Keri put them on. If Darci could only see her now, she thought. Actually *wearing* this guy's shoes! Tennis shoes, at that. Nothing fancy.

Jeremy was right. The shoes were too big, but she was happy to have them. She wiggled her toes, enjoying the space. "I think I'm ready," she said.

"Just click your feet together three times, and repeat 'there's no place like home—there's no place like home,'" Jeremy said.

She laughed. "It's not quite that easy."

Jeremy led her to the front door and they stepped out on the porch together. She squinted, the sun seeming unnaturally bright after the relative dimness within the home, then she turned eye to eye to Jeremy.

"I'll bring the clothes back as soon as I can, and we'll talk about the bookcase."

Jeremy nodded. "Sounds good."

Keri waved farewell and took off down the cobblestone path in her floppy shoes. When she returned to the road, she looked apprehensively both ways for any sign of Keith's vehicle returning, but no cars were in sight. Good!

Keri glanced back once at the house, and saw Jeremy still standing by the front door, watching her leave. Next to him, sitting calmly, sat Scalawag.

Chapter 6

"I can't pretend anymore, Darci," Steven said. His voice was grim. "I'm just not ready to be a father-figure yet, especially not to Nathan. He needs more attention than I could ever offer. I'm sorry."

Darci's lower lip wobbled as she watched Steven head to the front door. He walked slowly, but decisively. His back was ramrod straight as he turned around and set his cool gray eyes on her. "I hope you understand."

Darci said nothing. Every muscle in her body was rigid and her throat too swollen to speak. She gazed at him in frozen disbelief.

Steven's eyes averted from her, then looked off into space. "It's been fun, but it's over. Tell Nathan goodbye for me." With that, he opened the door, and without a backward glance, left. The door shut with a resounding thud.

Darci backed up slowly, and feeling the sofa against the back of her legs, fell into it. She stared ahead, still stiff with shock, at the closed door. It was many minutes later before tears came to her eyes. Soon, although she fought it, she was wracked with sobs.

She'd thought Steven was the best man she'd dated yet! No one had come this close to being as wonderful as Nathan's father, Jonathon, had been. Jonathon was gone. He'd left her even before Nathan was born. Said he was dangerous, had psychological problems and the baby wouldn't be safe around him. Darci had never seen any signs of emotional illness from Jonathon, at least not until she became pregnant. Then, he had changed. He became moody and silent with occasional outbursts, even slapped her around once—only once—then left. He'd moved to the west coast, saying it was for her own good, hers, and the child's. Until then, he'd been wonderful.

They'd had four special, very beautiful years together. They were to be married as soon as Jonathon got the promotion he'd been promised.

The promotion came, but the proposal did not. There were always excuses, good excuses for postponing the wedding, but never reasons good enough to schedule it.

It seemed a child wasn't a good enough reason. She had not, as he had implied, gotten pregnant to trap him. Having a baby had terrified her, too. She had grown up an only child and her parents were far away; there was no help. She didn't know how to handle a baby. Those first few years without Jonathon had been the most difficult of her life, but she'd gotten through them. Nathan was a handful, though; he needed a father figure.

Two hundred dollars a month in child support, express from California, could not buy her poor child a relationship with his father. The stinger was, two years ago, Jonathon had gotten married. He now had a one-year-old daughter and seemed to be doing fantastic.

New tears came to Darci's eyes. How unfair it all was! Maybe Jonathon hadn't been so great after all in those early years. Maybe William, Randy, Seth, and even Steven hadn't been, either.

Maybe *she* had been the problem. It seemed she couldn't pick a decent man if her life—or her son's—depended on it.

Darci collected herself as much as she could and finally got to her feet. She wiped away most of her tears and walked down the hallway of her plush condo and eased her son's bedroom door open. She peered in at him and slipped over to his bedside, staring down at the sleeping child.

He was deep asleep, snoring lightly because of a stuffed nose. He looked so sweet—a dark-haired, alabaster skinned cherub with a fluffy stuffed dog cuddled in his arms. He seemed so innocent, so helpless. And, he was. But he wasn't an easy child to care for.

He could be loud. He had tantrums. At six years old, he'd already had discipline problems in kindergarten. He wouldn't listen to the teacher, wanted to be his own boss. Wanted to be the boss of the other children in the class as well, so he bullied them.

"Oh, Nathan," Darci whispered, and tears once again formed in her eyes. "What am I supposed to do?"

She'd never had a maternal instinct, so to speak. She did her best, but knew she needed help. None of her many boyfriends had been much help, even the ones who'd been divorced and had kids of their own.

Why couldn't she find a decent man?

Darci stepped back out of the room and quietly closed the door. She folded her arms and wandered aimlessly around the condo, staring blankly at the walls, the furniture, the artwork and pottery. It was a lovely home, polished and modern, upscale. Just like the men she dated.

So what was wrong?

Maybe it was time to stop looking at shoes and wallets and look a little deeper, said something in her mind, but she had no idea what that meant.

She wasn't sure she was ready to know. What would Keri think of her?

Chapter 7

Andy was flat on his back under the car, changing the oil, when he noticed the feet standing next to him; jeans and worn hiking boots. He pushed the dolly out from under his car and looked up at the stranger.

"Excuse me," a young thirty-ish man said, "I was looking for Keri Ferrita. Do you know if she's home?"

Andy looked at the man's hopeful face, and noticed a gift-bag of some sort in his hand.

Oh no, the 'Man-Eat-a' has struck again, he thought. This guy probably didn't have a chance. Too short. Too 'tree huggerish.'

"She's here," said Andy, sitting up and wiping his brow. "Inside somewhere. I'll take you in. I need a drink, anyway." He got to his feet. "By the way, I'm Andy Wood, Keri's brother-in-law. I'd shake your hand, but I'm pretty grimy."

"I'm Jeremy Quinn."

"Oh—yeah! The guy who made the crib," Andy said. "We love it. We hope to have a baby in it within the next few days. You're quite talented."

"Thank you."

"So," Andy continued. "You're here to see Keri this time?"

"She stopped by a few days ago, needing a bookcase built." Jeremy held up the bag. "She accidentally left something at the house."

Andy looked at the bag, then at Jeremy. "She

wanted a bookcase?" he asked, surprised.

Jeremy simply smiled.

"Oh." Andy paused. He wiped his hands on his coveralls. *A bookcase?* Keri liked to read, but she already had furniture stored all over the country. He couldn't imagine her wanting anything else, especially since she was basically homeless at the moment. Where would she put it? It didn't make sense. His mind whirled as he looked at Jeremy. Maybe, just maybe, he thought. Maybe it was really *Jeremy* Keri was interested in. He didn't seem to be her type at all, but maybe that was a good sign. Her 'type' had certainly never worked out before. Suddenly, he smiled. "Come on," he said, "I'll take you inside." As they headed from the driveway to a side door, he added, "Keri's something, isn't she? Never seen someone with so much energy. I swear she has springs inside of her instead of bones."

Jeremy laughed. "She's unique," he said.

"She's so different from Kelly, my wife," said Andy. "Kelly is more laid back, logical. Keri is spur-of-the-moment, high-strung. It's hard to believe they're sisters."

"Opposites can complement each other," said Jeremy.

"Sure they can," said Andy. "But they can fight like cats and dogs, too."

Jeremy tilted his head oddly.

"It's kind of fun sometimes," Andy said in a knowing whisper.

A moment later, they reached the door and Andy stepped inside. "Kelly and Katie are out shopping, but Keri is around someplace," he said.

"Keri!" he called. "You have company!"

"Maybe she's busy," Jeremy said nervously. "I probably shouldn't have dropped by unannounced like this."

Andy waved that thought aside. “She likes spontaneity. It’s her middle name. Keri!” he shouted once more.

They waited.

Jeremy clutched the bag tighter. Maybe this hadn’t been a good idea; he probably should have called first, even if he was returning her…

“I’m here,” came Keri’s voice from somewhere below.

A second later, Jeremy heard footsteps rapidly coming up a staircase and then Keri appeared, a white towel wrapped around her head and an oversized, yellow robe wrapped around her body. She was visibly startled to see Jeremy.

Jeremy glanced at his watch, suddenly wondering if it was really morning or afternoon. Obviously, Keri had just come out of the shower.

It was two-thirty in the afternoon.

“Every time you see me I’m a mess!” said Keri. She came closer, obviously not too shy to talk to him, or to explain. “I was mowing the lawn and got hot and itchy. I’m surprised to see you here! Do you want your clothes back?”

Andy threw up his arms. “Whoa!” he said, “I don’t think I need to hear this… I’m leaving now. You two have fun!”

Jeremy felt his face grow hot as Andy went back outside, ignoring Keri’s cry of “It’s all very innocent!”

They just stood staring at each other.

“So,” Jeremy said after finally getting his mouth to work. “How… do you think the turtle is?”

Keri gave him a confused look, then suddenly brightened. “Oh! The one I rescued. I think he’s okay. There was another turtle near us when I fell. I’m sure they had a good reptilian chuckle over it.”

Jeremy gazed at her and grew flustered. He had no idea what to say. He wasn't usually this dopey, but she held a strange fascination for him, no matter how she looked. Covered in balloons, mud, or a floppy robe and towel.

"I have something for you," he suddenly blurted, and held out the hand with the bag.

Keri came closer and took it. "What is it?" She peered in, and her eyes grew huge. She put her hand in and drew the object out.

"It's my shoe!" she exclaimed. She looked at it in wonder, toyed with it, turned it up and down and over.

"Scalawag found it," Jeremy said. "He seemed to know right where to go. I cleaned it as much as I could."

"I can't believe how good it looks—it's like new!" Keri said. She looked at Jeremy, then the shoe, and back to Jeremy again.

"I hope you didn't throw its mate away," said Jeremy, and then looked down at the floor, wondering why he said that.

"No, no, it's around someplace. Probably with the rest of your stuff, which I did wash by the way."

"I'm in no hurry for it, that's not why I'm here," he managed to say. "I was just in the area, delivering something. I remembered I had the shoe so I stopped in."

"Oh," Keri said, "well then, want to stay a while? I'll go down and clean up, and we can talk about the bookshelf."

Jeremy gave her a puzzled look. "Bookshelf, or bookcase?"

Keri looked momentarily lost. Then, "Bookcase, I mean. Quite a difference, isn't there?"

Jeremy nodded politely. "Sometimes. But whatever you really need is fine." She smiled; she had a delightful smile, and Jeremy's knees grew rubbery.

"I live downstairs. In the *basement*," Keri said,

emphasizing the word 'basement' in a spooky way. "Why don't you come on down and relax while I change."

"That'd be fine."

Keri turned and led him through the kitchen and down a hallway, stopping to open a door. "Be careful," she said, "the stairs are steep." She switched on a light, and they headed down a bank of steps that were heavily carpeted, but seemed like they'd be a nightmare to climb up and down all day.

Keri held out her arms. "This is my domain when I'm in town. Kelly and Andy always let me stay here, long as I want, because I do a lot of work for them. I like to carry my weight."

"When you're in town?" Jeremy asked, looking around. It was no ordinary basement, but a well-furnished walkout with a living area, and kitchenette. Sun streamed in a huge picture window in front of a round table by the kitchenette, creating a warm, golden hue. The place seemed very comfortable.

Keri explained. "I'm kind of a gypsy, always moving around. I'm thankful I have someplace to hang my hat when I need to, though."

"This is nice," said Jeremy. "Everyone should have a place to return home to. How long do you plan on staying here?"

She shrugged. "Hard to tell. I've been here for a few months already. I should probably either look for a place of my own in the area, or get on with it."

"On with what?"

"Oh—life, I guess." Keri seemed eager to change the topic, as she folded her arms and looked at him. "By the way, that's quite a pretty little abode you live in too. I love all the plants and flowers, and that arbor is great! It feels like an enchanted forest over there."

"I love it," said Jeremy. "I grew up there. My folks

owned it. They're retired now and live in Georgia. I kind of took over the shop for my dad."

"Your dad was a wood-worker, too?"

"My dad and my grandfather. I guess it's in the blood."

"So," said Keri, "how does Keith fit in all this? He told me he's an actor. Now here he is, helping out his cousin in a woodshop in Michigan."

Jeremy shrugged. "He's just laying low, trying to reevaluate some things in his life. Although we're total opposites, we've always gotten along pretty well on the occasions we've seen each other."

"That's kind of like Kelly and me," said Keri. "I'm just hanging out, too. When—do you think Keith is going back to California—or is he?"

"Hard to tell. He's got a lot to work out first. Hey," Jeremy added, "why don't you go ahead and change into some clothes? You don't look too comfortable. I can hold my own for a little while. I promise I won't break or steal anything."

"I trust you," said Keri. "You trusted me alone in your home, and I trust you alone here in Kelly's." She went over to the table by the window. "There's a refrigerator right over there, help yourself to something to drink. I think the only food I have is cheese and pickles right now, but be my guest. You can root around for anything you might want. I'll be back in a few minutes."

"Thank you," said Jeremy. He watched Keri as she left, disappearing around the paneled corner of what he assumed to be a bedroom. He sighed happily, relishing the afterglow of her presence. It'd been a long time since he had felt this way, and though he wasn't quite sure what this 'way' was, it felt good. It was like being a kid again, when the world was exciting and full of possibilities and adventure. Maybe the dark days were finally over. He knew it was silly to be this optimistic all of a sudden—he remembered how fast things could change.

Still, it felt good for now, and he was glad for it.

Jeremy turned and looked out the window. He squinted, and the outdoors came into focus. A freshly cut lawn sloped down to a small barn and a few other outbuildings. Tall trees framed a large pasture area on one side of the barn; to the other side was a large vegetable garden. Rolling hills and woods filled in the distance. It was beautiful country, just like he loved.

Then Jeremy turned his attention to the refrigerator; he was a bit thirsty, and Keri did tell him to help himself. Normally, he'd feel odd rummaging through a stranger's icebox, but he had the feeling Keri expected him to and might be disappointed if he didn't. He opened it and chuckled, finding reasonably bare shelves with the exception of two jars of pickles, one Polish and one Kosher, and a variety of cheeses in different wrappers and containers. There were also a few cans of diet cola on the top shelf, which he thought odd. Keri was thin enough to be called skinny. Perhaps she preferred the taste of diet pop, maybe it tasted better with all her cheese.

He took out a can of pop and was just opening it when he heard her call to him.

"Sorry there's no beer. You'll have to ask Andy for that."

Jeremy turned toward her, and nearly dropped his can.

Keri was standing several yards away in a Raggedy-Ann outfit. "You've never seen me totally normal, so I thought I shouldn't break the trend now," Keri said, coming closer.

"Are you sure this isn't the read you, when you're not 'clowning around?'" Jeremy asked. He pulled a chair out and sat down, laughing. This lady was full of surprises!

"Actually, I wore it one Halloween," said Keri, pulling off the wig and flinging it over a sofa as she came and stood next to him. "The wig had to go. It was too close to being like my own hair."

Jeremy looked at her and grinned. Her eyes sparkled light green in the sunlight, and her smile was genuine. Even with giant red freckles drawn on her thin face and her hair flattened from the wig, she was beautiful. The denim pullover she wore over a pink polka-dot blouse created an intoxicatingly sweet image.

"Glad to see you helped yourself to a drink," Keri said, opening the fridge herself. "It bugs me when people are too timid to do anything."

Jeremy watched her pull out a jar of pickles, the Polish, and set them on the table. She twisted the lid open and sat down across from him.

"Want one?" she asked, plucking a dill from the jar. "These are the best."

"No thanks," said Jeremy. "I like pickles, but not with pop."

"Aw, come on—pickles taste good with everything." Keri popped the dill in her mouth and crunched off a bite. "What is your favorite kind?"

Without thinking, Jeremy replied, "Midgets."

She looked at him with a rather stunned expression. He could tell she was unsure if he was making a joke or not. She smiled, but said nothing, eyeing him carefully for a clue.

"I was called a midget all through school," Jeremy offered, "then I grew a few more inches, so I guess I've risen to the realms of dwarf now."

Keri shook her head and laughed. He laughed with her. He'd never been overly sensitive about his height, and he wasn't going to start now, even with her.

"You're not that short," said Keri. "I doubt you're shorter than me, and I'm five-five. I've seen shorter." She paused, and then added, "Come on, stand up. Let's check."

She got up and ushered Jeremy to his feet. She led him into the living area and pointed out a large mirror over a buffet. They both stood in front of it, staring at their image together from the waist up.

"See," said Keri, "we're the same size. You may even be a little taller than me."

"I've got boots on," said Jeremy.

"Take 'em off."

Jeremy shrugged, and kicked off the boots.

"Now, turn around," said Keri.

Jeremy turned away from her, and the next thing he knew, Keri was pressing her back against him. The shock of her touch was a pleasant surprise.

"Now we're cheek to cheek," said Keri, laughing. "Look in the mirror now!"

Jeremy looked, and blushed. Yes, they were definitely cheek to cheek, the floppy-haired Irishman and Raggedy Ann. They were also the same height, perfectly. Suddenly he felt uneasy and stepped away. He turned to her and smiled. Unsure of what to do, he bent and put his boots back on.

"You're kind of bashful, aren't you?" Keri said.

"Not normally, no," he replied.

"You certainly don't have to be shy with me," said Keri. "I'm an open book. Just relax. I feel comfortable with you, like we're old friends already. That's a different feeling for me, and I like it. I'm glad you're not weird about being short and that we can talk about it. Just loosen up a little more."

"I'll try."

"I know," said Keri, eyeing the discarded wig on the sofa. "Maybe this will make you taller." She grabbed the wig and hurried over to Jeremy, raising it in the air. "Try this on!"

Jeremy's eyes rounded. "Oh, no." He raised his arms. "I don't look good in braids."

"Oh, come on." She attempted to put it on his head, but Jeremy ducked. She tried again, and soon they were weaving around each other, laughing. Finally Jeremy broke away and ran to the kitchen table, but Keri was right behind him, wig held high. She chased him around the table a few times before he noticed the door and ran towards it. He was able to turn the knob and squeeze through before she could reach him. He then held the door firmly shut with both hands. He could feel Keri tugging on it. *My, she's strong!*

"I give up!" Keri called, "Come on, open up!"

"Not until you promise not to crown me with that thing!"

"I'll think about it."

A sudden growl behind Jeremy caused him to loosen his grip on the doorknob, and the door flung open. Keri stepped out just as he was frozen in place by a large dog baring his fangs, five feet away. Jeremy loved dogs and was used to them, but this one was huge, and obviously protective. "Calm down, fella," he said, looking down, making sure not to make eye contact. "I'm not hurting anyone."

"It's all right, Rover," Keri said, hurrying to the dog. "He's my buddy. His name is Jeremy." The dog visibly mellowed at her words, and slowly began to wag his bushy tail.

"Didn't something similar to this happen a few days ago, just in reverse?" Jeremy asked.

"Yes—Scalawag scared the liver out of me when I first saw him," she said, squatting to pet the dog. "Especially with only three legs, one eye, and one ear."

"He's not exactly the kind of pet they use for

children's therapy, although I've thought of it."

Keri straightened. "You have?"

Jeremy shrugged. He had thought of using Scalawag in that way. He'd seen things like that help before, but the dog might do more harm than good. He might actually scare kids. He carefully bent down to pet Rover.

"I think Scalawag's looks might set people back," he said. "Now, if he looked like Rover here, it might be okay, as long as he didn't get too protective of the kids."

"You've actually thought of using Scalawag as a therapy pet, but chickened out?" Keri asked.

"Chickened out?"

"I bet kids would connect with him. Especially kids in physical therapy. They'd see that he's been through the wringer, too."

Jeremy stood. "You think so? I've wondered about that, but I didn't want to frighten anyone."

"Sure, he'd help. You might have to sneak him in, though. Not everyone would agree with us." She paused, then added, "Maybe we could put a harness on him and sneak him in some hospital and say he's a guide dog."

Jeremy chuckled. "Now that'd truly be a case of the blind leading the blind."

"You never know, it might work." She finished petting the dog and sat down on a bench swing near the door. Rover sniffed Jeremy a few times, and then ambled away on one of his mysterious country-dog pursuits. Keri patted the bench next to her.

"Here, have a seat. It's fun."

Jeremy shrugged and sat next to her. They began to swing rhythmically in the sun, a slow, lazy pace.

"I'm still thinking about taking Scalawag to see the kids in rehab," Keri said. "It seems like an exciting idea. I've never done anything like that before, have you?"

Jeremy watched the ground slide back and forth

beneath them. His throat went tight all of a sudden and heaviness descended upon him. He couldn't speak, couldn't quite talk about what had happened yet. At least, not with someone like Keri, someone he wanted to get to know without burdening her with his memories.

"Yeah, I have," he finally said. "But it's been awhile."

Keri was studying his face, but Jeremy couldn't look at her; he felt his eyes dampening, ready to give him away. Suddenly he got to his feet.

"About this bookcase," he said, walking away, as if deep in thought. "When would you need it?"

Keri didn't answer right away. He could hear the creak of the swing still rocking; otherwise, silence. At last he turned to look at her.

"I'll go with you," she said. "We can take Scalawag to St. Therese's Rehabilitation Center, walk him around outside and let the people getting a breath of fresh air choose to come to him or not. Maybe he could even wear an eye-patch, like a pirate. I could dress up like something, too, and maybe even you…."

Jeremy lowered his head, and ran his hands across his face. Somehow he found himself smiling again. Maybe," he said. And, maybe he could. If Keri was with him, it might actually be fun, might work out okay.

Keri sighed, looked dreamily out at the countryside and motioned for Jeremy to sit next to her again. Without a problem, he did.

"Jeremy," she said, still gazing down at the barn as two horses came out and began to graze. "I don't think I really need a bookcase. I'm sorry. I guess I got too excited by your work. After Keith showed me that baby crib—the one with the canopy and all the carvings, I realized my wants were way out of my league with my needs. At least, for now. Until I'm more settled." She looked at him hopefully. "Do you understand?"

Jeremy relaxed more than he had all day. "Sure," he said, looking directly at her. "That's fine. I keep busy with a lot of small things. That mahogany crib was one of a kind. It was a lot of fun, but kind of a monstrosity when you think of it. The money those people spent on that could... well, could do a lot of good in a lot of different ways."

"That's for sure!" said Keri. "Keith said it was made out of some kind of special kind of wood, too. I can't remember what. Does he help you make furniture, too?"

"No, he's not handy in that way, but it's nice to have someone around for company, sometimes. Cats and dogs are fine, for a time, but people are what one needs for true companionship in the long run."

Jeremy took a deep breath, amazed that he had made such a feeling known. But, he had, and it was about time. It was about time for a lot of things. He looked back to Keri, and saw she was smiling slightly, leaning back on the bench in a casual manner. Not at all frightening or intimidating. She was a goofball, that was for certain, but having a childlike zest for life was a wonderful thing. He hadn't run across it many times, and it brought back something younger and fresher in him. How he'd like to see her more often, he thought. He began to imagine it, and felt boldness returning.

"Keri," he said, "I was wondering if—" But just as he managed the first few words, the sound of a window sliding open above cut him off.

"Keri!" someone called. "Oh, there you are."

Jeremy and Keri looked up to see Andy hanging half out of a window, a cell phone in his hand.

"Someone wants to talk to you, but it could be a salesman. Want to take the call?"

"Ask who it is," Keri called up.

Andy mumbled into the phone, listened a moment,

and called back down. "Says his name is Keith. Keith Quinn."

Jeremy's throat clutched as the words sank in, and he watched Keri's eyes brighten.

"Toss the phone down!" she said.

Andy dropped the phone, and Keri caught it easily. She turned to Jeremy. "We were just talking about him! Maybe he wants to talk to you—does he know you're here?"

Jeremy shrugged, unable to speak as Keri talked into the phone. "Hello? Yes, this is Keri. I remember! Sure. That party was some coincidence, wasn't it?"

As Keri talked on, Jeremy's former buoyancy began to ebb. Then a new heaviness crept in as he watched Keri's smile flash while she spoke to his cousin, as he saw her sit straighter in her seat. He looked away.

"Sounds good," Keri was saying, finishing the conversation. "I'll see you Saturday night, then. I've never been to that play. Yes, okay. Goodbye." With that, Keri clicked off the phone and set it in her lap.

"How about that," she said, looking at Jeremy. "Your cousin called *me*. That's coincidence, isn't it?"

Jeremy smiled. "Yes, I guess it is."

"We're going to see '*Les Misérables*' this Saturday night. That is, Keith says, if you don't have too much work for him to do."

Jeremy shook his head. "No—go have fun. He needs to get out more." He got to his feet, feeling weak and deflated, but he managed to smile. "I better go now. I have more errands to run."

"Oh—let me get your clothes first," said Keri, getting to her feet too. "I'll be right back." She went inside the house, and suddenly it became very lonely outside. Jeremy stared at the empty glider, rocking slowly and smoothly toward a stop. After the creaking stopped and the chair was still, he remained there;

motionless, practically invisible. Smaller than he'd felt since grade school.

Jeremy wasn't sure which chisel would work best to carve the acanthus leaves on the table leg before him. He sat on his stool, staring at his assortment of tools, and then chose another one. He positioned the walnut piece between his knees and the bench and began to chisel away, first with slow and precise movements, then faster and faster. A flurry of wood shavings fluttered to the floor.

"Jeremiah Quinn, it looks almost like you're attacking that wood instead of carving it," came a voice from behind.

Jeremy ignored Keith's observation and kept carving. He could sense Keith approaching, and soon his cousin was leaning against the workbench next to him, his arms folded.

"You think I sabotaged you, don't you?" he asked.

Jeremy stopped carving, but did not look straight at him. "You knew I was going to see Keri," he said.

"Yeah, to talk business, I assumed."

Jeremy made no reply.

"I'd been thinking of asking her out ever since I met her," Keith continued. "I had no idea you were interested. I mean, it's about time you did go out. It would be good for you. Hannah and Seth have been gone almost three years." He lowered his voice. "But Keri Ferrita is not your type. It's as plain as that."

Jeremy turned slowly on his stool and glared at his tanned, handsome cousin.

"Not my type?" he said. "I don't know how you think you know what my type is, and I have to wonder why you believe she's more your type."

Keith sighed and uncrossed his arms.

"Jeremy, open your eyes. Keri is out of your league.

She's high-maintenance and classy, she wouldn't understand or fit in your world."

"I'm not sure we're talking about the same person," said Jeremy. "A person who dresses up as a clown, rescues turtles off the street, and chases me around with a Raggedy Ann wig is more *your* type? You call that high-maintenance and classy?"

Keith eyed him speculatively, and just shook his head.

Jeremy knew what he was thinking, that Keri was just feeling sorry for him, humoring him. But Jeremy hadn't gotten that impression of Keri at all. She seemed *real.*

"I don't want to hurt you," said Keith. "Like they say, all is fair in love and war. If you want to date her too, be my guest, but I'm not giving in."

Jeremy eyed him coolly, waiting a long moment before finally replying. "I doubt Jamie thinks all is fair in love and war," he finally said.

Keith threw up his hands and rolled his eyes. "I knew it! I should have guessed. You're going to try to impose your morals on me. We don't think the same way, cousin, and let it go at that."

"I think Jamie and I think the same way."

"You don't really know her. Or the kids." Keith's face reddened. "We're separated. I wouldn't doubt she's filing for divorce as we speak. We can do what we want, whenever we want."

"And you think dating another woman while you're still legally married is going to ever help work things out again? Does Keri know about Jamie…or about little Amber and David?"

"It doesn't matter."

"I think it might matter to her."

"And because of your own goody-two-shoes morals, I bet you feel the need to tell her yourself," said

Keith. “Stay out of it. You’re just jealous. Always have been.”

“This has *nothing* to do with jealousy—and you know it. There isn’t a whole lot I admire about you, Keith, and Keri has nothing to do with it. I hoped to help you by letting you live here, letting you think this through. But all you’ve done is take advantage of me.”

“Take advantage of you? I work my tail off for you, and for what? Nothing!”

“Free food and board is nothing? And do you call helping me lift tables and cabinets into the truck for deliveries working your tail off?”

“I do more than that, and I was there when you needed me after Hannah died. I was there when Seth died. Didn’t that matter to you at all? Doesn’t it count for something?”

Jeremy whirled away from Keith and rested against the workbench. His arms trembled. His mind clouded as memories rushed in, rendering him unable to talk or defend himself. Eventually he felt Keith’s hand on his shoulder.

“I’m sorry,” Keith said, “I shouldn’t have brought all that up. I know you’ve been through hell. Now I’m going through a bit of my own personal hell, and I could use some support. I know you don’t agree with what I’m doing, but please, don’t sabotage it, either. I’ll tell Keri about my family if and when it becomes necessary. I promise.”

Slowly, Jeremy nodded. He felt drained all of a sudden. “Keri and I did talk about taking Scalawag to see the kids at the rehab together,” he said at last.

Keith looked confused. “You’re taking that flea-bitten wreck to see sick kids? Wouldn’t he scare them to death?”

“Keri thinks they’d identify with him.”

Keith was quiet a moment, then, “Well, whatever.

Be her friend, hang out a little, I don't care. I don't own her. Just stay cool about my circumstances, okay?"

Again, Jeremy nodded. "It's your business."

"It is. So—we're agreed?"

Jeremy sighed. "We're agreed."

"Good. See you later then, I've got some planning to do." Keith gave Jeremy a friendly punch on the shoulder and left the shop.

Jeremy turned back to his work.

Chapter 8

Keri stared at her reflection in the mirror for a long time before deciding she looked as good as she ever would. She smiled at herself, making sure her teeth looked bright beneath the chosen shade of lipstick. The new mascara made her lashes so long she could practically dust the room with them, and her hair gleamed in its flip-floppy, sassy manner. Irresistible.

She knew she was being vain—oh, so vain—but this night was going to be one of the most important nights in her life. The butterflies in her stomach spun faster than they ever had before a date. This should be a milestone.

She had even gone shopping for an outfit with Darci.

Darci had impeccable taste for clothes and fashion in general, and Keri knew she'd benefit from her friend's guidance. Yet, oddly, Darci had seemed quiet and distracted most of the time. At lunch, Keri had finally gotten her to open up. It hadn't been too much of a shock to Keri.

Steven had broken up with her. He said he wouldn't be a good father figure for Nathan.

Keri knew that it'd be difficult for most men to accept a boy as troubled as Nathan, let alone love him, and she knew Darci knew it, too. It was something they didn't talk about, though. It was just too depressing.

Keri left the bathroom and slipped into a slinky jade

green dress. Lacy black sandals finished the ensemble. She stopped to check herself in the full-length mirror on the bathroom door and wondered what she would do in Darci's position. Being beautiful, sharp-minded and bold was a plus for Darci, but having a young son as part of the package, especially a handful like Nathan, would make it nearly impossible to find that right man. She thought of how lucky she was to be dating Keith tonight—*the* one she'd been waiting for. She'd even told Darci that. Perhaps it would have been better if she'd kept that to herself, because afterward Darci's mood had grown somber. Finally Darci said the thing that Keri thought she'd never hear from her friend, something that kept coming back to Keri's mind.

"Keri… maybe I've been looking at the wrong kind of men. Maybe it's time to find someone less 'perfect,'" she'd said, rolling her eyes at the word 'perfect,' "and more down to earth. Maybe even someone chubby, or bald, or short, but someone with a good heart who would be a good dad for Nathan."

Keri had nearly fallen out of her chair.

To think Darci would allow herself to—in her own words—*settle*, stunned Keri, but she did have that little boy to think of. Would Keith date her if she had a child? Would it completely turn him off, or did he like kids? At this point, she had no idea. She liked to think she was irresistible, no matter what. A conceited thought, she knew, but a thought that she'd grown up with. A notion she'd never really had to test.

Poor Darci. And, poor Nathan. Keri wished she could help them somehow. She'd put her mind to it, later. For now, the doorbell was ringing! Keri snatched up her purse and hurried up the steep stairway to the main level of the house. She stood behind the closed door and waited; couldn't appear too eager. She heard the doorbell ring again, the door squeaked open and

Kelly invited someone in. Keri's nerves prickled as she looked at her watch: five-ten. Keith was a few minutes late. That was good he didn't want to appear too eager, either. He knew and recognized *the game*.

"Keri!" Kelly called, "Keith's here."

Keri waited a few moments before actually opening the door, then finally cracked it a little and called, "I'll be there in just a few more minutes." Then she stood and waited once more. When an appropriate time had passed, she held her breath, straightened, pushed the door opened and entered.

Sitting calmly at the kitchen table, Keith nearly took her breath away. He wore a pale blue shirt that matched his eyes, and they seemed to glow behind his tan. His white-blonde hair was combed smoothly back over his head in a smart, sexy style. His smile was, without question, magic as he greeted her.

"Hello again, Keri. You look like a million bucks."

"So do you."

Keith stood as Keri approached. He seemed taller than ever in dark blue slacks. A taupe belt matched his shoes, *expensive* shoes, she noted. Darci would approve.

"What time does the play start?" Kelly asked, waddling over to the table with her hands on her expanding belly.

"At eight," Keith said. "That'll give us time to stop for a bite in the big city, first, if you're interested," he added, raising his eyebrows at Keri.

"I'm always interested in food," Keri said.

"Well, let's be on our way, then."

Kelly bade them farewell as they exited the house and walked over to Keith's SUV.

"It's not as fancy as your Corvette over there," Keith said, eyeing Keri's car parked in a turnaround area of the driveway, "but at least it's masculine." He threw back his shoulders and puffed out his chest, making Keri laugh as he opened her door for her.

"You're either masculine in California, or you're a girly man," he added, sliding into the driver's seat. "I didn't want anyone to ever wonder about me."

"I wouldn't have," Keri said. "I'd lived out there long enough to tell the difference."

"That's right—you did. Seems we have a lot in common, doesn't it? Started out here in the Midwest, then turned our sights on bigger things."

"And now we're back 'home' again," said Keri.

"But not forever," Keith added.

The chit-chat on the way to the restaurant mostly revolved around each of their respective escapades with the rich and famous—or just the rich—in Los Angeles. Keri loved to bring up her knowledge of who-knows-who, and Keith loved to top it. It was an exciting ride. When they reached their destination, a new French restaurant, and were shown to their table, people eyed them as though they were celebrities. Of course, Keith did have some background in film, and a starry-eyed woman recognized him from his work on the cable show. He happily signed an autograph, which had even more customers eyeing him in that curious, awestruck manner.

Keri had been with well-recognized people before, but never so close to her hometown roots. The feeling was exhilarating. Keith ordered both of their meals in French, leaving Keri to wonder just what it was she was about to eat, but she wasn't about to complain since it wasn't the pickles and cheese that usually filled her own refrigerator.

Their dishes arrived shortly, and Keri discovered that far from french fries or french toast—she was looking at a smorgasbord of delights, complete with a long-forgotten favorite, crème brûlée.

She never felt so gloriously giddy in her life. Then

it was on to the show, where she could hardly keep her attention on the actors. Keith's masculine presence next to her made it impossible to think about anything else. She felt linked to him, somehow, and her hand itched for him to take and hold it. He kept it to himself, though, which was maddeningly sly of him. He did, however, whisper to her a few times during the performance and the feeling of his breath in her ear had her floating out of her seat until the end of the show.

By the time they reached the lobby, Keri was too enchanted to speak and found herself nodding in a wooden manner whenever Keith spoke to her. Her throat didn't relax until she excused herself to use the restroom to get a grip on reality. It was almost a relief to break away from him for a moment and allow herself to float back down to earth for a breather.

She was just about ready to leave when she felt the glare of a woman standing in the corner of the restroom. Keri was stunned to see such an expression on the woman…it was Darci.

Keri approached her hesitantly, and found the stony look in Darci's eyes was not one of wrath but rather one of someone fighting tears.

"How do you do it, Keri?" Darci asked. She slumped back against the sink and folded her arms. Her lower lip was visibly trembling. "Just how do you do it?"

"I don't know what you mean," Keri said. "Do what? Why are you acting so strange?"

Darci turned and faced the mirror and made subtle attempts at adjusting her hair before replying. "You know—how do you get guys so easily? I just saw you with Keith. Everyone was looking at him—and you. You have the most wonderful life. You make it all look so easy."

A small tear slipped from Darci's eye. She quickly

brushed it away and fumbled in her purse for her makeup.

Keri stiffened, unsure of how to reply, unsure if the statement was a compliment or an insult…but as she studied Darci's troubled face and remembered her recent breakup with Steven, she softened.

"I think I just finally got lucky," Keri said. "It hasn't always been easy to be me, like you say. Kelly thinks I have the saddest life in the world."

At that, Darci managed a weak grin. "Words only a true sister could say. One that has a great husband, a kid and another on the way."

"Any moment now."

Darci nodded and sniffed back another tear.

"Who are you with tonight?" Keri asked.

Darci made another faltering grin. "My mom and dad are home visiting. Dad is watching Nathan. Mom called today and thought it would be good for me to dress up and get out.

"That's nice of her. She's right, too. You don't always need some gorgeous man at your side to be happy."

Darci grimaced, and Keri quickly continued. "It's only luck I'm with Keith tonight, Darci. Most of the guys I date I end up not being able to tolerate. They drive me crazy. I don't know what it is, and I do get depressed sometimes." Keri paused, wondering where her words were coming from. "I do get lonely, really lonely. *Scary* lonely. Kelly thinks I'm my own worst enemy and I have some kind of kooky personality disorder. Well, maybe I do."

Darci looked Keri full in the face, fascinated. Keri held her full attention. She could feel her face redden and her throat grow tight once again, this time not from Keith, but from an awful truth.

"I've seen shrinks when I was away, Darci," she

said under her breath, "I've had times when I didn't think I could go on being me. I couldn't stand being alone. Sometimes I even…I even hated myself. So, please, don't think I've always had it all together, that I have it made. Tonight is the first night I've really felt hope in years."

Keri's voice trembled and she looked away. Tears blurred her eyes but she forced them away. She took a deep breath and turned back to her friend. "Nathan may have troubles, but he's *yours*. He'll always be your little boy. You'll always have someone who loves you and depends on you your whole life. And that's a lot, it's a whole lot. I've envied you over that for years. Soon you're going to find a nice man, a good man, and your life will be wonderful, light-years ahead of mine."

Darci blinked back a few tears as Keri stared at her. "I don't know what to say," she finally mumbled. "Keri… I never knew you felt that way."

"I do. You're going to be all right, kiddo. So go put on a happy face, and you'll grow into it. You deserve it."

Darci took a long breath and shook her head. Suddenly, she smiled. "I will. Thanks, Keri." She reached over and gently hugged her friend. "Now, I think it's about time to get back out there to my mom, and you to your hunk, before they both think we flushed ourselves to the world down under."

Keri grinned. Then both girls turned, arm in arm, and exited into the crowd.

Jeremy stood before what looked like a blank paneled wall, slowly lifted his arm and pushed on it. A perfectly disguised door eased open, and Jeremy slipped into the darkness.

He hadn't been in the secret room he'd transformed from a closet in months. He knew Scalawag still enjoyed sneaking in there to hide, and that was all right, but the room had a much more sentimental connection for Jeremy.

He paused and felt for the light switch, unsure if he really wanted to turn it on to face his past once again. He wasn't sure what drove him here in the first place. Maybe he'd been feeling a little sorry for himself, knowing Keith was out having fun tonight with Keri while he was, once again, home alone with a mutilated dog and a few zany kittens.

The animals had kept his head above water many times in the past, and he was grateful for it. But now, with a sadness dwelling inside that no animal could comfort, he flipped on the light to wallow in it. It only took a second as everything came into focus; the pictures on the walls, the letters fanned out across his desk, the toys and mementos scattered about the tiny enclosure. His shrine to Hannah and Seth. It overwhelmed him, and he was lost in the past once again.

Chapter 9

Keri was aghast.

"You're naming him *what?*"

Kelly beamed at Keri's obvious shock, and held her new baby tighter against her chest.

"His name is going to be Quentin."

"Quentin? But that's breaking tradition. It doesn't start with a 'K' like all the rest of us! Even his crib has a KW carved on it!"

"We couldn't agree on a 'K' name," Andy broke in. He leaned over and gently felt Quentin's tiny, fluffy-socked foot. "Besides, my name isn't a 'K' name. It's no big deal."

"Yes it is!" Keri exclaimed, then quickly quieted down, remembering where she was. A maternity ward in a hospital was no place to argue with her sister.

"What's mom think?" Keri asked.

"We'll see. She should be up here with Katie any moment."

"You're being so weird about this," Andy said, and Keri could tell he was irritated, but how could she explain? It would sound stupid—she knew it. How could she say, 'Well, Keith's name starts with a K, too, and it's a sign." One of the signs that finally meant this must be the man for her. Keri's toes curled just thinking of him. She looked down at Kelly's newest, red-faced arrival and tried to get Keith off her mind.

Quentin.

He looked like a normal, healthy, eight-pound little boy. She watched as both Kelly and Andy cooed over him, touched him, and spoke those sweet little meaningless words that parents murmur to their newborns. They held hands and Andy kissed Kelly's forehead. She smiled back at him and suddenly Kelly, Andy, and Quentin seemed like the only ones in the room and Keri was an outsider. She'd never considered herself a maternal person, but the feeling of not being included bothered her now.

What was going on?

A commotion at the door stirred her from her thoughts.

"Hello! Where is my new grandson hiding?" came a voice behind a wall of balloons and flowers.

"Mama!" Katie squealed beneath the balloons, and burst across the room to hug Kelly on the bed.

"How's my little Katie-did today?" Kelly asked, beaming as she enfolded the little girl in a one-armed hug. "Meet your new little brother, sweetie. Someday he'll be your best friend."

Katie's eyes bulged as she stared at the tiny, red-faced baby in Kelly's arms. Finally she turned to her dad.

"He's so *little!* When can he play with me?"

"In a few years," said Andy. "He'll grow like a weed, just like you did."

"Oh!" Katie said, still gazing in wonder at the baby.

"Hi, mom," Kelly called, and Mrs. Ferrita poked her head around the balloons to absorb the sight of her daughter and new grandson. Finally she set the balloons down and came around to the side of the bed, winking at Keri as she did.

"I almost thought you forgot about me for a moment there!"

"I can relate," said Keri with a quick grin.

Andy stepped back to let his mother-in-law reach down and gently collect the new baby in her arms.

"Oh! He's so precious," said Katherine. "Oh…what a marvelous little nose…and look at these little fingers and his little mouth and—"

"All the parts are there," Andy chuckled.

"Of course they are," Katherine cooed, and began to gently rock the baby in her arms. "He's so sweet, so tiny!"

"Mommy, what is his name?" asked Katie all of a sudden.

"Oh—oh, let us guess!" Katherine said. "It must start with a K, so we have to start there. Now, let's see. How about Kyle?"

"No, it's not Kyle," said Kelly, folding her hands together in her lap.

"Is it Kermit?" Katie asked, grinning broadly.

"Like the frog?" Kelly asked.

Katie nodded, her eyes sparkling.

"No, sweetie," Andy said, "it's not Kermit either. I don't think any of you are going to figure out this name."

"Oh, don't be silly," said Katherine. "How many K names can there be for a boy? Unless you named him one of those new, wild names like Katmandu or something as ridiculous."

"It's not ridiculous," said Kelly, a touch of anger in her voice.

Keri bit her lip from saying anything, and raised her eyebrows at her sister.

"It's…it's Kevin," said Katherine. "Or Korey, or Kramer…something like that."

"No—it's not anything like that," said Kelly.

Mrs. Ferrita began to look flustered.

"Well, how about Ken? Kenny? That's a perfectly respectable name. Come on, give me a hint."

"It's not Kenny, either," said Andy.

Katherine stopped rocking the baby and stared hard at him.

"This will be interesting," said Keri, mostly to herself.

"What's his name, mommy?" Katie asked.

Kelly and Andy looked at each other, then back to their daughter, careful not to look Katherine in the eye.

"It's Quentin, honey," Kelly said to Katie.

"Quentin," Katie repeated, not as a question but rather as a name she wanted to learn to pronounce.

Katherine gaped at Kelly.

"I told you," Keri mouthed silently to her sister.

"Kelly, dear," Katherine finally said quietly, forcing a smile, "what kind of name is that?"

"It's my grandfather's name," said Andy.

"Oh. Your *grandfather's* name." she turned to Kelly.

"Sweetie, *your* grandfather's name was Kurt. With a 'K.'"

"We like Quentin."

"And not Kurt?"

"Mo-om!"

"But we've *always* used K-names," said Katherine. "My mother, my grandmother, all down the line—for years. Your crib even has a K carved in it"

"Maybe I'm just a little tired of K's," Kelly said. "We can live with the crib."

"How about something like…" Katherine implored.

Kelly moaned. "His birth certificate already says Quentin, mom! Can't you just enjoy your grandson without getting upset? Honestly, you're just as weird about this as Keri is!"

Andy folded his arms. "Maybe even weirder."

Katie looked from her mother and father to her grandmother with a helpless expression.

"I like the name Kentin!" she said.

"Kent!" said Katherine. "How about Kent?"

"We're not naming our baby Kent!" Andy said firmly. "It's Quentin, Quentin Wood, and that's final."

"Give it up, mom," said Keri, "it is their baby."

Katherine looked at Keri with a dumbfounded expression.

"Keri, I'm surprised! Even your new boyfriend has a K-name. Keith, isn't it? Yes, that's it. There's something almost…almost magical about it, isn't there?"

Keri's eyebrows lifted. Yes, that's what she'd been thinking all along, silly as it was. All those signs pointing to Keith being *the* one. She hadn't mentioned her thoughts to anyone but Darci, and now her own mother was affirming them!

Maybe she wasn't so silly after all.

"So what if his name is Keith, it could just as well be George or Danny, because he'll soon be yesterday's news just like all the rest," said Kelly.

"You don't know that!" Keri interrupted. "This one is different."

"I doubt that."

"What do you know? You the family know-it-all?"

"Most of the time, I have to be! The rest of my family is nuts!"

"Kelly! Shame on you!" said Katherine.

Suddenly Quentin began to wail.

"Now look what's happened," said Andy. He walked around the bed to take the baby from Katherine. "I think it's time for you and Keri to leave."

"What?" asked Katherine, "I just got here!"

"Come on, mom, we'll come back later when we're all more civilized," said Keri, taking her mother's arm.

"I will not leave my grandson so soon!"

"Does Grandma really have to go?" Katie asked, wide-eyed.

"Just for a little while," said Andy, bouncing the baby and whispering to him, "Just until Quentin is settled down again. But you can stay, sweetie, and ride home with me."

The baby screamed louder.

"What's wrong with Ken-tin?" Katie cried.

"Nothing, honey," Kelly said, propping her pillows up higher, "he's just testing his lungs. Now come here, come see mama."

Katie eagerly crawled on the bed and snuggled next to her mom as Keri continued to tug Katherine's arm.

"Let's go, mom. Everything will be okay."

Reluctantly, Katherine let herself be led out the door. She blew a kiss to Katie, and Keri let go of her in the corridor.

"Honestly," said Katherine, staring into the room with her hands on her hips. "What's gotten into those two?"

With that, Andy softly shut the door. Quentin's cries became muffled, and then drained away into silence.

"Well, I never!" said Katherine.

"Let's go, mom," Keri said, gently tugging on her mother's arm. "I'll take you out to supper, and tell you all about my date with Keith—with a 'K.'"

Katherine reluctantly relented. Sighing, she said, "Well, at least someone has some sense."

Keri raised her eyebrows at that statement. Her? Having sense? It felt good to hear something like that after all these years. If it could only prove true.

Chapter 10

"Daddy—when are you coming back home to stay?" David asked, bouncing the basketball up and down on the sunny sidewalks of Los Angeles.

Keith swiped the ball from his tow-haired, seven-year old son and twirled in a circle. "I'm not sure yet," he said, expertly keeping the ball from his son. "But I wouldn't miss your birthday for the world; that's why I'm here now. Be patient, David. Everything will be okay, I promise."

With that, Keith lost his balance with the ball and David snatched it from him.

"Great steal!" Keith said, eyeing his son proudly.

"Thanks, Dad."

The two continued down the sidewalk toward home, side by side.

"Amber thinks you're staying home forever, now," David said quietly. "But she's only six. She doesn't understand these things."

Keith tousled David's hair. "But you do, don't you? You're my big man. The big man of the house when I'm not here."

"Yeah. I help mom a lot. Just like you're helping Uncle Jeremy."

"Yes. Uncle Jeremy needs my help really bad right now."

"Is he still real sad from when Aunt Hannah and Seth died? That was a long time ago. I was only four then."

Keith paused. "I think so, sometimes. He and Aunt Hannah were together since they were teenagers. He misses her a lot."

"Mom misses you a lot, too, when you're gone. I'm glad you're not dead, though."

"No, David, I plan on staying around for a while."

David's face brightened. "You are? Staying here?"

"Well—not here, not yet. Things aren't fixed enough to stay more than a few days. Your mom and I have a lot of things to talk about."

"You mean about Uncle Jeremy?"

Keith paused. "Yeah. About Uncle Jeremy."

"I hope he gets better soon, dad. I'm tired of you being gone all the time. Why doesn't Uncle Jeremy move out here, where it's warm? Mom says he doesn't like the cold and winter hurts him. He'd feel better out here."

Keith laughed at that. "Big cities would hurt him in a lot more ways than cold weather would. He's a country boy, through and through. Just like I was when I was a kid."

"You were?" David asked, incredulous.

"Oh, sure. We had dogs and cats and woods to play in. Our neighbors had a horse and a cow that shared the same pasture and were friends. I even helped bale hay one summer when I was fifteen. Sometimes I even cleaned poop out of barns for extra money."

"You cleaned up *poop*?"

"Yup. Poop as big as this basketball!" With that, Keith held the ball high in the air and twirled it on his index finger. "I didn't play ball with it, though!"

"And I bet it didn't bounce, either," said David.

"Oh, but it does. It bounces all over and you have to dodge it or get splattered."

David's eyes were huge as he stared up at his

father, a man he simply adored. "Poop does not bounce!" he finally stated.

"Well, they sure wouldn't show that part on TV westerns," said Keith, "it would make a big mess all over the camera lens."

David giggled. "Do you think you'll ever be in a western, dad? You'd be great as a cowboy. And you already know lots about horses and poop!"

Keith laughed too. "If that's all it took to get a part like that, I'd have it made."

"Look!" David suddenly said, "Mom's out in the yard. Let's tell her about the poop."

Keith looked at their small, over-priced Spanish style home and the miniscule yard Jamie was puttering around in. A stab of emotion struck him at the sight of his first love; Jamie, a tiny blonde woman with a round, cherubic face and sparkling brown eyes. She was wearing pink shorts and dopey flip-flops. Part of him longed to run to her and twirl her around in his arms, but a darker side made him slow his steps. Voices of agents and actors haunted his mind…*"She's a career immobilizer, Keith! She's plain and shy. She'll hinder you. You need the female audience to long for you—with your looks, you could be number one! You need women to believe that you're sexy, available and can attract the glamorous starlets."*

Jamie knew none of this, but it wouldn't be too much longer before she did. She wasn't stupid. She looked up and saw her husband and son approaching. She gave a forced smile.

"How did my two men do on the basketball court?"

David ran to her. "I did great, mom! Someday I'll be as tall as dad and be a star, just like he was in school." He turned to Keith. "Won't I, dad?"

"I have no doubts," Keith said, tossing the ball to him. David caught the ball easily.

"This ball is my best present," David said. "I'm going to save it forever!" He bounced it a few times on the driveway and added, "I'm going inside to play with the rest of my presents now and make sure Amber didn't break anything."

"Don't worry," said Jamie, "she's just coloring in another one of her unicorn books."

"Yuck," said David, making a face as he opened a side door into the garage and disappeared.

There was an awkward silence as Keith and Jamie stood before each other. Finally Jamie put her hands on her hips and sighed. "They grow up too fast—don't they?"

Keith raised his eyebrows. "Yeah. Seven years old now, twenty before we know it."

Jamie looked at the ground and poked at a dry patch of grass with her foot. "It was good of you to come home for his birthday. I wish you'd stay."

Keith took a long breath. "You know I can't, not yet. Jeremy needs me. I'll have to go back."

Jamie looked up. "*I* need you, and the kids need you. Jeremy is only your cousin, but we are your immediate family."

"I gave you enough money to get by for a few months. I can get you some more."

"This isn't about money!" Jamie blurted, her eyes growing moist. "What's *really* going on here, Keith? Why do you have to 'get away' so bad?"

"You know why. It's the work, it's driving me crazy. I needed to get back to my roots, to regroup. And Jeremy needs the help. It's a win-win situation."

"No. It's not a win-win situation."

Keith looked helplessly at his wife. "Sure it is."

"No, Keith." Jamie pointed at herself, then into the house. "When you're away, *I'm* the loser. Those two kids are the losers. We need you here!" A tear slid from her eye. She shook her head and looked away. "We could move, all of us, back to the Midwest. If acting is so hard, get out of it completely! We'd all be better off and the kids would be closer to their grandparents and cousins and…"

"No—no," said Keith. "I'll make it work here, somehow. Someday. I'm not sure how, but I don't want to move."

"Just what do you want?"

Keith could feel his face growing hot. "I don't know, I haven't figured it out yet. I'm working on it."

"What are the kids and I supposed to do while you're *working* on it?"

"I don't know, Jamie!" Keith ran a hand through his hair. "Take the kids to Disney, have some fun. Or, if you want, hire a sitter and pamper yourself for once. Go get a makeover."

"*A makeover?* What's wrong with how I look?"

"I didn't mean that."

Jamie looked at him suspiciously.

"Look," said Keith, "you're taking this too seriously. Things will work out, just be patient."

"Patient! I think I've been patient. You've been gone for weeks, and now you're going away again. I have half a mind to call Jeremy and tell him to just hire his own help. I can't believe he guilts you into staying away from your family for so long. He should be able to deal with Hannah and Seth by now. Something else is going on there, something I'm not sure I like at all."

"There you go," said Keith, "imagining things again! You always make a mountain out of a molehill, Jamie. No wonder I'm going crazy here. No wonder!" He turned abruptly and stalked back down the sidewalk, unaware of the two faces pressed against the picture window behind him.

Chapter 11

It's so good to finally be able to see my feet again! I'm feeling better every day. Quentin is such a little charmer and so far, Katie adores him and isn't jealous at all. Even mom has hushed up about his name not starting with that stupid K, although Katie still calls him 'Ken-tin.' (Mom looks smug when she hears Katie say it that way.) Even Keri is all goo goo over him, more so than when Katie was born. Keri looks at him in a way that makes me think she might actually want a child some day. Imagine that! Keri...a mother! It would go in the record book of unexplained phenomena. Well, maybe it isn't so crazy after all.

Keri thinks this guy Keith is the ONE. I think she's dreaming of getting married and having kids with him. I'm not sure what I think of this guy, though. Mom already adores him and he and Keri have only been dating a few weeks. Now he's out of town, back in L.A. I'm sure Keri would follow him right out there if he asked her to. The signs are all there, she says. Because he didn't chase her. She didn't have one of her crazy dreams about him, or—oh! His name starts with a 'K.' And he's also a leftie. Still, something about him bugs me. I'm not sure what it is, but I trust him about as far as I can throw a refrigerator. Andy and I think she'd be far better off with someone like Jeremy, but we both know that'd never happen. I wouldn't want someone as nice as Jeremy to go through one of Keri's turn-abouts, anyway. They sure seem to have become friends, though. I'm afraid of where that'll head while Keith's in the picture.

What's wrong with me? I've got to quit worrying about other people and take care of my own family! To have two healthy, well-adjusted kids and a happy hubby should be my main goal in life right now. Still, I wish everyone could be and stay as happy as I am. It's a curse always to sense when the boom is about to fall.

Keri hurried down the cobblestone walk and sprang up on Jeremy's little porch. She was excited—this was the day they'd do it…they'd actually take Scalawag to the children's rehab. It was an experimental situation; normally the hospital only allowed dogs in who were crucial to a child's condition after they were released to go home. Keri had convinced them that Scalawag's particular condition would give kids hope of a happy, productive life even when disabled. They would soon find out if it would work.

With Keith out of town, Keri was eager to keep busy. It felt odd to bang on the door for Jeremy instead of Keith, but she knew Keith understood and was comfortable with her relationship with his cousin. To have it any other way would have been unfortunate, for Keri had rarely felt as comfortable in a man's company as she did with Jeremy. She wasn't sure whether she thought of him as a brother or a long-lost buddy, but she was happy to have the humble little Irishman in her life. It felt good in her bones.

She stood with the sun warm on her shoulders, the air sweet with flowers in her nostrils, and she was happy. Life was good.

A moment later, the door clicked open, and Keri's jaw dropped as the person standing there came into focus. "Jeremy?" she asked, eyes wide.

"Thought it was about time to surprise *you* with an 'outfit,'" he said.

Keri bent over, laughing. There stood Jeremy, in a tall pirate's hat with skull and crossbones, a patch over his left eye, a billowing white shirt with leather vest, and dark blue trousers with buckled boots. Next to him, a skull and crossbones decorated the front of Scalawag's collar and a red bandana flapped at his chest.

"You look great!" Keri said. As silly as Jeremy looked, he also looked kind of sexy, and the lovable beat-up dog at his side only added to the appeal.

"The kids will love you. I should have dressed up too. I'd be a great pirate's wench," she said.

"I'd never think of you as a wench," said Jeremy.

Something about the way Jeremy said that made Keri blush. "Thank you—I guess," she said. "So, are you ready to go?"

"We both are," Jeremy replied, as he and the dog stepped out of the door to stand by her side.

It feels good," Jeremy said, "to try to help someone again."

"Again?" said Keri, as they walked toward Jeremy's pickup.

Jeremy shrugged. "I used to carve canes for the kids who had a hard time walking. Some liked unicorn heads, or dogs and kittens. One kid wanted a snake. *That* was interesting to make."

"And you quit doing it?" Keri asked.

Jeremy nodded. "Yeah, a few years ago." He was unnaturally silent as they climbed into the truck. Scalawag, for only having three good legs, scampered in easily and sat between them, his tail wagging like a windshield wiper. Jeremy took off his hat so it wouldn't get crushed against the roof and Keri offered to hold it for him. Then they buckled up, and off they went.

The ride to the hospital went a little better as

Jeremy's silence lifted. By the time they got there, the cloud over his head had all but dissipated, and Keri had him laughing so hard with her kooky banter that he had to pull over and catch his breath. Even Scalawag seemed to be wearing a huge doggy smile, making his pathetic muzzle seem less pitiful. A few moments later, the odd troupe headed into the administration building to get their passes. Soon, they were passing gawking nurses, candy stripers and wide-eyed visitors. After navigating a dizzying array of corridors that Jeremy seemed to know by heart, the boring walls were suddenly festooned with brightly colored flowers, cartoon animals, funny bugs, sunny fields and trees. The murals were glorious.

"This is great!" said Keri, running her hand over a giant, blue bird with rolling eyes sitting on top of a gate. Overhead, painted vines dripped with a wide variety of animals sticking out their heads, along with squirrels, lizards and possums, and even one mysterious monkey tail. As Keri stared at the mural, she tilted her head, puzzled. Something about it seemed familiar.

Suddenly, she thought she knew what it was. Jeremy's arbor! She found herself poring over the mural to look for the artist's signature.

"It's not there," said Jeremy, straightening his hat as a nurse walked by, laughing at them. Scalawag thumped his tail.

Keri whirled to him. "You painted these, didn't you!" she said.

Jeremy nodded.

"This is *wonderful!*" Keri gushed, spreading her arms. "You, Jeremy, are a man of many talents."

"Thank you."

"What drives you to carve canes and paint murals in children's wards?" Keri asked as Jeremy gently ushered them on.

Before Jeremy could reply, a stout, red-haired nurse

nearly bowled him over with a bear hug. "JQ!" she announced so loudly that several other nurses came scurrying. "You're back! It's been so long. Love the hat!" After releasing Jeremy, she glanced down at the unusually well behaved Scalawag. "Now, who is *this* big guy? He's had a few hard knocks, hasn't he?"

"Hello, Dora," Jeremy said with a grin, his face flushed as several other nurses crowded in and gushed over him and the dog. Keri stepped quietly out of the ring, folding her arms in wonder as Jeremy explained about Scalawag and greeted people he'd obviously known quite well at one time.

Finally Keri could hear her name being called from inside the 'inner circle,' and could see Jeremy's billowing white-shirted arm beckoning to her. She eased into the little mob.

"This is my friend, Keri Ferrita," Jeremy said, looking at her with sparkling eyes. "She's the one who convinced me to take Scalawag up here and see if he can brighten up some of the kids' days."

Next thing Keri knew, the nurses were gushing over her, too.

"What's *that*?" asked a high-pitched voice behind then, and Keri turned to see a big-eyed little boy in a wheelchair, gazing in wonder at Scalawag. Keri blinked at the little boy a few times before realizing that he had no legs below his knees. A second later, another kid in a wheelchair appeared, a little girl about eight with a crippled arm and leathery red burns on the left side of her face. She also wheeled in to stare at the excited dog with awe. Scalawag's doggy smile was enormous as he basked in the attention, and he softly yipped and whined in glee. It was almost like he sensed, somehow, that these kids had something very much in common with him, just as Keri had predicted.

Jeremy raised his eyebrows and gave Keri a little

smile before bending down to talk and joke with the kids. Soon, more and more kids were appearing, some in wheelchairs, some with canes, some pale-faced with unknown illnesses, but all of them with bright eyes for the pirate and his mangy, crippled dog.

"We're a hit!" Keri whispered to herself. Then, feeling bolder, she joined in the hubbub, wishing she'd worn her clown outfit, or opera lady dress, or Raggedy Ann get-up, but, there was always next time, and, she decided, there would be a next time! Her heart swelled as she laughed and joined in the merriment...she'd found her niche.

It was over three hours later before Keri, Jeremy and a completely exhausted shaggy dog were settled back at Jeremy's house, flopped across the sofa. There was a glow on Jeremy's face as he laid his head back on the sofa with eyes closed, his bootless feet splayed out across a coffee table. Keri sat sideways on the couch next to him, leaning back over the armrest with her arms folded behind her head. Scalawag spread out on the floor below them, crashed out under the coffee table, quietly snoring. A kitten came and folded his furry little body into Scalawag's stomach and took a kitty nap.

It was all so calm, so peaceful and idyllic that Keri found herself slipping away into la-la land herself.

Chapter 12

"You've *got* to show up, Darci!" Keri said into her cell phone as she greeted yet another young couple at the open house.

She pulled herself away from the phone. "Just take a look around, I'll be right here if you have any questions," she said to the couple as they began to glance around, heads turning right and left in the kitchen.

Keri lifted the cell phone again. "It's next Saturday, the fourth of July. Andy and Kelly always have a great party, a nice bonfire, tons of food and the best fireworks you can stand."

"I'm still not sure I'd fit in," came Darci's voice at the other end of the phone. "I'm not exactly the outdoorsy type, Keri."

"I'm going to make sure Jeremy is there!" Keri said. "You've *got* to meet him, Darci! He's great with kids and has the heart of gold you want. He'd be great with Nathan."

"But isn't he the… the short one?"

Keri shook her head in frustration, then smiled and gestured another couple in the door. She turned her head and whispered hotly into the phone, "Darci! Snap out of it. You told me you were changing your mind on what kind of guys to date and I've found a keeper for you!"

"I know, but—"

"Darci! Be there."

"But you're going to be with this big move-star hunk, Keith, and I'll get the sidekick."

"Jeremy is not a sidekick. It's all different now that I'm getting to know him. He's a *wonderful* guy, and I think you'd like him if you gave him half a chance."

"Well, maybe. As long as he's not only half a guy."

"He's *not*. And you *will* like him."

"Oh—all right. I'll be there. Just don't tell him about me, let me look him over first. If we meet, it will be totally by 'accident'…know what I mean?"

"I know what you mean."

"Say—how's the open house going? That old white elephant's been on the market for months."

"I've already met a couple wanting to make an offer," said Keri, bouncing on her feet. "Maybe there'll be more. I've still got an hour to go."

"I've never met anyone who can sell homes the way you can!" Darci laughed. "You must have some kind of charm."

"Must have," said Keri.

"Must have! My goodness, you're dating a Greek god, Keri. There's something about you, I'm not sure what it is."

"Yeah, yeah…Keri Ferrita, the Man-Eat-a," Keri mumbled.

"What?"

"Oh, nothing. Just something Kelly's husband dreamed up a long time ago."

"Oh. How's the little baby?"

"Great! He looks like dad did as a baby."

"That's nice. I guess. Is it hard on your mom?"

"No, not really. Dad's been gone so long that she can handle it."

"I can't believe they named him Quentin. Sounds like something out of an old movie, but it doesn't start with a K, Keri. Something's up. Just be glad your new hunk is named Keith. Some things just have to fit, you know."

Keri nodded, but said nothing into the phone. She'd surprised herself that she'd blabbed so many of her secret 'signs' away in the last few weeks to a variety of different people. It unnerved her now. Maybe that in itself wasn't a good sign.

She tried not to think of it, it was too awful to contemplate.

"You still thinking of buying that fixer-upper on Forest Street?" Darci asked.

"I'm thinking of it, but it'd be quite a commitment," said Keri. "I'm never sure how long I'll be around."

"So, just fix it up and sell it at a great profit, like you always do."

"I'm not sure I'd have the time to fix it up."

"Why? What do you mean—" There was a pause on the other end of the phone, then: "Keri, is there something you're not telling me? You've been with Keith for six weeks now. That's a lot of time for you. Has he asked you to move with him?"

Keri didn't reply right away. How could she explain herself? Keith hadn't said anything about moving back to Los Angeles, but she knew he thought about it a great deal, and she wondered if she was holding him back from his career. He acted strange sometimes, a little distant, and she wondered if the hills of 'Hollyweird' were calling to him from afar. Like her, she sensed he was getting restless again. They were so much alike. Maybe that's why she wasn't getting tired of him. In fact, she couldn't get enough of him. She was used to having guys chase her, and this one had barely kissed her. When he had, it almost seemed an accident—but a delicious accident. He'd apologized and left her alone for the rest of the evening, which left her craving for more. There was a mystery surrounding him that made him even more irresistible. He was moody and contemplative and hard to figure out.

Actors. What a bunch.

"Keri?" came the voice in the phone again, jarring her back to reality. "What's wrong? You still there?"

"Yup. I've got to go, though," Keri said. "I'll talk to you Saturday. Just be there, okay? I'll make sure Jeremy is, too."

Jeremy was doing the final sanding on a beautiful walnut cane with a carved rabbit head when the phone rang. He reached over to the shop phone and answered, continuing his task.

"Hello?" he asked.

"Jeremy, it's Keri."

His heart skipped a beat. "Hi Keri. Keith's not here right now, want me to take a message?"

"Actually, I wanted to talk to you about something."

Jeremy stopped sanding and sat up a little straighter. "Sure. Is everything all right?"

"Everything is great. We still on for going to the hospital this Sunday?"

"Sure are," Jeremy smiled. "It's been great for the kids, hasn't it? And Scalawag seems to have a renewed sense of purpose now. Actually," he paused, then added softly, "I think I do, too."

"Me too," said Keri. "It is fun. But I have something else to ask you. You busy Saturday night?"

Jeremy sat up even straighter, and froze. "Am *I* busy?"

"Yeah. My sister and her husband—the ones you made the crib for—are having a Fourth of July party. A bonfire, fireworks, food, the whole shebang. It's usually a lot of fun—when the police don't show up. I was wondering if you'd like to go."

Jeremy blinked, felt the hand holding the phone start to shake. "But what about Keith?"

"Let's not worry about Keith right now. He'll understand."

"He will?"

"Yes. I've got it covered. Can you be there, let's say, about seven-thirty or so?"

"I guess so. I mean, sure I can. Sounds like fun."

"It will be. I guarantee it! See you Saturday!"

"Okay—it's a date." Jeremy hung up the receiver and stared at it like he'd just fallen asleep and dreamed the whole conversation. He felt breathless and a little out of himself. Keri wanted to be with *him?* It was unbelievable. He needed to pinch himself. Obviously, something had happened between her and Keith for this to take place.

He didn't know what was up, and didn't really care. Keith never talked to him about Keri anymore, and the relationship between Jeremy and his cousin had become somewhat strained. Maybe Keith was finally coming to his senses, though, and was thinking about reuniting with his family. Maybe he'd finally told Keri about them. If so, it could be that Keri was just feeling bitter or hurt and hoping Jeremy could be there to pick up the pieces.

That was fine with him. He hadn't allowed himself to even imagine the possibility to its fullest extent before, but now here it seemed to be, smacking him right in the face.

Feeling warm, and almost giddy, Jeremy began to finish sanding the cane once again. Then he began to whistle.

Chapter 13

"It feels good to just hang out," said Keri as she wandered hand-in-hand along the beach with Keith.

This was a remote place, secluded by the looming sand dunes that this section of the Lake Michigan shoreline was renowned for. They'd left their blankets and coolers so far back they could no longer see them along the shore, but they had no fear of anyone taking them.

"It *is* nice here," Keith agreed, squeezing her hand. "I forgot how the lake looked so much like the ocean. Sounds like it, too."

"Just doesn't smell like it," said Keri, staring out at seemingly ceaseless waves stretching into the horizon. "I can't smell salt, but I can usually smell the dead fish."

Suddenly, she froze. Dead fish? Why had she said such a stupid thing? If Keith had been feeling at all romantic, that thought could certainly curtail it.

But Keith just laughed. "Yeah, I remember that smell from when I was a kid. Glad most all the alewives are gone."

"Me too," Keri said, glancing at him. She could almost watch his tan getting deeper beneath the midday sun. Hers needed work, major work. She'd slathered on sunscreen so she wouldn't burn, as her skin was sensitive and prone to rash if she wasn't careful. She remembered overhearing a remark her sister had said once, that Keri would look good in any weather. She'd filed the compliment away and remembered it on such occasions.

She thought of the striking contrast she and Keith made: he, tall, lean and tan in his faded cut-offs, and she, petite and delicately pale in her lime-green bikini.

Paparazzi, she thought, where are you? She let go of his hand, leaned in, and wrapped both of her hands around his arm as they continued to stroll.

"This isn't quite California, is it?" she asked.

"No. Sometimes, it's better. Except for the snow and ice, of course."

"I sure don't miss that when I'm away," Keri agreed. She paused, then added carefully, "I'll probably be leaving again before snow hits this winter."

Keith looked at her. "Where to?"

"Well," Keri shrugged, "I can handle smog more easily than snow. Maybe I'll head back to L.A., I've got contacts out there."

"L.A., huh?"

"Maybe. We'll see what happens."

"Oh."

Keri glanced at him, then away. There was a period of silence between them. She desperately wished he'd ask her more questions, but he appeared lost in thought. Maybe he was weighing the possibilities of them both returning to the city. Maybe it was hard for him to believe it could actually work out. The providence was probably just too good to be true.

"Wouldn't you miss the kids at the hospital?" Keith said suddenly, "and all the goofy dressing up you could do?"

Keri faltered. "Dressing up? What do you mean?"

"Jeremy said you two sometimes dress up to entertain the kids. I can't believe he does it himself, it's so unlike him. But, I guess if it's a worthy cause, it'd make sense."

Keri's heart thumped. "Yes—it is a worthy cause." She laughed slightly. "Why else would we do it? It's not like…like I *like* to put on weird clothes or anything."

"I didn't think so," Keith said, "That would be too strange. Sometimes I think Jeremy and I know you as two different people. He's kind of a dreamer, though, can exaggerate a bit."

"Does he talk about me a lot?" Keri asked.

Keith shrugged. "Not really. We don't talk about anything a lot these days. It's getting awkward over there."

"What do you mean?"

"Jeremy and I have different opinions on things, so it's easier for us to just keep them to ourselves most of the time. I probably won't be staying there much longer. Not if we want to remain friends as well as cousins."

Keri contemplated the remark. Maybe Keith *was* just a little jealous of her and Jeremy's relationship, and maybe, just maybe, that was a good thing. She tried to think of the reasoning. It would mean that he actually thought of her as *his*, in that odd, guy sort of way. Keri didn't usually like being thought of as 'property', although it wasn't quite like that, but if someone like Keith wanted to think of her as *his*, maybe she should be flattered. A blush came to her face.

"And where would you go if you leave?" she asked.

Keith shrugged. "I'm not sure. I've been doing a lot of thinking about that."

Suddenly he stopped walking, turned to Keri, and rested his big hands on her shoulders. His eyes gleamed like lasers in the sunlight and the breeze whipped at his white-blonde hair. His gaze was steady, and made Keri's knees weak. "I'm thinking of going back to L.A., too. Resume my career. Rescue it before it slips away from me. But there are a lot of complications I've been trying to work out. It's not going to be easy."

"What sort of complications?" Keri asked. "Maybe I can help."

"I doubt that." Keith smiled limply, and looked away. He pulled his hands away from her, put them on his hips and stared at the dunes.

"Keith," she asked, "what is it?" She walked around him and pulled his hands into hers. "Come on, tell me. I still have a lot of connections out there. Are you in trouble with the law? I know a great lawyer…sold his house in three weeks. He knows a lot about agent-actor contract type things too, if that's a problem. We can work things out."

Keith looked at her, and nodded. "Yes, we probably could work things out, but it won't be a joy ride. There are some things you don't know about me yet, Keri. In time, though, you will. And everything will all work out, I'm sure of it."

"Of course it will! With two great brains and talents like ours, how could we go wrong?"

"That's right," he replied, locking his jaw firmly. "That's right."

"So then," said Keri. "Tell me. What's the problem? What can we fix together?"

"You know, I'm getting *hot*," he said suddenly. "How about you? Think it's time for a little dip in the lake?"

Keri was about to protest when Keith grabbed her around the waist and hoisted her up over his shoulder.

"*Keith!*" she squealed, but he merely laughed and trotted into the water. Soon he was up to mid-thigh, Keri still laughing and squealing.

"It's cold in here!" Keith said, but continued to head toward deeper water.

"If you throw me in I'll deck you!" Keri warned.

"Deck me, huh?" Keith laughed. "You sound like such a bruiser for a sophisticated little thing. Don't worry, I'm not going to toss you."

When he was chest high and her lower legs were dragging in the water, he slowly slid her down into the water in front of him.

"Cold-cold-cold!" Keri cried as the water came nearly up to her neck. "Oh—you're a demented one, Keith Quinn!"

"Demented, am I?" Keith asked as she finally got a good foot grip on the sandy bottom and relaxed. Then he lowered himself in the water until he was face-to-face with her. "I'll show you how demented I am."

With that, Keith cupped Keri's face in his hands, leaned in, and kissed her. It was their first true, deliberate, bona fide kiss, and Keith's passion and determination surprised Keri—at first.

But not for long.

A moment later, she was an eager participant

Chapter 14

"I've got to let you in on a little secret," Keri said, tapping Keith on the shoulder. He turned away from the picnic table where he'd been piling his plate with grilled chicken and pasta salads, and looked to where she was discreetly pointing.

"See that pretty girl sitting at the end of the round table—the one with the thick red hair?"

"Yeah…"

"I'm setting her up with Jeremy."

Keith tried not to stare. "You are? Haven't I met her before?"

"Yeah, on our first date when we went to the theater. Her name is Darci. I invited Jeremy here tonight, but he has no idea I'm trying to fix him up. I told him to come around seven-thirty so that I'd be sure Darci was here first."

Keith nodded, then continued filling his plate. "Looks to me like she's already made a connection."

Keri looked critically at a man sitting across from Darci, talking to her in an animated manner. She didn't recognize him, and assumed he was one of Andy's friends. He certainly didn't seem Darci's type; with thinning brown hair, a roundish face and a thick torso, he was obviously too ordinary for someone like Keri's finicky friend, even if she was trying to change her taste in men. Keri glanced at her watch as Keith helped himself to a beer out of a huge barrel filled with ice.

Jeremy should be there at any time.

"Come on, let's go sit with them. I haven't had a chance to talk to her today," prompted Keri.

"Could it be because we spent so much time at the beach?" Keith asked. "I never even made it home. Lucky I had a clean shirt with me."

Keri stared approvingly at Keith's bright, Hawaiian-style shirt. It showed off his tan and good looks more than ever. Many people were staring at him, and Keri introduced him to the ones she knew. The others, well, they could just stare. She took his arm and led him over to Darci's table.

"There you are!" said Darci, "I've been looking for you. There's quite a crowd here."

"I've been in the house," said Keri. "We just got back from the beach a little while ago."

"I can tell," Darci said, gesturing. "Your nose is a little sunburned."

Keri lifted her hand to her face. "It is?"

"It's okay—it looks good." Darci's eyes grew big. "Keri, let me introduce you to someone I just met." Her smile grew wider. "This is Daniel Lambert. He's a *child psychologist*." She went on. "Daniel, this is my good friend, Keri Ferrita. She lives here with her sister and brother-in-law, and this is her boyfriend, Keith."

Keri looked grimly at Darci as Keith and Daniel shook hands. Darci seemed suddenly overly interested in this Daniel guy, this *child psychologist*.

"Uh, Darci…" Keri said. "Can I talk to you a moment?"

"Sure." Darci got up, and Keith took a seat by Daniel and started to eat.

Keri drew Darci out of hearing range and sputtered, "What are you doing with that guy? Jeremy will be here any moment. This one doesn't seem like your type."

"Neither does Jeremy, Keri," Darci said flatly. "But

at least *this* one seems more Nathan's type. Daniel is a child psychologist, for crying out loud! What more could I ask for?"

Keri sighed and put her face in her hand. "Okay, okay. Maybe he would be better for Nathan. But please, at least give Jeremy a chance, or I'll feel rotten for inviting him."

"Oh, come on," said Darci. "Look around. There are other single girls here. I'm hanging on to Daniel before they zone in on him. If Jeremy is so great, he won't have any problems connecting with someone."

Keri nodded, and looked past Darci toward a bank that sloped around from the front of the house. Her heart did a little flip-flop as she saw Jeremy making his way down the hill toward the crowd. He looked great in a faded denim shirt and jeans, similar to what she was wearing, his dark, curly hair bouncing across his shoulders as he walked.

"Don't look—but here comes Jeremy, walking down the hill," Keri said.

Ignoring the warning, Darci turned to look. She twisted her head a few times to look around people before spotting him.

"Hmmm," she shrugged. "He is kind of cute."

"Told you!" said Keri.

"But—too short," said Darci. "I'm heading back to Daniel."

"Darci!" Keri wailed, but her friend ignored her and returned to her table.

Keri rolled her eyes and groaned, then, feeling guilty, threaded through the crowd to find Jeremy. When he saw her, his face lit up.

"Hi," he said. "I wasn't sure if you'd be yourself or dressed like Uncle Sam tonight, but I can see we're actually dressed kind of the same."

Keri laughed and folded her arms. "Yes, we are.

And we even know, through Swamp-Thing kind of situations, that we wear about the same size, too."

"That's true," said Jeremy. "Seems like we've known each other for years, but it was only a few months ago that you rescued that turtle and fell into my swamp."

"True," said Keri.

"There must be a hundred people here," said Jeremy. "Where'd you guys get all the food and tables?"

"Kelly borrows the tables from friends every year, just for this event," said Keri. "And everyone brings food. It's kind of a pot-luck."

Jeremy made a crestfallen face. "I didn't bring anything."

"That's okay—usually only the wives do, or guys with girlfriends. I mean," Keri paused, "well, you know what I mean, I hope."

"I think I do," Jeremy said, and grinned.

"Just wait 'til it gets dark," Keri said, "They'll light the fireworks—don't ask where they come from—then start the bonfire. It's a blast!"

"I bet it is. I'm kind of excited. I've been thinking about it all day."

"Great!" said Keri. "Hey, come this way, there are people I'd like you to meet."

Jeremy nodded as Keri led him through the crowd to where Darci had been sitting. Keith was still there, but Darci and Daniel were gone.

"Where's Darci?" Keri asked Keith.

Keith waved his hand. "She and that guy went for a walk or something. Hey—how you doing, cuz?" he added, smiling at Jeremy.

When Jeremy didn't reply, Keri turned to look at him. His face was ashen.

"Jeremy—you okay?" she asked.

Jeremy remained motionless as he stared at Keith.

Then he seemed to snap out of it. "Yeah—I'm fine. Hi Keith. Haven't seen you all day."

"We've been at the beach," said Keith, and motioned over to the food table. "Hey, go make yourself a plate. This food is incredible!"

Jeremy looked to Keri, and back to Keith. "Think I will," he said, putting his hands in his pockets and walking away.

Keri gazed after him, and slowly sat down next to Keith.

"I think he knew," said Keith.

"Knew what?" asked Keri.

"That you were setting him up. I think he's figured out that the girl took off."

"I can't believe she did that!" Keri fumed. "Now poor Jeremy is stuck by himself. I feel like a moron."

"It's okay. Your heart was in the right place," Keith assured her. "Don't beat yourself up over it. Jeremy is a grown man. It's time for him to get out and meet someone and he can do it all by himself."

"Well…I know. I just feel bad for him."

"You'll get over it."

"I hope so."

"C'mon, lighten up. Come here." Keri leaned in toward Keith, and he put his arm around her, drew her close, and kissed her forehead.

"Smile, now. That's my girl. Enjoy yourself."

"You're right," said Keri, feeling warm inside at Keith's attention. "I tried. Now it's time to have fun."

"That's right."

Soon Jeremy came back to the table, and sat down with a plate of food that would barely feed a small child.

"Aren't you hungry?" Keith asked, "The food is great."

"I lost my appetite," said Jeremy, glancing peculiarly at him. He began to pick at his food, and didn't say anything more for awhile. When he did speak, it was in short sentences. He tried to smile, but it was easy to tell something was bothering him.

"It is kind of boring here now, but it'll get better later," Keri tried to offer, snuggling next to Keith. "It'll be easier to mingle when it's dark and the fire is roaring."

"And everyone is three-sheets to the wind," Keith added, taking a long drink of his beer.

They made small talk for some time, and Kelly and Andy both made an appearance to show off the new baby. Katie was staying with their mom for the night. Kelly said it was just too busy and loud for a little girl.

Jeremy asked about Rover. Apparently the dog was shut inside the house until the party was over since he was unpredictable around strangers. Keri remembered how Jeremy had witnessed this first-hand when he brought back her shoe. They reminisced and had a good laugh over that incident, while Keith just sat back and listened, too mellow to be curious.

As dusk set in, Jeremy got up and wandered around a little bit. Later, Keri caught sight of him talking to a cute brunette shorter than he was. She was glad for him—relieved, actually. Something about the girl annoyed her and Keri couldn't put her finger on what it was. Soon she and Keith also began to mingle, and, with Keith at her side, Keri soon forgot about her unease.

All was going well until the cell phone in Keith's pocket rang.

He turned his head and clicked on the phone, covering an ear to drown out the chatter of the crowd and loud music. Keri watched him curiously as he spoke into the phone.

"Yes?" he said, "What?" Long pause. "Say that again? When?" There was another long pause, and Keith became agitated. He glanced at Keri, and then turned his back on her and whispered urgently into the receiver, his words indistinguishable. At last Keri heard him say goodbye. He clicked off the phone and stuffed it back into his pocket. He straightened and looked blankly out at his surroundings.

"Keith?" Keri asked, "is everything okay?" When Keith didn't reply, Keri gently tugged on his arm. "Keith, what's wrong?"

At last Keith turned around, and it took a moment for his eyes to focus on her. His distraction was unnerving. "Sorry, Keri," he said, and began to fidget. "But something's come up. I have to go."

"You do? So soon?"

"Yeah. It's kind of an emergency."

Keri's eyes widened. "What happened? Can I help?"

"No. I have to go. I'll call you later."

With that, Keith began to walk off toward the front of the house. Keri scurried after him, ignoring people's stares.

"Keith! Let me come with you. Maybe I can help."

Keith ignored her, and began to walk faster.

"Keith!" Keri said, frustrated, "Talk to me!"

Suddenly Keith whirled in his tracks. His face was red and flushed. "Would you stop being so clingy?" he shouted, then spun back around and walked away.

Keri froze in her tracks, thunderstruck. "Clingy?" she murmured. Blood rushed to her ears, and she turned in a circle, glancing at the shadowy faces of people gawking at her predicament. Feeling disoriented, Keri scurried down the gently sloping yard to the comforting darkness of the barn, where she'd taken refuge once before. No one else would be down there, since it was considered off-limits to anyone but family.

Keri brushed inside the door, looking for the comfort of one of the horses' friendly heads hanging over the stalls. But the horses weren't there; Andy had taken them to a neighbor's barn earlier in the day so the fireworks wouldn't frighten them. The stalls were silent and empty, almost forlorn.

Keri sighed, walked around in circles, and brushed tears off of her cheeks. She found herself straightening some of the bridles and halters on the walls, and the shelves of saddle soap and fly repellents. It was surprising how messy the place was. She could tell, even in the darkness, that it hadn't been cleaned lately. What was wrong with Andy and Kelly, anyway? How could they let the barn become such a…a pit? They had small children to set an example for—this was a disgrace! Keri continued to mutter and to clean, to clean and to mutter, tears straining down her face.

"He's always been moody," a voice said behind her.

Keri stopped rummaging, and stood still, listening. She did not turn around.

"Sorry about how Keith acted," came the voice again—*Jeremy's* voice. "Try not to take it personally. You'll work it out later."

Keri turned to find Jeremy's small, sweet form silhouetted in the door, the stars in the deepening night carpeting the sky behind him. He moved inside, and the faint light coming from one of the barn windows coursed gently over his face and made his eyes seem to glow.

"It's nice in here," Jeremy said, looking around. "I love how old barns smell. Hay, leather, horses, dust. It's relaxing. Like stepping into the arms of an old friend."

"It is," said Keri, wiping the remains of tears from her cheeks.

Jeremy nodded, then slowly walked to the back of the barn where more of the tack was stored. He regarded each item with a comment on its use or beauty.

Keri followed him numbly, nodding at his remarks, unable to clear her mind of what Keith had just said to her. It echoed over and over in her head like a broken record, *Would you quit being so clingy...so clingy...so clingy?"* Her heart felt like a sandbag as she stood next to Jeremy.

"So, where are the horses?" Jeremy asked.

Keri told him about Andy taking them to the neighbors.

"That's a good idea. I hate to see horses spooked. They can hurt themselves or people around them."

"You grew up with horses?" Keri asked.

"Actually, I grew up where I live now," Jeremy reminded her, taking a seat on a bale of hay. He folded his hands together. "But I had good friends with horses. Good old Bob Hartman and his mom always encouraged me to become a jockey. I guess I had other plans."

Keri nodded, and sat next to him. The hay crunched against her backside and a wisp of its sweet, dusty smell filled her head and eased her mind a little.

They sat together quietly for a few minutes.

"Why was Keith so rude?" Keri suddenly asked. "I mean, all I did was want to help. He gets so weird at times."

Jeremy glanced solemnly at her. "Don't take it personally. He has… what do they call it these days… *issues*, I guess."

"But he won't let me in on them," she replied. "He changes the subject and becomes distant. I don't understand him at all. He embarrassed me in front of all those people tonight." She tried to laugh. "I guess I'm not used to that."

"It happens to the best of us."

"Do you know why he had to leave tonight?" Keri asked.

Jeremy lowered his eyes. "Not exactly, but I have an idea."

"Can you tell me?"

Jeremy lifted his eyes and settled his gaze firmly on her. There was a strange look on his face, almost a longing, but he didn't say anything. At last he sighed, and looked away.

"You know something," said Keri.

"There are things I wish I *didn't* know even more," Jeremy said. "But I can't talk about them, and that's the way it has to be. You'll have to talk to Keith about all his… his issues. I made a promise to stay out of it."

Keri looked steadily at him. She could tell it was painful for him not to reveal anything, but she asked anyway. "Please? Tell me?"

He shook his head. "I can't. Talk to Keith."

Keri sighed and slumped down. "All right. I understand."

Jeremy nodded. "Thank you."

Suddenly there was a huge bang outside, and a trail of lights filtered down past a dusty window.

"The fireworks have begun," said Keri. "They'll be lighting the fire any moment now, too."

"I saw that pile of old wood and skids out in the field," said Jeremy. "Is that where it'll be?"

"It is."

Another bang seemed to shake the barn, and more colored light fell past the window.

"Some night this turned out to be, didn't it?" said Keri.

Jeremy shrugged and stared ahead, smiling limply. "I'm just sorry to see you hurt."

"I'm probably overdue for it," said Keri.

"Nobody is overdue for that."

"If you only knew my history, you'd think I was," Keri said. She straightened, and tried to grin, "I deserve it, and probably worse."

"Don't say that," said Jeremy. "It isn't true."

"Okay—if you say so," Keri relented. She stared

ahead into a shadowy corner of the barn where old shovels, pitchforks, fence-posts and things she could barely make out where jumbled together with scraps of lumber. She hadn't been this far back in the barn in a long time. Suddenly something behind the pile caught her eye, something shapeless and tan draped over a board. Drawing her eyebrows together, she slowly stood up to peer closer into the gloom.

"Is everything all right?" Jeremy asked.

"I think so." Keri began. "I just have to check something out a moment." She walked to the corner, and pulled some of the junk aside to reach the thing she'd spotted. Her heart beat faster as she reached in and touched a soft, filthy cloth. Then she grasped it, pulled it out of the pile, and stared at the large, tan and green striped rag in her hands.

"I can't believe it." she mumbled. Her eyes widened, and she shook her head. "It's still here."

"What is? Keri?"

Keri turned, dazed, and walked back to Jeremy. She quickly sat back next to him on the hay before her rubbery legs could give out on her. She spread the cloth across her lap and smoothed it lovingly with trembling hands. Her eyes became damp.

Jeremy reached over and touched her hand. "What is it?"

She tried to chuckle, but all that came out was a tiny gasp. "This dirty old rag," she said. "It used to be… it used to be my old barn coat. I've had it since I was eleven. I thought it was lost years ago."

She glanced at Jeremy and his look implored her to continue. She turned the rag over, where tufts of ratty gray cotton lining still remained, and began to caress that, too. More fireworks crackled across the sky above them, but she could barely hear them. She'd been transported into another time.

"I was always such a tomboy," Keri finally continued, struggling to keep her words audible. "When I was eleven, dad bought me a pony. Just a tiny, shaggy little thing I named Little Red. I swear, that little guy had the heart of a thoroughbred, though. He could outrun any full-grown horse for miles. We became so close that when I rode him all I had to do was lean a certain way for him to turn or scrunch slightly forwards for him to run." She paused, and added with a sob. "Little Red was my best friend."

Keri's throat grew tighter and she couldn't speak for a while. Jeremy reached over and held her hand, squeezing it in empathy.

"Anyway," Keri finally said, glancing at Jeremy. "I was out in the barn so much, that dad bought me this coat. He knew it wasn't beautiful, and he didn't make me wear it to school, but it was so warm and comfortable that I wore it for years. I always kept it on a special hook, but the hook is long gone. Until now, I'd forgotten about the coat, and I haven't really thought of Little Red in years."

"What happened to him?" Jeremy asked softly.

Keri drew a deep breath. "Well, I grew up. I got taller, and Little Red got smaller. I started to hang out with boys and Little Red started to hang out by himself. Kelly was quite girly back then, and had no real use for him. I was Red's only real friend—and I abandoned him. I didn't see it that way at the time, though. I grew up, and Red just grew old. And lonely."

Suddenly Keri began to sob. "I let dad down. Little Red—and this—this coat were his gifts to me, and I didn't appreciate them."

"It's okay," said Jeremy. He drew his arm around Keri's shoulders, and she pushed her tear-streaked face into his shirt. He began to rock her. "I'm sure your dad understood that his little girl had to grow up. He knew how much you loved your pony, and the coat."

"You don't understand," Keri sobbed, then paused as she tried to find the words. "A few months after he got me the coat, I got strep throat and he took me to the doctor. The doctor looked at me and said I'd be fine, but he looked at dad and said he was the one who was sick. There must have been something about the way dad's eyes or skin looked, I don't know. But just as he started to go in for tests, he died. So, he never knew, he never really saw—" Keri looked up at Jeremy. "He never really saw all the good times and how much I did love Little Red, and this coat. I guess I just grew out of it all. Twelve years ago I came home for a weekend from college and never even went out to the barn. Mom had to tell me that Little Red had died, too. Alone. Frozen in the snow out in the pasture."

It took a moment for Jeremy to digest the shock of that. "What a horrible time for you," he finally said.

"It was," Keri sniffed. "It was awful! I tried to pretend it didn't bother me that much, and no one ever suggested that I'd neglected Little Red, but it was there. Oh, but the guilt was there."

"It was a long time ago," said Jeremy.

"Yeah, it was," said Keri. "Sounds kind of stupid, now, I guess. Here I am, a grown woman who's been all around the world, and I find myself bawling over some dirty rag like a little kid who'd lost his blankie. Silly, huh?"

"No," Jeremy said. "It's not silly at all. You should save that piece of coat, Keri. It's part of you. You need it."

"I do? You don't think it'd be silly?"

Jeremy pulled away from her. Keri could see his eyes shining. "Let me show you something," he said, and stood up. He reached in his pocket and pulled out what looked like a long, wrinkled red and white handkerchief. It looked as old and ratty as the scrap of Keri's old coat.

Jeremy lifted the handkerchief in the air. "This," he said, "was my grandfather's. He used it as a bandana when he was woodworking. He, too, had a special hook for it. This thing was usually grimy and covered with sweat. But it was his, and it was special to him."

Keri stared hard at Jeremy.

"That man had the best attitude of anyone I'd ever met," said Jeremy. "He had a bad leg; he was wounded at Normandy in the war. There was a lot of shrapnel in it that couldn't be removed. You could tell when the weather was going to change by how much grandpa limped. I knew that leg tormented him, but he never complained. He always told me that it's not what happens to you in life that counts, but it's your attitude toward what happens to you that matters. He lived that perspective to the day he died, about ten years ago."

"And you've kept that bandana ever since?" Keri asked.

Jeremy nodded. "Ever since. I always keep it with me in my pocket, as kind of a memento. It gives me strength, sometimes…and a peace of some sort." He paused, then lowered himself back down on the bale. "So, I guess you can see why I don't think keeping that rag is stupid. You *should* keep it. It's dear."

Jeremy folded the bandana, stared at it a few moments, then pushed it back into his pocket.

Keri watched Jeremy as he stared ahead in thought. She put the remains of her coat on a wooden rail behind her and sighed, putting her chin in her hands.

"We're a lot the same," she said. "We—and our rags. I doubt Keith would understand about my coat like you do. You won't tell him, will you?"

Jeremy looked at her. "Of course not."

"Thanks."

Speaking of Keith brought Keri's former misery back, adding to her grief over what had happened to Little Red and her father. Jeremy's presence helped, but she was unable to pull herself out of her doldrums. She was tired, and felt almost feverish. To make matters worse, an annoying pain that had been plaguing her on and off throughout the day had returned. She held her hand behind her ear and groaned faintly, closing her eyes, trying to will depressing thoughts away.

"Are you all right?" Jeremy asked.

Keri grinned in exhaustion. "It's a shame you've had to ask me that so many times tonight. I've been such a wimp. It's not like me. Thanks for caring, though." She put her hand on his knee and squeezed it. "You're just about my best friend now, Jeremy. I don't know what I'd do without you."

Jeremy smiled at that, and turned away.

"You know—I really don't feel very good," Keri managed to admit. "I think I've got a fever from too much sun, and those fireworks are giving me a headache. Would you mind if I went up to the house? I think I need to lie down and pull myself together."

"You could probably use a long night's rest," Jeremy said. "Go ahead, don't worry about me. I'd like to sit here alone for a while and think. I like it out here."

"Go ahead," said Keri. "Just watch out for the occasional horsey-poo that might be lingering."

"I will."

With that, Keri got to her feet, stretched, and sighed a last huge sigh.

"I'll see you soon," she said. "Thanks for being here, pal." Keri leaned down, gave Jeremy a big hug, then turned and left the barn.

Jeremy folded his hands together as he watched Keri leave. "Pal," he said to himself.

He sighed and stared ahead in the gloom. As sad and sentimental as the atmosphere in the barn had become, it had also been enchanting. He loved being able to comfort Keri as much as he had. But with Keri now gone, the atmosphere took on a different kind of sadness. There was now an emptiness, as well.

He should have known.

When he'd first arrived at the picnic and realized Keri was still with Keith, he understood, at last, that she had invited him to the party as a friend, not a date. *Keith* was the date. Jeremy's heart hurt. He tried to tell himself that just being Keri's friend should be good enough, that it was all he needed. He was her *pal*, and she didn't know what she'd do without him; she'd said so.

Wonderful. It should be wonderful, anyway.

But Jeremy felt lost and disoriented as he sat alone on the bale of hay, slumped over in the darkness, hands clasped in a silent form of resignation.

Her *pal*.

He sat alone for a while, until he could no longer hear fireworks going off. He listened to the rambling murmur of people's voices outside. Outside… a place where he ought to be if he could just pull himself out of this self-induced misery and rejoin humanity. He remembered the dark-haired girl named Janet he'd met earlier. He felt no real connection with her, although she'd been pleasant enough and seemed interested.

He was the one who wasn't interested.

What was wrong with him?

Jeremy shook his head and pulled himself to his feet. He knew he had to get on the move before he drowned in self pity. He mustered the courage at last and left the barn. He wandered aimlessly among people, hands thrust in his pockets, joining in here and there on little snippets of conversation. He watched the bonfire as it flickered orange across the faces of people mingling nearby, but he didn't spot Janet in the crowd. That was all right, for the stars were bright overhead and the smell of earth and vegetation out in the country was replacing his former gloom with a quiet, peaceful feeling. At last he sat down on the lawn beneath a maple tree, a short distance from the fire, and tried to meditate on the beauty of the night.

But his eyes kept drawing away from the fire, the people, and the stars overhead toward the house, where Keri was. He wondered what she was doing. Was she in bed sleeping, or maybe watching an old movie? Maybe she was up there quietly peering out the window at the party below, wishing she felt better, wishing she could rejoin…probably wishing Keith hadn't had to leave.

At that thought, Jeremy's heart sank. He forced himself to look away from the house back toward the bonfire. It had simmered down somewhat, but still covered the area about the size of a small car. It was hot enough to keep people back at least ten feet, yet people still were adding scraps of wood, beaten-up lawn furniture and other miscellaneous objects to make the flames grow higher. Jeremy saw Andy pushing his way through the crowd with a wheelbarrow full of junk, probably from the barn or other outbuildings, to add to the blaze. People moved out of his way as he propped the wheelbarrow before the fire and began to haul out armfuls of scrap, tossing it into the fire in a theatrical manner. Jeremy laughed at the antics…until something dangling off the back of the wheelbarrow caught his eye just as Andy snatched it.

Jeremy leaped to his feet. "No!"

He rushed towards the fire, hurtling past wide-eyed faces and gaping mouths—just as the rag that was once Keri's beloved old coat landed in flames.

Without thinking, Jeremy jumped into the fire. He kicked at the rag and tripped, ignoring the shrieks of onlookers as he rose to his feet and continued kicking at the smoldering fabric until it flattened out on the lawn. People backed away as he tumbled out of the fire and stomped at the flames still licking at the rag. Then Andy broke away from the crowd, tore off his shirt and tackled Jeremy, wrapping his shirt around Jeremy's legs to suffocate the flames climbing Jeremy's jeans and boots. The two men rolled in the grass, Andy refusing to free Jeremy until the flames on his clothes were out, and Jeremy refusing to release the rag until it, too, was extinguished. Then the two lay face up on the grass, panting, and an eerie hush settled in around them.

At last Andy turned his face to look at Jeremy.

"What in the hell were you doing?" he asked.

Jeremy said nothing. He lifted himself on his elbows, picked up the still smoldering fabric, and gazed at it.

Then, amidst the silence, he got to his feet, wincing slightly from undisclosed wounds, and left. People parted as the bedraggled figure passed through, and disappeared into the shadows over the hilltop.

Chapter 15

The banging on the door was hard enough to shake the house, and still no one came to answer it.

"Open up! Jeremy, Keith!" Keri shouted, and banged again. She heard Scalawag barking on the other side of the door and heard the scrape of his toenails against the wood.

All at once, the door clicked open. Keith stood there stoically, his face flushed, obviously upset.

"This is ridiculous, Keri!" he said. "Why can't you just leave me alone for a little while to take care of my problems? I told you last night I'd call."

"You oaf!" Keri shouted, and brushed past him. "Not everything is about you, Keith! Where is Jeremy?"

"Jeremy?" he asked as Keri bent over to pet the dog.

"Yes—Jeremy. I need to see him."

Keith's angry demeanor vanished. "I'm not sure. I haven't seen him this morning."

"He's not here?"

"I don't think he ever came home last night," Keith added. "Why, what's going on?"

"He never made it home?"

"I don't know. I looked for him earlier."

"Oh no," Keri put her hands against the sides of her head and began to pace the living room. "What have I done? What did my stupid blubbering cause?"

Keith looked at Keri, confused. "What are you

talking about?"

"I think Jeremy had some kind of accident at the party last night," Keri said. "It was after I went to bed so I don't know the whole situation. All I do know is that he may have gotten burned by the bonfire."

Keith's eyebrows shot up. "Burned?"

"I think he sorta...fell in, or tripped. But my brother-in-law said he just left the party."

Keith shook his head. "He must have been drinking. He can't hold his liquor, even if he is Irish. Crazy guy. I hope he's all right."

"I don't think he was drinking," said Keri.

"So why would he fall into the fire?"

Keri turned her head, tears blurring her eyes. She'd heard about the 'rag' from Andy. No one understood what he was doing, but once Keri heard the story, she raced to the barn to search for her old coat scrap and found it missing, and then she knew. Her throat tightened. Jeremy had saved it for her and no one else in the world, especially Keith, would understand why.

So where was he? At a hospital somewhere? Maybe she should start calling around, maybe—she felt Keith's hand massaging her shoulders. She jerked away from him, frustrated. She could never tell all of this to Keith, especially after how he'd treated her last night.

"Keri, baby," Keith said, "I've never seen you so upset! Talk to me. Let me help."

"Oh, now *that* sounds familiar," said Keri sarcastically. "If you want to help, you'd be out looking for your cousin right now." Her tone softened as she noticed the look in Keith's eyes. "Maybe we could go look for him together."

At that, Keith hung his head and sighed, and then looked away.

"I can't."

That was when Keri first noticed Keith's attire. It

was eight o'clock on a Sunday morning, and he was wearing tan dress pants and a dress shirt. Keri was certain he wasn't on his way to church, but he was on his way somewhere.

"Where are you going?" she asked. Then her eyes wandered past the living room into the kitchen. She spotted a suitcase lying against a cupboard and her eyes darted sharply back to him.

"Yes," he said, "I'm flying out. I have to leave now, to catch a plane for Los Angeles."

"But *why*? Why now, when Jeremy may be hurt!"

Keith's jaw tightened and he glanced away. "Because," he finally said, "a very close friend of mine was in an accident out there." He looked back to her. "I have to go. It's important I show my support. I can't explain it all right now, but I will when I get back. Trust me."

"Trust you? Why should I? You make me sick!" Keri seethed. She spun around and flung herself on the couch. "I can't even look at you right now."

"Now, now—quit moping," said Keith, following. He eased down on the sofa next to her. "Keri. Look at me! Jeremy will be fine." He reached out and turned Keri's face toward him. "Everything will work out. When I get back, I'll make it all up to you. I promise. Just give me the chance. Will you give me the chance—please?"

Keri reluctantly looked into Keith's imploring eyes and her resolve to ignore him dissolved. "I don't know," she said.

"Please." Keith pulled her toward him and kissed her forehead. "You can wait here for Jeremy, or use the phone to call around, whatever. You have my cell phone number, let me know as soon as you find anything out."

"I can't call you if you're on a plane."

"I won't be on one forever."

"I guess not. Maybe, just maybe, I'll call."

"That's my girl."

Keith kissed her softly on the mouth, then hurried to his feet. "I really have to go," he said, checking his watch. "I'll talk to you soon, okay?"

Keri made no reply. Even Scalawag stared dolefully at Keith as he backed into the kitchen to get his suitcase. "I'll talk to you. Just hang in there," Keith added as he grabbed his suitcase. He began to leave out the back door, then turned his head, and gave her *the wink*.

"Love ya," he said, then he went out the door and was gone.

Keri's head popped up. "Love ya?" she whispered to herself. She shook her head and felt more disoriented than she had in days. She patted Scalawag on the head and talked to him. "I don't know what to do, Scally," she said. "I don't know how to feel. I don't know what's going on with me!"

Tears streamed down her cheeks as the silence of the house, Jeremy's quaint little house, settled in. She was alone now. Frightfully, mournfully alone.

Except, of course, for the poor mutt sitting next to her with his head in her lap. Keri patted his muzzle, caressed the ruined eye and flaps of skin where the ear had been torn off. He looked at her with his good soft brown doggy-eye, and Keri knew that Scalawag, somehow, understood her pain, just as he understood the physical and emotional pain of the kids at the hospitals they'd visited.

"You're a good old boy," she said softly, sniffing. "You've got a big heart, just like your master. Why did he risk burning himself just to get my coat? It wasn't worth getting hurt. Your master is a strange man, Scalawag. Wherever he is. Maybe I will stay here a while and wait. He's got to come home sometime. He couldn't have walked away like he did if he was hurt badly—right? He has to be okay. Just driving around somewhere, probably. I bet he has all kinds of spots to go to. It'd be like him to hole up somewhere private, somewhere woodsy. Maybe he needs to be alone."

Keri leaned back on the couch, and visualized Jeremy as he'd looked in his pirate's outfit that first day after they'd visited the hospital. She smiled to herself. What a wonderful day that had been. So fulfilling, so sweet. And now she felt so empty, and alone. Her heart ached, and she didn't understand it at all.

"Jeremy, where are you?" she mumbled, and closed her eyes. She drifted into a restless sleep, and didn't awaken until a soft whining brought her back to her senses. She glanced around to find the sound coming from Scalawag, who was sitting on the floor in front of the den.

"I know, boy, you miss your master. I miss him too," said Keri.

Scalawag whimpered once more, looked at her, and went into the den. Keri stared after him, but didn't move. Soon she saw the dog stick his head out from the doorway and look at her again. Then he disappeared inside.

"What is it?" Keri asked, realizing, finally, that the dog was beckoning her. She pulled herself to her feet and went to the doorway and peered inside.

The hairs on the back of her neck prickled.

Scalawag was nowhere in sight.

"He *is* a ghost dog," Keri mumbled, backing away. This had happened before, and she'd dismissed it as her crazy imagination and forgotten it, but now, the creepiness came back full force. Her heart began to race. Maybe Scalawag really *had* been killed in that farm accident! She backed a little more, her hand clasped over her mouth, when he suddenly appeared from behind a paneled wall at the back of the den.

"What the…." Keri muttered, as a door, camouflaged within the paneling, swung silently shut as the dog came forward.

Keri's eyes rounded as Scalawag came to her, put his cool snout in her hand, and stared up at her face.

"It's a secret room!" Keri whispered. "You aren't a ghost dog after all."

Frightened, yet intrigued, Keri tiptoed over to where she'd seen the door come open. She stood before the wall, dumbfounded. There was absolutely no way to tell there was an opening if you didn't know about it. Scalawag stood next to her, then poked his nose into the wall. He pushed the hidden door open and disappeared into the darkened slit as the door swung smoothly shut behind him.

"Wow," was all Keri could say.

She looked over her shoulder, then around the room, feeling shamefully nosy but so curious she couldn't stand it. Gathering her courage, she held her breath and gently pushed open the door. She poked her head inside, but it was too dark to focus. She stepped in and the door closed silently behind her.

She found herself inside a room about the size of a small walk-in closet. She bent down to pat Scalawag's head as her eyes began to adjust to the darkness. A small desk sat against the wall, covered with books, knick-knacks, and photographs of people she couldn't make out in the dim light coming from beneath the door. Other photos, in varying sizes, were taped to the walls. Keri's heart thumped as she gazed around, blinking, trying to take it all in.

It took a few moments for her to notice there was something on the floor off to her left.

Moving towards it, Keri was confused to find what looked like a pile of clothes scrunched up in the corner. "What the heck…" she murmured, eyes wide.

Then the clump moved.

Keri would have bolted out of the room but every muscle in her body was paralyzed. Her jaw dropped as the object moved once more. Scalawag brushed past her to nose it, then lay down.

"Hi Scally," murmured a low, exhausted voice.

Keri gasped. "Jeremy?"

The pile of clothes slowly took on a human form and sat up.

Keri had never seen Jeremy so disheveled. A blanket fell off his shoulder to reveal wrinkled clothing, matted hair, and a sad, haggard look on his face. His eyes, always huge, looked out at her with a sense of resignation which was almost too heartbreaking to bear. A bandage was wrapped around his right hand, which he tried unsuccessfully to conceal beneath the blanket.

Keri crouched down next to the dog and gazed at Jeremy in sorrow. Neither said a word.

At last Scalawag sat up, and pawed awkwardly at Jeremy.

Jeremy looked away from Keri, and patted the dog. A thin smile came to his lips.

"Good old dog," he said.

"Oh, Jeremy," Keri finally said, her voice quivering. "What have I done to you?"

Jeremy looked at her with an odd expression, but said nothing.

"Can you forgive me?" Keri asked. "I heard what happened. You never would have gotten burned to save my old coat, if I hadn't been such a baby last night. I feel awful." Her eyes began to burn and she lowered her head and put her face in her hands. She was sick and disgusted with herself.

"It's not your fault," said Jeremy.

"Yes. Yes, it is." Keri did not lift her head. She tightened into a smaller ball, hoping to shrink away.

"Don't worry about me," said Jeremy in a soft voice. "I'm a resilient little guy. I didn't get burned that badly. It'll heal."

Keri slowly looked up at him. "I've been worrying about you. I didn't know where you were, and neither did Keith." She straightened slightly and began to look about the room. "I'm *still* not sure where we are." She noted a nightlight by the photographs and asked if she could switch it on. Jeremy agreed, and the photos came alive. There was one of a pretty, red-haired lady of about twenty-five sitting on a tree swing, another of the same woman laughing, close up, her red tresses flying out behind her in the breeze, and yet another of the same woman standing next to a little dark-haired boy on a bicycle. Keri's gaze wandered farther, past various other photos of the little boy or the lady or both, then suddenly stopped on an eight-by-ten framed portrait on the desk.

She froze.

Smiling out at the camera was the mysterious woman, the little boy, and Jeremy. She couldn't speak.

"That was my family," said Jeremy. "My wife, Hannah, and Seth. My son."

He spoke so calmly, so matter-of-factly, that Keri found it hard to accept what he was implying. Her throat closed up.

"They're gone," Jeremy continued.

Keri turned to him, tears streaming down her face. "You never told me," she said.

Jeremy looked up at the photos, from one to another, with a distant look in his eyes. "I know," was all he said.

"Why?"

Jeremy shook his head. "I'm not sure. It was a long time ago," he paused, then added, "and sometimes, not so long ago."

Questions flooded Keri's mind...*how* long ago?

How did they die—or did they leave? How long were Jeremy and Hannah married? Had they lived here? What had happened to them? And why this sad, secret shrine? As she looked at Jeremy's tormented face, she could not ask. Words would be worthless now.

Slowly, awkwardly, she scooted next to him. She picked up the blanket, glanced at his bandaged hand, then pulled the blanket up over them both. She leaned her head on his shoulder, as she'd done the night before in the barn, and snuggled next to him. He leaned his head back on hers, and a loose curl of his hair tickled Keri's nose. She held his arm in her hands, careful not to touch the bandages, Scalawag flumped down across their legs, and there they sat quietly in the secret, lonely room.

Chapter 16

Jamie lifted her eyes from the book she was reading and peered into the kitchen where her husband was making dinner. David was standing on a chair next to his dad, happily peeling carrots for the roast, and Amber was hunched over the table, arranging vegetables for a tossed salad.

Jamie tried to smile at the scene, a scene so sweet but so rare these days. Keith turned, as if sensing her stare, and winked at her. That wink still gave her the shivers, and made her blush for the first time in many months. She arched her eyebrows at her husband, then pretended to read once again.

It wasn't easy to spend so much of her day sitting in a wheelchair. Her rear was sore and her back ached. How could people who've spent their whole lives seated bear it? She was fortunate; in a few weeks she would graduate to crutches, then later, a cane. The fall down the stairs had broken her right ankle, and badly bruised her left foot, but she would recover.

It could have been so much worse, people had been paralyzed over such tumbles. It'd been so stupid! Where had her mind been? To fall down a flight of stairs at the local courthouse and in front of—of all people—her lawyer.

She'd been prepared to file for a legal separation. Jamie had met with the lawyer to go over details and was on her way out of the building to go home, while he on his way out of the building for lunch, when the mishap occurred.

Jamie laughed to herself at how her lawyer so aggressively searched the steps for ill repair or faults while she lay hurting at the bottom. He didn't even bother to call, so concerned was he with a possible lawsuit. She fired him on the spot, and now here she was.

She was glad she hadn't actually filed for the separation. It was funny how things worked out, because, at least for now, her husband was finally back home and behaving himself better than he had in years.

They had a wonderful, relaxed dinner together, and Jamie had never seen the kids so happy or well-behaved. David was almost too angelic. It was like he'd thought his dad had left because of him, and now that Keith was back, he was paranoid of making a mistake. They'd have to talk to him about that. On the other hand, Amber was her normal, squirmy, fussy self, but much less animated than usual. Everything was so calm and idyllic, almost dreamlike, that Jamie had the odd sensation she'd stepped into the fantasy world of June and Ward Cleaver. She wanted to accept it, and enjoy it, but a tingle of unreality gnawed at her. It grew stronger and, after supper, Keith asked the kids to go to their rooms to do their homework so he could have some time alone to talk to mom. She held her breath as he looked at her.

"How was the meal?" was the first thing he asked her.

"Great," Jamie said. "It felt like one of our old Sunday dinners. I could get used to this every day."

Keith laughed. "I don't think I could get used to the cleanup, though."

"I'm not *totally* helpless," Jamie said. "I think I could manage to stack the dishwasher."

"I'll take care of it. Don't worry about anything."

The way that Keith said ‘anything’ gave Jamie reason for hope.

“*Anything?*” she asked slyly, grinning.

And then, his face darkened. The proverbial ball fell. He didn’t say anything, but stared at the wall and clasped his hands together beneath his chin, thinking.

“What is it?” Jamie asked, wheeling her chair a little closer to him. “Look me in the face, Keith.”

Slowly, he looked at her. A limp smile formed on his mouth, but he could not hold eye contact.

Jamie sighed, and her heart grew heavy. So long, ‘Leave It To Beaver’ world. Her eyes dropped and she began to fiddle with the dishes in front of her. Maybe she didn’t want to talk to Keith after all, about anything. On further thought, she was certain of it.

As the silence between them thickened, Jamie grew even more uncomfortable. She turned the wheelchair and headed toward the living room. She heard the scrape of Keith’s chair as he got up to follow.

“Jamie,” he said, “we have to talk.”

“No, we don’t. Not now.”

“But you always want to talk. Especially when it’s about us.”

“Not this time.”

“Please.”

“Leave me alone, Keith.”

There was a short silence, then Jamie heard Keith take a seat in an easy chair. “Why were you at the courthouse?” he asked.

Jamie, facing a wall, did not reply.

“I have to know,” Keith said.

Suddenly Jamie spun to face him. “Do you? Do you really?”

He nodded. She stared hard at him, and her throat grew tight. Her eyes began to sting as she gazed at her handsome, but oh-so unpredictable and irresponsible husband. She wiped at a tear. "I was going to file for a legal separation," she managed to choke. "But, I didn't. Because of this accident. This accident may have saved us. Saved our future. We're together now, Keith. It's as it should be. It's as it's meant to be."

"I wish I was always as certain of that," Keith said.

That comment didn't surprise Jamie any, but it still hurt. "Stick around for a while, and you will be more sure of it," Jamie replied. "We need you."

Keith sighed, frustrated. "You need me, the kids need me, my agent needs me, Jeremy needs me, Keri needs…" at that, his voice dropped off.

"What?" Jamie asked. "Who needs you?" Her heart thumped as Keith refused to reply.

"Keith. Jeremy and *who* needs you?"

"Keri," Keith finally said. "Okay? Keri. A friend of Jeremy's."

"So why does a friend of Jeremy's need *you*?"

"Because—well, because she's a friend of both of ours."

Jamie doubted that this 'Keri' was some middle-aged school-marm who needed to have her lawn mowed or her sink fixed on occasion. "Who is she to you, and why does she need you?" Jamie asked, folding her arms.

"She's just a person I help out now and then."

Jamie nodded. "I see. And how old is she? Is she married?"

Keith became defensive. "I've no idea how old she is. I never ask a woman that kind of question."

"*About* how old, then? Fifty?"

Keith said nothing, but made a face and shook his head.

"Sixty?"

Again, he shook his head.

"Older or younger?" Jamie asked.

Suddenly Keith stood. "What is with you?" he

asked, "This interrogation is ridiculous!"

"Older or younger than sixty!" Jamie yelled.

"Younger! She's probably, oh, I don't know—thirty or so. And no—she's not married. I've heard she never sticks with just one guy for very long. I wonder if she even likes guys."

At that, Jamie's eyebrows arched. "So, what is it that you do to help her? Are you trying to change her mind about liking men? I should think the challenge would be irresistible to you!"

Keith put his hand on his forehead and looked away.

"Oh brother," he groaned. "This is getting absurd."

Jamie sat silently, chest heaving, tears trailing down her cheeks. She prayed the kids weren't hearing this. She didn't believe a word of what Keith was saying.

All at once the look on Keith's face softened. He walked over to Jamie, knelt down and took her hand in his.

"I'm not sleeping with her," he said. "She's just a strange, needy lady. Jeremy spends a lot of time with her and that's how I got involved, too. Actually, I think she may be a little screwed up. It seems like we each know a different person. Maybe she's bi-polar."

"Actually, I've wondered that about you," Jamie said, forcing herself to keep her voice calm.

Keith backed away and stood, letting her hand fall limp against the wheelchair.

"That isn't funny," he said.

"I didn't mean it to be. You're a very moody person too, Keith, and it's gotten worse over the last few years. There were times when I was… was afraid for the kids."

"Oh, for crying out loud," Keith said, raising his arms. "I'm an actor, Jamie! I don't have mood swings, I'm usually just trying to get into the mindset of a character. Not being in the business, you wouldn't understand that."

"I understand what the kids see, and it scares them sometimes."

"You're just jealous. You don't want me to be an actor because it makes you seem so ordinary. This has nothing to do with the kids. You don't like my career, and never have. It threatens you."

"What career, Keith? You haven't worked in months. No one is standing in line to offer you parts. I think you're having some kind of crisis, and your agent knows it and is *afraid* to get you out there again. Or, maybe, *you're* afraid to work again."

"Afraid? What would I be afraid of?"

Jamie bit her lip, then said, "Failure."

Keith sighed and sat down, putting his face in his hands.

"That's ludicrous. Afraid of failure? Just ludicrous!"

"Is it?"

Keith looked at her between spread fingers. "Yes. It is. I never set out expecting to be the most famous actor in Hollywood. Not even the hundredth most famous—or most talented. I just love the work. I love pretending to be someone else. I always have. I love it because…" he paused, thinking, "Well, I don't know, because…"

Jamie finished for him. "Because it's easier than being yourself when you don't know who you are."

Keith sat up straight. His face adjusted from a sneer to a bemused chuckle.

"That's a good one—that I don't know who I am. That's classic, Jamie. Maybe I ought to go see a shrink or go sit on top of a mountain to truly 'find myself.' Where do you get these ideas, anyway? You read too many of those women's magazines."

"You used to know who you were," Jamie said, ignoring his statements. "I married a man who had his feet firmly planted on the ground. He was a man who wanted a wife, a home, and children to carry on his name. He genuinely wanted to be the best husband and parent he could be, because his *own* parents were the worst they could be. It was a noble plan. At one time, you didn't notice or care that I wasn't flashy and popular. You loved me for me, and you said that would never change."

Jamie wheeled closer to Keith, who sat eerily still. She watched the color drain from his face as she continued.

"Let's get back to that, Keith, it's what's *real*, it's what matters. I still say, let's get out of here! Out of this… this phony Hollywood atmosphere and find a place where we can be ourselves again. You could work in landscape design like you always wanted to back in high school. You could coach Little League, go fishing in a clear stream, have a lawn big enough to need a riding lawn mower. It's all still possible! We're still young, and it'd be great for the kids."

Again, Keith put his head in his hands. He made no comment as Jamie wheeled right next to him and put her hand on his arm.

"C'mon, Keith, *think* about it. Think about us, about the kids. We can be happy again, all of us. We deserve it."

Slowly, Keith looked up. His eyes were red-rimmed. His voice was hoarse. "A few days ago you were in court ready to file for legal separation."

"I know. I was," Jamie admitted. "Then," she added as she looked down at her wounded legs, "*this* happened. Who knows why it happened. Maybe it's the best thing that could have happened. Maybe there was a reason for it that needed to be driven into our heads."

"A reason?"

Jamie nodded. "Yes. A reason for you to come

home once again."

Keith nodded. "Well, it certainly did that."

"And a reason for you to come home—to stay. If you ever leave again, I want us all to leave together. We can do it, Keith. Let's try again. It's worth it." She paused. "What do you say?"

Keith seemed to shrink into himself. He stared at his lap. He said nothing more, but when he finally lifted his eyes, David and Amber were leaning on the back of Jamie's wheelchair, hanging onto their mother and staring at him as though their very lives depended on his reply.

Chapter 17

How could people be so unrealistic?

Keri flung herself on her bed, feeling tired and out of sorts, and gazed at the ceiling.

The Vandenbergs were driving her crazy.

She'd shown them through twelve houses in three different towns, all beautiful homes—yet not one seemed good enough.

They wanted bigger. Better. *They couldn't afford bigger or better!*

Sure, the mortgage company had pre-qualified them for an absurd amount, and they could possibly make the payments for a home like that…if they lived on canned soup and crackers for thirty years and never left the house except to ride their bicycles to work each day.

Keri grabbed a pillow and pulled it over her face. The coolness felt wonderful on her skin. She'd been feeling crummy for the last few days, vestiges of a summer cold, she guessed. And there was that rotten, gnawing emptiness inside that she knew she wouldn't be able to kick until she finally—*finally* heard from Keith.

He'd been gone four days, and she'd heard not a word from him.

Neither had Jeremy.

Thinking of Jeremy, Keri pulled the pillow from her face and stared past the footboard of her bed to her dresser. She could see the edge of a piece of fabric resting against the wood, an old, weathered piece of fabric she'd lovingly cleaned and now used as a kind of ragged doily beneath her lamp.

Keri intended to keep that scrap of coat Jeremy had saved forever. First, because it reminded her of the reason her father bought that coat so many years ago, and second, for the care and the...the...she could scarcely think the word, the *love* Jeremy had shown her by rescuing it.

Rescuing it to the point of burning himself in the process.

Keri crushed the pillow over her face once again.

Jeremy *had* shown a certain kind of love for her in what he'd done, but it was the kind of love of a friend for a friend. It had to be. To think anything else would be too unsettling to consider. Too awkward.

But... said a little voice in her mind, she and Keith were more than friends, would Keith have leaped into the fire like that for her? Would it even have dawned on him as an act necessary in any way, or would he just have seen the coat as a stupid old rag hanging out of a wheelbarrow?

"No," Keri moaned to herself beneath the pillow, "he'd have gotten the coat out of the fire, too!" But a little image of her own face rolling her eyes and smirking "yeah, right," flashed across her mind.

"It doesn't matter!" Keri grumbled. She couldn't compare the cousins like that. Each had his own faults—and strengths. Keith could be remote to the point of rude sometimes, egotistical, and a little thoughtless. And Jeremy himself could be...well....

Keri's mind went blank. He had faults, of *course* he had faults! But nothing came to mind.

"He's not perfect, for crying out loud," Keri murmured. She'd have to think harder about it, some other time. Right now she was too pooped. Exhausted, really. It wasn't like her, usually she had enough energy for two people.

She rolled on her side, sighed, and stared at the telephone on the nightstand. “Ring,” she whispered, trying to will the machine into action.

She couldn’t, and wouldn’t, contact Keith, and Jeremy was of no help in reaching him. It was all so secretive, so cloak and dagger. It was so cruel of Keith to leave her as he had. Didn’t he even wonder where Jeremy had been last Sunday morning? Didn’t he wonder if Jeremy was seriously hurt in the fire? Didn’t he wonder if Keri was seriously hurt by his actions?

“Ring!” Keri groaned.

Her hair nearly stood up straight when it suddenly rang. She came to life and snatched the receiver. “Hello?”

“Hello, Keri,” said the well-known voice on the other end of the line.

“Keith!” Keri said. “I’ve been worried about you!”

“And not totally ticked at me?” he asked.

Keri paused. “Well—yes I was. For a while. Then I realized it must have been pretty urgent for you to leave as fast as you did.”

“It was.”

“Is everything okay for your friend?”

“It’s better now. Complicated, but better.”

“Can you tell me what happened?”

There was a silence on the other end of the line. “Keith?”

Keri said.

“So—how is Jeremy?” Keith asked.

Keri’s shoulders sagged. So, he was still being mysterious. At least he remembered, and was concerned about Jeremy.

“He’s hurt,” Keri said. “Burned his hand and wrist, but it’ll heal. It’ll slow down his woodworking, though. He’ll need help. You coming back soon?”

"Keri," Keith said, and Keri did not like the tone of his voice, "we have to talk."

A dull humming began to fill Keri's ears. "I'm listening."

"You mean so much to me," Keith said. "I know we're great friends, but…"

"Friends?" Keri asked, suddenly unable to feel the receiver in her hand. She began to feel numb as Keith continued.

"Yes—friends. Really great friends, Keri. And we always will be. But…"

"But?" Keri managed to repeat.

"But I'm not coming back," said Keith.

Keri shook her head to try and whirl away the fog.

"Not coming back… for how long?" she asked. "A few weeks?"

There was no reply. "Months?"

"Not for a long, long time," said Keith. "If ever."

Keri pulled herself to the edge of the bed and began to rock back and forth, the phone suddenly feeling like a foreign object in her grip.

"Keri?" Keith asked. "You there? Are you all right?"

"But Jeremy needs you," said Keri.

"Jeremy has you," said Keith.

Keri shot straight up. "Me? What do you mean by that?"

"I think he thinks of you as his best friend."

"Oh no. No, no," said Keri. "I'm the person he should hate. I'm the one that hurts him, and burns him."

"Nonsense," said Keith. "He needs you."

"But I need you!" Keri said. "Come home, Keith!"

"Keri, don't you get it?" said Keith. "I am home. This is where I belong. I have my friends and my career over here. You've always known that."

"I know, I know. But I thought things had

changed."

"They have. I'm staying here."

Suddenly an idea struck Keri. "Then let me come out there… let *me* be the one that moves! I'm always on the go, anyway, and I know Los Angeles. I still have a few contacts, I can get my old realtor position back. It'll work. Yes, it'll work!"

"Keri," Keith said, but Keri refused to listen, and rattled on.

"We can be together, like we should be. In the City of Angels. It'll be great! We can go to those crazy parties together, hang out in all the right places, stay up until dawn, and watch the sunrise through the smog. As long as we're together, everything will be fine. It'll be better than fine, it'll be perfect!"

"Keri…"

"We're destined to be together, you know? I have a list of all the reasons why. And now here's another. I stared at the phone and willed it to ring—and it did!"

"Keri, you're sounding weird…"

"I wanted it to be you, and it was!"

"Keri…"

"We're soul mates, Keith. Don't you feel it?"

"Get a grip on yourself!" Keith suddenly shouted, and Keri's jaw snapped shut.

"Just take a breath, relax, and listen to me," Keith said. "I've got things to do out here, complicated things to take care of and a lot of old issues to resolve. I can't leave. It'd be running away and I don't want to run anymore. I'm sick and tired of it. And don't say you can help me, because you can't. I don't *want* you to. I need to start taking care of things myself. You'll be fine, Keri. You're so strong, and independent. It's what I've always liked about you. Go on with your life and be happy."

Keri couldn't believe what she was hearing. Go on with her life and be happy? Who said things like that?

Except, of course, she did, on occasion—but only to guys she had dumped.

Her blood ran cold. Her voice was a squeak. "Are you dumping me?"

"Keri, we never really had anything to…"

"Are you dumping me?" she demanded.

"I wouldn't call it that. We'll always be friends."

"So. When and where can I contact you?" Keri asked, "if we're such great friends. If I'm not getting dumped!"

"I don't know. I'll call again. Later. Maybe after things calm down."

"Keith, how can I reach you?"

"I have to go now, Keri. I really do."

"Keith!"

"Goodbye, Keri. I hope Jeremy will be okay. He'll take care of you."

"But Keith…"

Click.

Keri stared wide-eyed at the phone, the beast now dead in her hand. Her fingers popped open, and it dropped to the floor.

Slowly, she sank back on the bed. Dazed, she lay back down, stretched out, and stared at the ceiling. There were a few cobwebs scattered in the corners. She should get them, clean them, but how could she when she suddenly realized she couldn't feel her body. She was weightless. Numb. Just a pair of big green eyes floating above her bed.

So this is what it feels like to be dumped. Soon she wasn't feeling much at all.

"It can't be over between us, all the signs were there for you to finally be the right one for me," Keri insisted.

"What signs?" Keith asked.

Keri stared into his shadowy face. Clinging tatters

of mist drifted across it, obliterating his eyes for one moment, his mouth the next moment. The fog was cool and clammy on her skin in the dismal mist.

"The signs," said Keri. "You know, the *signs*." But, suddenly, she couldn't think of even one.

He turned his back on her, and began to fade into the distance.

"Keith, come back!" Keri said. "I'll remember them, I know I will. It'll make a difference!"

But Keith continued to shrink into the fog. Soon he was only a dark patch in the distance, amid the wisps of lonely swirling mist.

Keri was left in silence. A silent world of emptiness and chill.

"Keith…" she whimpered, "come back, I need you…." Only silence.

Keri heard her heart beating against her chest.

"Keith." she whispered, tears trailing down her cheeks. Her knees went weak, and she sank to the ground. "Don't leave me, I need you, don't leave me."

"Straighten up, Keri," came a voice behind her.

"What—who?" Keri asked, and slowly turning her head.

It was clearer where he stood, almost as though the sun was ready to break through the mist that was strangely falling away from him.

Jeremy.

"Please, stand up," Jeremy said again. Something about the tone of his voice, oddly authoritative yet gentle at the same time, made Keri gather her strength and stand.

"Come here," Jeremy said, and held out his hand.

"Keith left me," Keri sobbed, but found herself drawing nearer to Jeremy. He seemed spectral as she stared at his outstretched hand, his comforting hand, as she stepped toward him. When she reached him, she took his hand, and he pulled her close.

A jolt of something indescribable, joy mixed with peace and an incredible calmness pulsed through her at Jeremy's touch. He held her hand tighter, pulling her closer, and Keri began to quiver as she found herself face to face with Jeremy, gazing into wonderful eyes radiating a calm assurance and wisdom she had never before encountered. Heat raced through her and her legs became weak.

Jeremy's eyes glimmered. It paralyzed her to stare into them. Those eyes seemed to search into hers, gently probing, as though trying to connect with her soul. Keri became lightheaded, intoxicated, the poison of Keith's rejection now drained away.

"You're going to be all right now," Jeremy said, and his voice seemed to roll like thunder and yet felt a breathy whisper at the same time. It echoed as he continued, and suddenly the fog parted and a warming blaze of sun fell across them.

"I'll stay with you," said Jeremy. "You don't have to be afraid anymore. You can finally be yourself."

Those words flowed through Keri in cascades of relief. Finally, finally she felt it. She couldn't quite grasp what it all meant, but a weight had lifted.

"Thank you, thank you, Jeremy," Keri said, gulping in great breaths of air. "What would I do without you? You're the one I need, you're the one I was meant for all along."

At those words, Jeremy smiled. Keri's eyes strayed toward his lips, and lingered there. His mouth smiled, his eyes smiled, and Keri was sure his heart smiled, too.

And so did she. Keri let go of his hand, and slowly wrapped her arms around his neck. He put his arms around her shoulders and drew her tighter to him. When they fully connected, the warmth of their touch was explosive, and Keri could scarcely control herself. She closed her eyes and suddenly, tantalizingly, his lips were pressed against hers. She gasped inwardly as the warmth and movement of his kiss sent shivers down her spine and into her toes. At first Jeremy's kiss was sweet and gentle, but as it became more urgent, its passion leached all of the strength from Keri's limbs until she was practically hanging limp in his embrace.

All she could think was—*how did he learn to kiss like this?* Was it the way it was supposed to be when two people were genuinely… in love?

No—it couldn't be! Jeremy was just her dear friend, like a brother, really.

Yet…

"Aunt Keri, get up!" said a wee voice far, far away. "You promised to play opera lady with me this morning."

"What?" Keri moaned.

There was a soft shaking on her shoulders. "Aunt Keri, Keri, get up, sleepyhead! Take the pillow off your face."

Reality crawled back to Keri in a lazy wave. Jeremy's embrace vanished, and the scene dissipated into fragments as Keri awoke, reluctantly pulling herself from the dream. Only a dream.

"Jutht a minute, Kate," Keri mumbled. "Have thum patienth."

"What?" Katie asked. "You sound weird."

"It'th the pirrow on ma face," Keri said, rising slowly as she removed the pillow. "I like ta thleep like dat."

Keri noticed the oddity just as Katie's eyes bulged at her.

"What's wrong with your face?" Katie cried.

Keri's hand flew to the right side of her face, which felt heavy and numb. It seemed dragged down, contorted. She could barely see out of her right eye.

"There's drool coming out of your mouth, just like Rover's," said Katie. "I think your pillow got too heavy! It melted your face!"

Keri tried to gasp, but her mouth would not work correctly. It seemed weights were pulling her lip down on the right side, making it lopsided.

Dear Lord… *had she had a stroke?*

She flung off her blankets, twisted to the side of her bed, and sat up. It seemed her right arm worked fine, as well as her leg. And she could think clearly. But the horrified look on her niece's face confirmed the frightening fact that something was drastically wrong.

"I'm going to get Mom," said Katie as Keri pulled herself off the bed and rose, testing her legs.

"Mom!" Katie bellowed.

She ignored her niece and, after finding her legs quite sturdy, raced into the bathroom. Her heart pounded as she flicked on the light and looked into the mirror.

Her hands rose to her face in horror.

The mirror was warped, it had to be! Or water was on it, or something, anything!

She did not look like a monster!

As children, she and Kelly and friends used to use this bathroom to play "Mary Worth." Spin around in the dark enough times, repeating the name, and when you stopped and looked in the mirror, you were supposed to see a witch. Of course, no one really had.

Until now.

"I'm a flreek!" Keri sputtered out the left side of her mouth.

As Katie had said, the right side of her face seemed to have fallen, or melted. Her eyelid drooped and she was unable to open it, unable to move it at all. And worse, the right side of her mouth was drawn down into a horrid frown, and any way she tried to move her mouth merely resulted in a disfiguring grimace.

She had to be still dreaming. She *had* to!

Suddenly Kelly burst into the door, with Katie just behind her.

"What's going on…what's the matt—" Kelly gasped and her eyes bulged. "What happened?"

"You tell me!" Keri said, tears running from her one good eye. "I woke up like thiz."

Kelly took a moment to collect herself, and massaged her frightened daughter's neck to comfort her.

"Are you dizzy…is your side paralyzed?" Kelly asked.

Keri shook her head. "I feel fan, exthept for this!" she moaned, pointing at her face.

"Is Aunt Keri going to die?" Katie whimpered.

"No—no," Kelly said, trying to control her breathing and sound calm. "I think I know what's going on."

Keri looked sharply at her. "You do?"

"A co-worker's brother had the same thing happen to him last year. I think it's Bell's Palsy."

"Did Aunt Keri get hit by a bell?" Katie asked, tears brimming.

"No, honey, it's just the name of the man who invented it. I mean, named it," Kelly said. "A big nerve in your face goes funny, and this happens. But," she hastened to say, sounding brighter, "it almost always goes away. His did."

"How long until it gothz away?" Keri sputtered, still trying to work her mouth. But it was no use; the whole right side of her face felt like the terrible after-effects of a dental numbing disaster. And there actually *was* a little drool sliding from her mouth!

Keri looked away and put her hands over her face.

"I don't know how long it takes. I suppose it's different with every case," Kelly said.

"Like maybe a day, or two?" Katie asked, and Keri

glanced hopefully at her sister for the reply.

"I don't know." Kelly paused. "I think it's more like weeks, or maybe months."

"Nooo!" Keri wailed.

"Just control yourself, you're scaring Katie!" Kelly warned. "You'll be okay. But, let's get you to the doctor, just to be sure."

She turned to look at Katie. "Now Katie, honey, you stay here with daddy. Tell him mommy had to take Aunt Keri to the doctor and we'll be back as soon as we can. Can you do that for me, sweetie?"

Katie, trying to be strong, wiped her tears and nodded.

"Let's go," said Kelly to Keri.

"Bat I'm in mah pajamaz," she said.

"As long as you're not in your birthday suit, we're going!" Kelly said, and pulled her away from the mirror.

"Katie, go let daddy know what's going on, okay?"

"Tell him that Aunt Keri has Mr. Bell's face?"

"Sort of," said Kelly. "Go on now—we have to go to the hospital."

With that, Katie scurried upstairs, and Kelly dragged Keri out the back door.

Two to three weeks at the very earliest, but three to four months, was more probable. That's how long it could take for Keri's facial nerve to heal, if in fact it healed at all. Ninety percent of all cases heal just fine, the doctor had assured her. He prescribed a short duration of oral steroids, rest, and a patch for her eye at night. She'd also have to put drops in her bad eye several times a day to lubricate it.

That was all they could do until time ran its course.

It was unfathomable. A disaster.

She could never leave the house until this was over.

How had this happened? The doctor said stress, combined with a cold or a virus could have done it, but no one knew for sure.

Keri kept wondering about her dream.

She'd been unfaithful to Keith in that dream. Even though he'd said he didn't want to see her anymore, she didn't believe him. He'd get things worked out, and they'd be together again. So why did she have that crazy dream about kissing Jeremy?

Keri pounded the kitchen table in frustration.

It was the dream that did this. Her guilt! Thinking of Jeremy like that! How could she?

One thing she was certain of, though, was how glad she was she wouldn't be seeing Keith for a while. He'd never get past how she looked.

A deformed hag.

"Can you get that soup down all right?" Kelly asked, puttering around in the kitchen nearby.

"If I conthentrate," Keri mumbled, staring darkly at the bowl of chicken broth before her. Even eating was a trial, now.

Suddenly the front door burst open and in dashed their mother, her eyes wild. She spotted Keri hunched over the tableand raced to her side. "Honey! Are you okay? I just heard the news. Let me see you!"

Keri glumly lifted her face to show her mother.

"Oh, sweetie. How awful for you!" Keri's mother cupped her hands around Keri's face and tilted her head, gazing into her daughter's eyes.

"It'll go away, soon, I'm sure of it. My friend Sharon's son's daughter had it, too, a few years ago. And she's fine today!"

"How long?" Keri mumbled.

Her mother looked at her questioningly.

"How long did thee have it?" she asked again, wiping chicken soup from her chin.

"Well, I'm not sure."

"No one's ever thure."

"You're going to heal fast," Mrs. Ferrita said, smiling in the well-meaning but condescending way that mothers do. "I just know it." She took a seat at the table, and put her hand over Keri's. "You'll be fine, soon, just wait and see."

A moment later, Katie came out of her room and ran to greet her grandmother.

"Katie-did, sweetheart, how are you?" Mrs. Ferrita said, hugging the child.

"Did you come to see Aunt Keri's face?" Katie asked.

"Uh, no, I just stopped by to see you."

"But look at her face!" Katie said innocently.

"Katie, that's not nice!" Kelly said, coming over to join them at the table. "Hi, mom. Great to have you stop in."

"What's all the commotion?" came a voice from down the hallway, and soon Andy appeared, holding baby Quentin in his arms.

"Oh, hi, Mom," he said.

"Hello Andrew, and also hello there, baby Quentin!" She held out her arms to take the baby. Andy relented and carefully handed him down to her, then pulled out a chair and sat down too. Kelly gave him a quick kiss on the cheek, sighed, and sat down next to him.

Suddenly everything was quiet as Keri slurped on her soup.

Everyone was trying so hard *not* to look at her. How was she going to live like this?

The silence continued, comical yet uncomfortable at the same time.

"Why don't you all jutht get one good look, and eat your own lunth," Keri said, tossing her spoon in her bowl.

"Yeah—look!" said Katie.

Just then a knocking came at the door.

"I'll get it," said Andy. Halfway to the door, he could see who it was through a side window. He turned hesitantly toward Keri. "Keri, it's Darci."

Keri's face fell even more. Oh no! She was supposed to be at an open house today! She'd forgotten all about it. She glanced at her watch. It was already one thirty-five.

She'd never make it. She *couldn't* make it.

Disfigured monstrosities don't sell houses!

Before she knew it, Darci was walking over to her. Keri buried her face in her hands.

"Keri? Are you sick? I tried to call, is your cell phone off? They had to cancel your open house! Your boss called and asked me to check on you because I live nearby. What's going on? No one can reach you."

Keri sighed, then slowly looked up and faced Darci, eye-to-eye.

Darci shrieked and Keri smirked. After what Darci had done to Jeremy at the party last weekend, she deserved a little payback.

"Nithe to thee you again," she said. Gloating at Darci's discomfort, Keri forced a smile that she knew twisted her face into an even more ghastly grimace. Darci stepped back, put her hand over her heart, and leaned against a counter for support. Her wide eyes never left Keri's face.

"For heaven's sakes," said Kelly, coming to the rescue, "it's not like she went face-first into a wood chipper, Darci."

"Aunt Keri's face is stuck," Katie chirped in. "Mr. Bell gave it to her."

"Katie, we told you, no one gave it to her," said Andy. "It's just a bad nerve. It'll heal soon."

"And Aunt Keri will look just fine again," said Mrs. Ferrita, in a manner Keri thought was touched with uncertainty.

Darci slowly broke from her daze. "You poor thing," she said. "You poor thing!" She paused, then, "What will Keith think?"

Silence struck again.

Keri lowered her head and pushed away her soup bowl. "He'th in California," she said.

Darci's eyebrows rose. "Oh—that's right. Maybe that's a good thing right now."

"Darci!" Kelly said.

"Well, I'm sorry, but you know what I mean," Darci defended herself. "I'm not sure Keith would understand."

"Says a lot about Mr. Keith," Andy sneered.

"Oh, I'm sure he'd understand!" Mrs. Ferrita said. "He's a good boy."

"He's a creep," said Andy.

"He's not a creep," said Darci. "He just, well, he has standards is all."

"Like Keri won't match up to his standards because something like this happened, something totally out of her control?" Kelly said bitterly. "If that's so, then I agree, he is a jerk."

Suddenly Keri stood, hurt and fuming. "He won't be seeing my face for a long time."

Everyone stared at her.

"We broke up." Everyone gaped at her. Darci was the first one to break the hush.

"How did he see you? Does he have one of those picture phones?"

Keri spun around to her. "You assume that he broke up with me because he saw my face?" she asked, incredulous.

"*He* broke up—with *you?*" Darci asked, even more

incredulous.

"You're kidding!" Andy said.

"That can't be so," said their mom, shaking her head and holding Quentin against her chest as though comforting herself. "That just can't be." She patted the baby's back. "No one breaks up with my Keri."

Keri moaned as everyone began talking at once. Their voices became a buzz in her ears and her head began to ache.

"I have to go back downstairs," she said.

"But why?" Katie asked.

"I need to find an old towel to cut up. I'm going to cut one eyehole out of it and wear it over my head like the elephant man!"

Then she stomped off.

"Who is the elephant man?" she heard Katie ask.

Chapter 18

Jeremy was surprised at how fast Andy scurried him toward the basement to check on Keri. Andy seemed past frustration, moving toward hostility.

"I hope you can get through to her, Jeremy," he said. "I'm getting ready to wring her neck. I've had to hold Kelly back from doing so more than once this week."

"It can't be easy for Keri to live with a condition like that," Jeremy said as Andy herded him toward the stairway.

"It isn't easy for us, either," said Andy. "Straighten her out, Jeremy. She'll listen to you. If you don't, we're shipping her to Siberia in a barrel with no return postage."

"That bad?"

Andy nodded and rolled his eyes. "Just do your best. If you can't do it, it can't be done."

"Why do you say that?" Jeremy asked, genuinely confused.

"Because she relaxes around you. She can finally be herself. No airs."

"I think we're talking about a different person."

"I never said she wasn't drifty, Jeremy. She doesn't always know who she is." At that, Andy whispered "good luck" and gently closed the door to the stairway behind him.

Jeremy shook his head, grasped the rail, and

carefully went down the steep steps into Keri's domain. She didn't know he was coming, and that's how Kelly had thought it should be. Jeremy was still amazed that Kelly had thought to call him to help. Did she think he had that big of an influence over Keri, and, if so, why?

Jeremy felt a sudden heat in his cheeks.

Or...were his feelings for Keri more obvious than he'd thought?

Before he reached the bottom of the stairs he quietly called Keri's name. He didn't want her to be shocked by his unexpected appearance. It was mid-afternoon, and although he doubted she'd still be running around in her pajamas, Kelly had said she was behaving oddly. Jeremy had seen her covered in balloons, covered in mud, even dressed up like Raggedy Ann, but he didn't quite know what he'd encounter under these circumstances.

"Keri?" he called again, taking the final step and peering around the corner. "It's Jeremy. Can I talk to you?"

Still no reply.

He stepped into the dining area. No one was around. The basement was quiet and still, yet he knew Keri was down here—possibly in bed. He walked over to the bedroom door, and, with a deep breath, knocked. "Keri. It's Jeremy. Can I please talk to you?"

"It's not a good time," came a mumbled response.

"When will be a good time?"

"Try this time next year."

Jeremy shook his head and sighed. "Keri, I know what happened to you. Nothing will shock me."

"That's what you think."

"Please—may I come in? I won't stay long."

There was a pause.

"I guess so," came the reply at last.

Jeremy gently opened the door and slipped inside.

His heart was in his throat as he gazed over at the bed, where Keri lay in a wad with the covers pulled up over her head. He went over and sat beside the vaguely human-shaped pile of sheets.

"It's got to be hot in there," Jeremy said.

"Sorta," came the muffled response.

"Come on," Jeremy said, "take off the sheets. Let's go outside and take a walk."

There was no reply.

"It won't take long," said Jeremy, reassuring her again.

"Will anyone thee me?" Keri asked.

"Maybe Rover and the horses. No one else is out there."

"Well—maybe." But she didn't move.

"Let me help you," said Jeremy. With his good hand, he found the tip of the sheet by Keri's head and gently pulled it down…

…to see that Keri had a pillow plastered over her face.

"The pillow has got to go, too," said Jeremy.

"I kind of like it," said Keri.

"C'mon—I'm removing it."

Keri lifted an arm as if to refuse, but slowly let the arm fall as Jeremy took the pillow off.

Jeremy's eyes widened. Now she had a baseball cap pulled over her face.

"You're being difficult," he said.

"I don't think I'm ready for this," Keri mumbled, and, putting her hand over the cap on her face, turned sideways away from Jeremy.

"It's going to be all right," said Jeremy. "This will pass, Keri, and become a distant memory someday. But you have to get on with your life now."

"Get on with my life? How long did it take *you* to get on with your life after what happened to your family?" she asked.

That stung. Jeremy sat up straighter. He didn't say anything and could think of nothing to do.

Keri was right. How long had it taken for him to get on with it after what happened to Hannah and Seth? Still, that was different. Not the same at all.

"You're not going to die from this," he said, shocked that it came out of his mouth.

"Oh Jeremy—I'm sorry," Keri said all of a sudden, lifting herself to grasp his hand, but in her hurry, she accidentally grasped his bandaged hand just as her cap flopped off. Jeremy sputtered a gulp of pain as he caught sight of Keri's face.

Keri's good eye widened. "Sorry again!" she said, releasing his hand and turning away. "I always make such a mess of things!"

Jeremy shut his eyes against the pain, willing it to subside. Keri's face didn't look bad to him at all, just different, maybe. But it didn't shock him—the throbbing and stinging in his hand was more distracting than her condition.

"Keri, you don't mess things up any more than the rest of us," he said. "I deserved what just happened."

"You don't deserve what I said about your family," Keri said. "I don't know what's wrong with me—besides the obvious." She slowly turned back to him. "There. Take a good look. Let it repulse you and then leave. I'd only hurt you more, anyhow, if you stay."

"I'm not worried about it," Jeremy said, sighing. "I live with Scalawag, remember? Your face isn't that unusual to me. And if you hurt me somehow, I've been warned. But I'm a pretty strong guy for a shrimp."

"You're *not* a shrimp," she said, looking him full in the face.

Jeremy looked into Keri's eyes, one wide open and glazed with tears, the other half shut and drooped. Her mouth was drawn into an unnatural frown on one side. A heartbreaking aura of sadness radiated from her.

"You're beautiful," Jeremy said all of a sudden.

Keri's good eye widened before an expression of puzzlement came over her. Jeremy felt his cheeks burn again. Why had he said that? He always seemed to spout out things like that in her presence—even in the most absurd moments. Still, what he'd said was true.

"I mean it," he said, growing bolder. "Keri, I've seen you dressed like a clown with—with—what did your niece call those balloons sticking out of your neck?"

"Ham-rods. Her way of saying hemorrhoids."

Jeremy's eyebrows raised. "Oh—so *that's* what she meant. I always wondered."

Keri smiled ever so slightly as he continued. "I've seen you covered in mud, I've seen you dressed like Raggedy Ann and a bunch of other things. But nothing is as interesting or wonderful as your true face, even like this."

"Why do you say things like that?" she asked, shaking her head. "I don't deserve it. I'm a nutcase. People call me 'Scary Keri,' or, 'Keri Ferrita, 'the Man-Eat-a.' I've always been flighty and maybe just a little self-centered. What do you see in me that no one else sees?"

She was crying now, and Jeremy's heart went out to her. He relaxed, and sighed softly.

"I see a woman who will risk falling into a stinking bog just to help a turtle cross the street. I see a woman who isn't repulsed by Scalawag's face. I see a woman who loves to dress up and help make sick children laugh for the first time in days—maybe even weeks. I see the *real* you, Keri, because, for some odd reason, you let me."

Keri looked at him, a strange mix of emotions and

turmoil criss-crossing her weary face. Jeremy lowered his eyes, not wanting to frighten her in some way with his confessions, yet knowing he had to tell her now he felt or he'd regret it one day. He glanced around the small room with its sunny yellow paint and cheery pictures on the walls. This was decorated to be a happy place, a haven. Then he stiffened as his eye caught on something hanging from the top of her dresser, a weathered raggedy piece of fabric, so out of place with the rest of the room.

It was Keri's old scrap of a coat.

"I want to keep it in sight," Keri said. "It reminds me of who I am. Sometimes it's good, sometimes not."

Jeremy looked back at her and found her staring at his bandaged hand. She tried to smile.

"You've got a heart of gold, Jeremy," she said. "I could never thank you enough for saving that rag for me, but look what happened to you because of it."

"It will heal," Jeremy said. He began to subconsciously rub his lower leg, where he'd also been burned, though not nearly as severely. It was more like a bad sunburn.

"I still don't know why you did it," Keri said. She rose higher on the bed and pulled her legs over the side and sat next to him. She was wearing a loose-fitting white short outfit and her legs were smooth and creamy. Her toenails were painted a shimmery pink. The warmth of her skin next to his made him tremble.

"I did it because it meant a lot to you," he said. "It reminded you of your dad, and of your pony. Your *youth*."

"No one else would have cared."

"I'm not sure about that."

Suddenly Keri stood up. She walked to the dresser and began to finger the fabric longingly.

"No, they wouldn't have cared," she said, then

paused. "Keith wouldn't have cared," she added bitterly.

Jeremy rubbed the back of his neck, uncomfortable at hearing Keith's name. He said nothing, allowing her to vent. A part of him that he didn't like enjoyed hearing her anger, as long as it was aimed at his cousin. Keith deserved it, he was certain of that. Still…

"I didn't even dare call him to tell him what happened," Keri said. "I slurred so bad in those first few days before I had learned how to work my mouth again, I sounded as much a freak as I looked. Even after he gave me the kiss-off, I didn't want him to think there was something really, physically wrong with me."

Jeremy's heart jumped. *Kiss-off?* Keith hadn't told him about that. Jeremy knew Keith had returned to take care of Jamie, as he should, but he'd finally broken it off with Keri? How much had he told her? Did Keri finally know her Romeo had a wife and two kids begging for his attention?

"Keith likes everything to be perfect," Keri continued. "I never feel like myself around him. Yet, I can't stand *not* to be around him. I don't know what's wrong with me! Why can't I feel like I do whenever I'm with you, Jeremy, when I'm with him?"

Jeremy could hardly breathe. A shiver went down his back. "How do you feel around me?" he managed to ask.

Keri turned to him. "Comfortable," she said. "Myself. No airs, no games. I know you don't critique me. You don't compare me to others. I sometimes feel like I'm in a show and everything I say and do is getting analyzed and used against me. I don't know why—but I don't know how to lose that feeling."

"But you don't have that feeling with me?"

"No! That's what's so great about it," Keri said, raising her arms. "I think you're teaching me something, Jeremy. Slowly, maybe. But that it's okay to be me. It's okay to feel relaxed and comfortable in my own skin. I'm learning to like it… just a tiny bit. When this, this *face* problem goes away, maybe I'll be a better person for it."

"I think you're all right, right now."

"That's because you see the real me," said Keri. "As you said, I *let* you see the real me. Few people do. I can be a jerk, but not as much of one when I'm not always 'on.' I want to be a better, more normal person, Jeremy, I really, really do."

Jeremy stood. "Well, I'm grateful you think I've had a hand in it if you're feeling better about yourself. That's quite a compliment."

"You have the biggest hand in it!" Keri said, walking over to him. "Ten minutes ago I didn't even want you to see me—and now I feel better. You seem to bring out the best in me."

Jeremy was glowing. He didn't know what to say. His toes were curling in his boots, and all he could do was stare numbly at Keri, a lump in his throat.

"And you know, maybe it's not so much Keith's fault he blew me off," Keri said. "He never knew the real me. Maybe someday, he will. When I'm better, when I'm more, more *me*."

The words jolted Jeremy so much he sat back down on the edge of the bed.

"What do you mean?" he asked, heart beating furiously against his chest. "You want to actually see him again?"

"Maybe when I'm better. When I'm healed and stronger."

"But why? After all he's done?" It became obvious that Keith hadn't told Keri about Jamie and the kids. There was no way she'd want to see him again if he had. Frustration brewed in Jeremy's stomach and boiled into his throat. He wanted so badly to spit it out—so badly did he want to blast out all Keith kept hidden. But Keith had made him promise not to—a promise made on the basis of how loyal and helpful he'd been when Hannah died, and later, Seth. It'd be like a betrayal to them if he blabbed Keith's secrets, wouldn't it? Keri was so close to him now, so within reach!

But she was also extremely vulnerable.

Jeremy put his face in his good hand. If he told Keri, she'd be so devastated, she might never truly recover, especially in her condition now. This wasn't the right time. It seemed it was never the right time! Jeremy felt himself sinking. The weight on his shoulders was unbearable. He felt, more than ever, that he was playing a role in Keith's deception and he had no idea how to free himself of it without hurting Keri even more.

Suddenly Keri was sitting next to him again.

"Jeremy! Are you okay?" Her words seemed a thousand miles away. Muffled and faint.

"I'm fine. Just a little dizzy," he heard himself lie. "I haven't eaten yet today."

"Are you hypoglycemic?" came the far away voice. "Let me get you something. I probably just have pickles and cheese, but it'll help."

The weight lifted off the mattress next to him as Keri left. Jeremy fell back on the bed, trying to ignore Keri's scent on the sheets.

What was he to do?

He took Keri's pillow and crushed it over his own face in frustration.

There was no way to win in this. If he told Keri about Keith, he'd lose. If he didn't, he'd lose. Keri was heading for a big shock one of these days, if she continued to think it would ever work out with Keith. Why was she so insistent on gaining that man's love and respect? Maybe it was some crazy flaw in Keri's character. But, maybe not.

Keith was tall. Charismatic. Handsome.

And vain, dishonest, and selfish.

And who was he? Little old Jeremy, the cabinet-maker with his little old house in the woods and his deformed dog? No money, no connections, no glamour.

Jeremy hadn't felt this insecure in a long time. What did he have to offer Keri? How could he make her happy?

But she did say that he made her happy—a better person.

He was paving the way for someone else to win her heart is what he was doing. Whether it was Keith or someone else.

Could he live with that?

Suddenly the extra weight was back on the mattress. "Jeremy! Sit up. I found you some cheese, crackers, and deli chicken. I made some little sandwiches for us."

This time it was Keri pulling the pillow off of Jeremy's face.

"Didn't this just happen—in reverse?" she said. She set a plate of food down on the bed and leaned down over him, put an arm beneath his neck and pulled him up. Jeremy relished her touch and didn't think he could stand it if she ever let him go.

"Come on," she said, leaning next to him, her arm still around his neck. Her warmth was intoxicating. Even her breath was sweet. He stared into her face and couldn't move. She began to feed him her little sandwiches and he was helpless in her embrace.

"C'mon—eat. You'll feel better. I always do." She paused. "Don't know what I'd ever do without you, Jeremiah Quinn. Don't you ever leave me, okay?"

Jeremy chewed on the sandwiches, and stared into her eyes. He was always just going to be her friend. Always. Could he really live with that?

“Someday I’m going to repay you for all the kindness you’ve given me,” said Keri. “I promise. You won’t regret it.” She gave him a friendly kiss on the cheek, and picked up another one of her little sandwiches.

Just maybe he could live with that.

At least, for a little longer.

Kelly was about to lightly tap on the door to tell Keri she had a phone call from a client when she caught sight of Keri feeding Jeremy the sandwiches. “Oh, no,” she whispered under her breath, backing away. “Poor Jeremy. Poor, poor Jeremy.”

Chapter 19

Keri tipped the rim of her hat up enough to take a good, long gaze at the sky. The sun glowed against the golden leaves swaying on the branches above her, creating a striking contrast against a sky so big and blue it nearly took her breath away.

At last she looked down, and continued to rake. She loved the scent and rustle of the fall leaves. She hadn't been sure she'd be able to enjoy it this year, but she was. She raked harder, faster, relishing the physical workout. Jeremy would be arriving soon, and she wanted to impress him with the huge pile of leaves she'd created. Big as a minivan! She knew it wouldn't last, though. She could picture what would happen once Jeremy arrived. They'd clutch hands like little kids, run toward the pile, then yell like banshees before leaping in and scattering leaves everywhere.

Maybe they'd even make leaf forts and pillage and plunder each other's domain.

Her heart swelled with joy. She hadn't felt this good in months… maybe even years. She'd been learning to let down her guard around people, and not be as afraid of what they'd think of her facial distortion. Something was working, because the paralysis was slowly losing its grip on her muscles, and she looked a little more like herself every day. She didn't even have to wear a hat when she was out anymore, although she was beginning to enjoy them now that she didn't have to tip them down over her face.

Life had become bearable again. Even fun.

"That's quite a pile," a voice said behind her.

Keri turned to see Kelly walking down the driveway toward her, baby Quentin bundled in a stroller. Keri leaned on her rake, proud of her work.

"It's almost as big as the ones we made when we were kids—remember that?" she asked.

Kelly laughed and pushed the stroller close. "Sure do. Remember when you were hiding under a pile and Jim VanderVeen rode his bike through it and ran over your legs?"

"It was my butt. How could I forget!"

"Could have been worse."

"A lot of things could have."

"Hey, you don't tell Katie about all of those things, do you?" Kelly asked, scrunching her eyebrows. "Don't want her to get ideas."

"C'mon, you know I'd never give Katie… *ideas*."

"Yeah—right," Kelly said. "Oh, by the way, one of your clients called. Wants to make an offer on the old Hanlon house. You're doing well, Keri. I'm proud of you."

"Thanks. I'm really 'raking it in' again," Keri laughed, swishing at a few more leaves. "Thanks for letting clients call the house while my cell phone is recharging, Kelly. Keeps me on top of things."

"You're welcome."

Kelly was starting to push Quentin on, when she stopped and looked back.

"Why *are* you making it so big, anyway? We can't burn it like that."

"Jeremy's coming over to play."

"Oh. Oh! That's nice."

Keri cocked her head oddly at her sister. "Why did you say that so funny?"

"Funny? What do you mean?"

"It's like it bothers you that he comes over so much. It is your house, Kelly, and if he bugs you, let me know. I don't want to take advantage of all you've done for me. We can go other places to hang out."

"Don't be silly. Both Andy and I love Jeremy. He's a doll. And he's great with the kids."

"Okay. Just wanted to make sure."

Kelly smiled, a little uneasily, though, and began to move away. Keri stared after her as Kelly slowed to a stop once again, and looked down.

"What is it?" Keri asked.

Kelly sighed. "Oh, nothing really. It's not important. Just

have fun."

"No—what is it?" Keri asked, dropping the rake. "You can tell me, sis." She walked over to Kelly and looked her in the face. "What's bothering you?"

Kelly looked flustered. "I don't know how to say it."

"Then just say it."

Kelly rolled her eyes, shook her head, then spat it out. "Do you realize just how head over heels Jeremy is in love with you?"

Keri's jaw dropped.

"He is," Kelly said. "It's all over his face. When you walk into a room it's like he shines, like he gets taller."

"He—well, he might love me, as a friend," Keri said, "I don't think it's like what you think!"

"Then you're in denial."

"No, I'm not in denial. We're just great friends. Kindred spirits."

"If you say so." Kelly turned to move on.

"Why would it bother you if he was—not that he is—in love with me?" Keri asked.

Kelly stopped again. She seemed to have a hard time finding the words to say. She watched a leaf twirl to the ground and stared at it.

"Kelly…" Keri said.

"I guess it's because you've always been so used to having guys in love with you that you either don't see it anymore, or it doesn't mean much to you," Kelly said. "I usually don't care, but I'm a little concerned this time. So is Andy."

"But why?" Keri asked.

"Well, because we still know you're infatuated with Keith, even though you haven't heard from him in a few months, and we're afraid Jeremy is going to get hurt. He's the best guy you've ever dated, I mean, hung around with. He's great. He's good for you, too. But we're just not sure that…" she paused, "sure that…"

"Sure of what?"

"Well, sure that you're good for *him*."

Keri rubbed her eyes and looked away. She couldn't believe she was hearing this! "Am I some kind of monster or something?" she asked, genuinely hurt. "I'm trying to be a better person. I don't want to go around messing with people's feelings."

"But you still have to learn to *sense* what they're feeling before you can figure out if you're hurting them."

"And I don't do that?"

"Not if you can't see that Jeremy is in love with you."

Keri looked down at the ground, numb. Finally, she asked, "He *shines* when I walk into a room?"

Kelly nodded.

"And it's like he gets taller?"

She nodded again.

"Wow. I don't know what to think."

"Just be careful," Kelly said. "Don't lead him on.

As long as he knows where he stands with you, he'll be fine." She paused. "He does know where he stands with you—doesn't he?"

When Keri didn't reply, Kelly stared at her hard. "Do *you* even know where he stands with you, Keri?"

Keri moaned. "I don't know. I have to think about all this. Take your walk, Kelly, have fun. Thanks for the input."

Kelly shrugged. "Okay. See you later."

Keri watched as she walked away, happy and content in her little hobby-farm world with her cute little baby in his cute little blue stroller. A strange feeling of sadness washed over her—she was so confused all of a sudden! Sighing, she backed toward the leaf pile, then flopped into its crispy, cushiony embrace. She closed her eyes against the flutter of leaves covering her face, the heady aroma filling her senses with its earthiness. "Now what do I do?" she murmured.

Jeremy. In love with her. Couldn't be.

She wasn't his type, she was certain of it. He didn't even really know her.

He knows me better than Keith does, said a little voice in her head. Well, maybe Jeremy did know her. More than most, anyway, but she was working on that. She was changing.

She was going to reunite with Keith one day, she'd promised herself that. Show him her true self. That was probably the biggest problem they'd had between them. They'd both put on airs, and tried to look and act more important than they really were or felt. Maybe if Keith saw that she could relax, then he could relax, too.

But, oddly, she wasn't thinking of Keith that much anymore. Sometimes, she could barely remember his face, and when she did, it was the memory of his angry face yelling at her for being so 'clingy' the night of the Fourth of July party so long ago.

The night Jeremy had burned his hand.

Keri shook her head, trying to resurrect better thoughts. Leaf tidbits tickled into her ears and mouth. She decided it was nice inside this leaf pile. Cozy. Hidden. Kind of dreamy. Like falling back into a sweet memory.

And then, she remembered the dream where Jeremy had kissed her so passionately.

Keri gasped. It felt so real. Just as the dream had been. She could feel Jeremy holding her, pressing his lips against hers, and all thoughts of him being just a friend were washed away.

Gone.

But how could that be? Something was at war within her. She couldn't be with Jeremy, he was too…too…

Too what?

Too short? He was a little taller than she was. Still a bit short, though.

People would stare. Cute couple. Couple of munchkins. *So what!*

She thought deeper about this. No, unexpectedly, his height wasn't the problem. He was just too…too…nice? Too good to her? And guys who were nice and good were usually dull, and any attraction she'd ever felt for them faded away after the first few kisses had become routine.

She knew this about herself. It was a pattern, it'd been a pattern her whole life. So far, Keith had been the only one different. The only one with all the signs, crazy as they might be, that he was the ultimate one for her. Mrs. Keith Quinn. Keri Quinn. She'd even found herself doodling it here and there on occasion, and she liked how it sounded.

Keri Quinn.

"Is there a body attached to those feet?" came a

voice from the outside world.

Keri shot up, leaves trailing off of her, to find Jeremy standing in front of the pile, laughing. "You snuck up on me!" she sputtered.

"No, I just wandered over to see whose feet were sticking out of the pile"

Keri couldn't help but grin. Jeremy did brighten her world with his intelligent, clear eyes, his ready smile and floppy, scrunchable brown hair. Today he had a shadow of a beard and moustache, and Keri wondered if he was growing it out for the coming winter. It'd probably make him seem older, more masculine and less elf-like. Still, he looked good in khaki pants, a tasteful green and yellow plaid shirt and his faithful buckled boots.

He'd blend right in with the leaf pile.

The thought of him diving in with her and then snuggling in the leaves together rushed across Keri's mind, and she felt her cheeks grow warm.

Who'd know? Kelly was out for a walk with Quentin, probably to Wendy Weber's house to talk baby talk together for hours, and Andy had taken Katie to see a kids' movie. No one would be around for a while.

Should she test it? Should she see if Jeremy really did love her like Kelly suggested?

"Keri? What's wrong?" Jeremy asked.

"What?"

"You seemed really deep in thought there for a moment."

"I did?"

He nodded.

Suddenly Keri didn't know what to say or do. It became uncomfortable to look at Jeremy without seeming to give her thoughts away. What thoughts, kooky ones, too.

But—maybe she could kiss him, somehow, just for fun and see what happened. See how he reacted. Find out how *she* reacted.

"Don't lose your hat," said Jeremy.

"My hat?"

"It's behind you—sticking out of the leaves."

Keri turned. "Mercy sakes, it is. Forgot about it. I guess I'm not hiding as much from the world these days."

One of Jeremy's eyebrows shot up and he gave her a goofy smile. After all, she was half-buried in a huge pile of leaves. *Should she test Kelly's observation?* Keri kept staring at her hat. Finally she tugged it out of the pile and brushed the leaves off. She put it on, a cream-colored hat with a floppy brim and vine-patterned ribbon, and turned back to Jeremy.

"It's cozy in here," she heard herself say. She moved over a bit and patted the pile next to her. "C'mon, dive in."

"Dive in?"

"Well, at least jump in. I made this pile just for us to mess up."

"Are you sure?" Jeremy asked.

"Positive. Now, come on. Back up and take a running leap. I promise there are no hidden sticks or stones or old ladies to land on."

"Old ladies?"

"Or sticks or stones."

"In that case…." Jeremy paused, then began to back up. He stopped about twenty or thirty feet away, then yelled, "Cowabunga!" and raced toward the pile.

Keri laughed, and scooted over a little farther.

For a small guy, Jeremy's burst into the pile created an explosion. When all the leaves settled, there was an indent where he'd leapt in, but no sound and no further movement.

"Jeremy, where are you?" Keri said. "Come out, or I'll have to root you out myself!"

When the only reply was a muffled, "Find me," Keri tossed off her hat, brushed some leaves aside with her arms, and began to bore through the loose leaves with eyes closed, feeling for him.

Now was her chance! Jeremy was asking for it, asking for an 'accidental' collision which could lead almost anywhere.

In the darkness and damp, Keri kept her eyes clenched tight against leaf grit and continued to work the leaves with her arms. Nothing. Was he moving away from her? Teasing her? She sputtered a few leaves out of her mouth, continuing to arc her arms, grasping for fabric.

And suddenly, she felt flannel. "Aha!" she murmured.

It could be Jeremy's arm or back or chest, she didn't know, but continued to grasp and feel the fabric until she heard Jeremy laugh.

"That tickles!"

So, of course, Keri tickled on purpose. Jeremy laughed again, and Keri knew she had him in the stomach. She went after him, both hands tickling now, and he laughed harder. Suddenly her right hand was in his strong grip, stifling her play, and the next thing she knew, her left hand was captured too.

But where was his face?

All was darkness, the smell of earth and the warm sensation of the blanket of leaves covering her. Covering them both, like two gophers in a den.

Keri tried, but not too hard, to pull out of Jeremy's grip but he only held firmer. She tossed, and began to roll over, squealing at him that he was in trouble, really going to get it now, and all at once she felt the weight of his body against hers. They rolled a few more times, kicking and playing, until they suddenly burst out of one end of the pile and lay together in the grass.

Jeremy was pinning her down, laughing, his hair a mop of leaves. "What will the neighbors think?" he asked, the charming smile never once leaving his face. His eyes were bright with joy, a little mischief… and more.

Now was Keri's chance.

"I don't see any neighbors," she said, looking around, "Nope, no neighbors for a mile. We're alone."

"Alone?" Jeremy said, his voice slightly husky.

"Alone," Keri whispered, staring up at him.

Jeremy's smile faded, and his expression became more serious. His weight seemed luxurious to Keri, and her legs began to quiver as he stared at her. She looked into his eyes, then down past his nose to his mouth, and all strength drained from her.

He was going to kiss her—and she wanted him to. *But…but…but…*said her conscience. *It'll ruin everything! If this doesn't last, you can't even be his friend! You'll be together only, then you'll get sick of him, just like all the rest, and everything will be ruined! You'll both go your own way and never see each other again.*

Keri gasped.

The thought of never seeing Jeremy again was unbearable. She turned her head just as Jeremy's mouth came close. "I can't!" she said, instantly destroying the magic.

Jeremy rolled off, his face stricken.

"I'm sorry," Keri said, "but I don't want to know you only for a short time!"

Jeremy sat back, blinking, dazed, leaves sticking out all over him.

Oh no, what had she done? Keri could fix it. She sat up, brushed leaves from her hair, and stared at him. She could do it. Tackle him. Sit on him and smother him with kisses. She really wanted to—oh, how she longed to hold him!

She leaned toward him, body taut, ready to spring.

"I don't know what came over me," Jeremy said suddenly. His voice was remorseful. "I'm so sorry. I usually have better control."

"It's okay, nothing happened," said Keri.

Jeremy got to his feet, leaves fluttering off him. "I'd better go."

Keri shot to her feet. "No, don't go! It was only an almost-kiss between friends."

Jeremy looked at her solemnly. "Keri, I've laughed with friends. I've cried with friends. At times, I've hugged friends. But I've never, ever tried to kiss just—a friend." He turned away. "I do have to go." He shambled away toward his truck, pulling leaves out of his hair and clothes.

Keri's heart pounded as she stared after him. She didn't know what to do as he got into the truck without even looking at her, and started the engine.

"Are we still on for going up to the hospital this Saturday?" she called out.

Jeremy paused before backing out. When he replied, he barely looked at her. "I'll let you know. Scalawag hasn't been feeling himself lately." With that, he backed out and drove away.

Jeremy walked through his front door, shut it behind him, and leaned against it for support. He was shaking. He couldn't think. He wiped at his eyes with his good hand, ignoring the ugly red scars on the other. How long was he going to torment himself?

Keri didn't feel the same way about him as he felt about her, and it'd become obvious that day. She'd turned away from him.

What had she said… that she didn't want to know him for only a short time? What did that mean?

He knew.

If they became more than friends, Keri felt it would never last. She still wasn't over Keith, and Jeremy had allowed himself to believe, somehow, that he could replace his tall, Hollywood cousin.

Jeremy stared around at his cute little home, his father's home and his grandfather's before it, and everything became lonely and bleak to him. It was silent, dark. The kittens were gone now, he'd given them to friends, and Scalawag—where was he?

"Scalawag?" he called. "Where are you?"

Hair tickled across his forehead, and Jeremy pulled another leaf from it and set it on the table, not looking at it. Sighing, he pulled his grandfather's bandana out of his pocket and tied it around his head. He'd go work out in the shop, clear his mind.

"Scalawag?" he continued to call, looking around. Still, no sign of the dog. A shiver drained down his spine. Scalawag usually showed up by now. Jeremy continued to hunt around the house, and finally, on weak-kneed legs, went into his den and turned on the light.

Still nothing.

Jeremy's heart beat faster. He had no idea how old his faithful companion had been when he'd found him in the field, but he hadn't been a young animal even then. And, he had been slowing down this past summer.

Still...

With his heart in his mouth, Jeremy pushed open the secret paneled door to his hidden room.

"Scalawag?"

As the darkness eased, Jeremy saw him. Sprawled on the floor, motionless below the photos of Hannah and Seth.

"Oh no—not now," he moaned. "Scally," he cried, cowering over the shaggy body of his dog. "Scally, wake up."

And then, slowly, the tail began to wag.

"You waited for me, didn't you?" said Jeremy, sinking to his knees. He cradled the dog's ruined face in his lap and Scalawag gazed up at him with his one, good, adoring eye. If it had to come to this, Jeremy was glad he'd been was home. He continued to pet his dog, to love him and talk to him, until the good eye dulled into a peaceful sleep.

Chapter 20

Another backup on the freeway. What was it this time?

Keith clenched his eyes and tightened his grip on the steering wheel, even though traffic was standing completely still. The air was thick with humidity. Sweat rolled from under his newly dyed brown hair and down his face and neck. Where did all these motorists come from? Where were they going?

He wasn't even sure where he was going.

Keith had just been sent to his sixth casting call that week, his twelfth in less than two weeks, and still nothing. He'd been sent away, passed over like trash discarded by a well-fed dog, And it'd only been for a tiny, fifteen-second commercial for laundry soap this time.

He knew what Jamie would say. Give it up. Leave this crazy, dog-eat-dog world. Move somewhere more relaxed, less frantic. Her idea of adventure was to sneak up some sunny hillside to explore an old castle in Europe, or to backpack deep into a primeval forest and not come out for days.

They were so different, he and Jamie. It hadn't always been that way, though. Jamie hadn't changed, he had. He knew it, but he was trying to hold things together, keep the marriage intact. Even though she didn't seem to recognize or appreciate what he was trying to do for this family.

Keith looked around at the people trapped in their

cars. Bored, ornery people in sunglasses surrounded him. Their faces were drained of all expression except disgust or impatience. Many were chatting into their cell phones in one hand, leaning their heads in the other hand. Most were sweating. Maybe they were low on gas, as Keith was, and were afraid to run their air conditioning. They were trapped, all of them, in more than just another traffic jam on the freeway.

Keith sighed deeply and tried to relax, but he felt torn inside. The trapped feeling overwhelmed him, and the miserable, stuffy air in the vehicle had made him uneasy. If he could only break loose, he'd float above the thousands of disgruntled motorists, shoot out over the hills and into cleaner, cooler air and head west to the ocean.

Or, maybe East, to the Midwest. Talk to people who knew him better, understood him. Looked up to him.

Without thinking twice about it, Keith pulled out his cell phone and punched in Keri Ferrita's phone number. It was three hours later there, but she should still be out and about, selling some house or another. He honestly didn't know if she even still lived with her sister and brother-in-law, but he was going to find out just what she was up to these days.

Keri heard the voice on her cell phone and felt nauseous. She pulled her car to the side of the road and hung her head out the window to get some air.

Jeremy's message had been short and to the point. He'd be unable to make it to the hospital that day. Scalawag had had some kind of doggie stroke a few days ago, and needed intense medical attention. Jeremy wasn't able to face the kids just yet.

Why hadn't he told her about Scalawag earlier?

Grief flooded Keri for the dog, as well as for his master. Jeremy had to be feeling terrible. But why hadn't he called her for support? Was it really so weird between them now that he could no longer talk to her about such a crushing event? She finally pulled her head in and leaned back against the headrest.

She should go to him. Cheer him up. Somehow. Anything. But the last thing Jeremy's message had said was for her not to worry about him. He'd be all right, but he wasn't ready to face her again.

Was she really bad for him, as Kelly had suspected? Couldn't she sense other people's feelings yet? Was she that naive? That cold? Who was she? Suddenly her cell phone rang, startling her. She grasped it immediately. "Jeremy?" she asked, hoping against hope.

"It's not Jeremy. It's the other Quinn. Keith."

"Keith?"

"Yes. Remember me? I know it's been a while."

"It's been months. A lot has changed."

"Are you still living with Kelly and Andy?"

"Yes."

"Still hanging with my cousin, I see."

Keri sighed. "Scalawag is really sick, Keith. Jeremy isn't doing so well right now."

"Oh no. What happened?"

Keri shook her head. It was hard to speak past the knot in her throat. "He had a stroke… and seizures," she said. "Look, Keith, it's not a good time. I have to go help Jeremy, even if he doesn't want me to."

"What do you mean he doesn't want you to?"

"It's complicated," was all Keri could say. What she really wanted to add was that Keith hadn't wanted her help, either, and now he was hundreds of miles away, leading some mysterious new life. She couldn't let that happen with Jeremy. Still, along with the bitterness of hearing Keith's voice, a little bit of the old thrill edged into Keri's bones. She tried to suppress it.

"Why did you call, Keith? Since I'm not allowed to

call you, it must be important. Get a part in a big new movie or something?"

"Working on it."

"Is your friend who was in that accident better?"

"Yes, she's up and walking with a cane."

"Hmm." Keri paused. She hadn't even known the 'friend' was female.

"I have to go," Keri said.

"No—wait!" Keith sounded almost frantic.

Keri sighed and waited.

"I know I haven't always been up-front with you. You deserved better. I want to apologize."

"Why now?"

"Because it's been haunting me. To tell you the truth, things are a little crappy out here. I don't like how people are treating me, and it's making me realize how people might have felt when I treated them the same way."

Keri sat straighter as she digested those words. Could it be? Could it be that Keith was going through the same type of growing experience she was still reeling from? Could it be even *Keith* was letting go of his ego enough to finally sense other people's emotions?

"Keri—you still there?"

"I am."

"Good. I don't want to keep you from whatever you have to do for Jeremy and Scalawag. I just wanted to let you know I was thinking of you, and that there are some things I regret about our relationship. Things I did. And I also hope you're doing well."

"I'm fine. I'm changing a little bit, too," Keri said. "Maybe we can talk more about it at another time."

"Sounds great. I'll call back."

"Can I call you?"

There was a hesitation. Then, "Sure."

"Maybe I will, then."

"Goodbye, Keri."

"Goodbye, Keith." Keri clicked off her phone, then looked at it oddly. Had that call really just happened? Or had she imagined it? Keith—apologizing? Keith—changing?

Who could tell what life still had in store.

Still, Keri didn't have time to dwell on it. If Jeremy wasn't ready to see her, she knew someone who was ready to see her. And it wasn't Keith this time.

Keri smiled to herself as she walked through the hallway, gazing at the beautiful vines and animals on Jeremy's mural. She knew the painting cheered a lot of sick kids. It even cheered her. She'd need to hold onto that feeling to talk to little Matthew Bender this afternoon. He was one of the few kids left who hadn't yet gotten well enough to go home and still he looked forward to regular visits from Scalawag.

She had to let him know, somehow, that Scalawag wouldn't be visiting anymore.

Poor Matthew, at age nine, had fallen out of a tree house and broken his back. He was paralyzed from the waist down, and had also lost an eye from hitting a branch. He'd connected with Scalawag right away. After getting to know this little boy, half-blind and confined to a wheelchair, Keri learned that maybe her own Bell's Palsy hadn't been the horrendous fate she'd originally thought it to be. It'd been kind of funny, actually, when she, with her droopy face, Jeremy with his bandaged hand, and Scalawag with his missing parts, all trooped into the hospital like old war victims.

She'd actually miss that. Keri stopped at Matthew's room and peered into the partially open doorway. An aide was just coming out after giving Matt his supper, pushing her trays past Keri. "Where are your buddies?" she asked.

"That's what I have to explain to Matt," Keri said softly. "It's a long story."

The aide lifted her eyebrows. "Ah. Good luck, then. He's been in a gloomy mood all day."

"Oh boy. This'll be interesting."

As the aide left, Keri slipped inside, wondering just how to tell Matt what had happened. She was able to stand and think quietly a few minutes while he was eating in bed, intently watching a cartoon. When he saw her, a huge grin spread across his face.

"Keri!"

"Hi, Matt the rug-rat! Didn't want to interrupt your meal..."

"It's kinda icky. The macaroni and cheese smells like fish."

"Fish!"

"Or something weird. Not mac and cheese."

Keri walked over to the side of the bed where the little sandy-haired, brown-eyed boy lay. "Hmm—hope it's not macaroni and *fleas!* Or macaroni and sleaze!" Keri said.

"Or, macaroni and bees!" Matt said, giggling.

Keri studied his plate. "Nope—looks like mac and cheese to me. Nothing interesting. I guess you should probably just eat it."

"I guess. Hey, where's Scalawag? Where's Jermie?" Matt asked, craning his head around Keri to see if they were in the hallway.

Keri stared at the little kid with his bandaged eye and lifeless legs and sighed. She pulled a chair next to him and flopped in. "Jeremy is feeling a little sad today," she said. "Scalawag is very sick."

"What's wrong with him?"

Keri leaned her chin into her hands. How to explain this? "He's very old, and very weak. He needs a lot of rest right now."

"He's sleepy?"

"Yup," said Keri. "I'm not sure how long he'll be sick. He might not have the strength to come back up here anymore. We just don't know, but we don't want to poop him out, do we?"

"No, I guess not." His eyes became moist. "Is he going to die?"

Keri's voice trembled. "I don't know, I hope not. Then her tone brightened as a thought stirred within her. "But, he did send you a message."

"He did?"

"Yes… it's this." Keri let out a series of barks, whimpers and growls that would put any real dog to shame.

"Woah!" said Matt. "He said that? What does it mean?"

"I had to go to the library and look it up in a doggie translation book," said Keri. "I think it means that he's sorry that he can't visit, and that he'll miss you. But he wants you to be happy, and get well."

"Oh," Matt said quietly. "I miss him too." His lips began to tremble and tears welled.

"And there's something else," Keri added.

"There is? What?"

"He said that…" Keri looked around as though to make sure that no one was listening, "he says to make sure that you never—*ever*—poop in poison ivy!"

Matt laughed at that, and Keri joined in. Maybe they'd both be okay, after all.

Jeremy leaned against the doorway into Matt's room and had to smile. He couldn't have explained Scalawag's disappearance any better than Keri had. He thought of joining them, but something stopped him. She and Matt had a connection going, something marvelous to see, and he didn't want to risk interrupting that.

And maybe, just maybe, Scalawag, unconscious and dreaming, was in a place where it was warm and sunny right now. A place where he had two good eyes, two good ears and four good legs. It was worth believing.

Jeremy slipped his hands into his pockets and walked away.

Chapter 21

Daniel closed his eyes and rested his forehead in his hand. "Darci," he said, "I'm sorry, but this is just not working out."

Darci clenched her teeth at the sounds of Nathan screaming and carrying on behind the door of his bedroom. Even a psychologist…a *child* psychologist… wasn't able to crack through to Nathan. What else could she do? She was desperate.

"He'll be fine. Just give Nathan some more time," Darci pleaded, holding Daniel's arm and leaning against him on the sofa. "He'll straighten out. I know he will!"

"Darci," Daniel said, looking her in the eye. "The only thing that can straighten him out is you. You need to love him, but love him enough to discipline him. You feel sorry for him so you pamper him. You need to focus extra attention on him, but without spoiling him. You don't need a man to do that."

Darci sat back, stunned. She let go of Daniel's arm and her own arms fell limp.

"I think, I truly think, that that's the way to help him," Daniel added. "When he's a little older, a little more confident and secure, *then* start dating again, but this just isn't right. I've seen it too much. I hate to say it, but you've got to forget about me for a while and focus on your own little man."

"How can you say that?" Darci asked, straightening. "A boy always needs a man's influence around him to grow up normal and healthy. I've heard that all my life!"

"That's what the Big Brothers are for."

"The Big Brothers?"

"Yes. He'll get all the male attention he needs to pattern himself after, without hating him because he's taking his mommy away."

Darci shook her head. "That can't be true. Why couldn't you have told me this earlier? We've been dating for months!"

"I'd hoped Nathan might be an exception. Some boys adapt better than others to these situations. I'd hoped, in vain, that it would work out, but it was for my own selfish reasons, Darci, so I could be with you. I see now, that it just can't work out. I'm sorry, but it's best for the boy."

As Daniel got to his feet, preparing to leave, Darci's demeanor changed.

"Do you know how often this happens?" she said, trying to keep her voice low, but it was heated as she choked back sobs, "that a man leaves and says he can't stand my little boy? Do you know how often? Don't you think Nathan figures it out? I thought you were different!"

Daniel lowered his eyes and sighed. "You just nailed it on the head," he said quietly. "It happens way too often. You *let* it happen by getting involved too often. You have to learn to love yourself, Darci, and be strong and independent so you don't need a man around."

"I don't need a man around!"

"Yes, you do. You're *too* needy."

"No, I'm not! I'm with you because I thought you'd be someone good for Nathan, not for me! I wasn't thinking of myself this time."

Daniel's face fell. "I see."

"I didn't mean it that way!" Darci said. "It came out funny. You're not like the guys I usually date, that's true, but it's a good thing!"

"My advice to you, no matter what your rationalizing is, is not to date at all," he replied. "Not until you get a grip on who you are when you're all by yourself." Daniel turned and walked out the door.

"But…." Darci whispered as she watched yet another man leave. "I don't like the company when I'm by myself." She fell back into the sofa, dazed. Was what Daniel said true? Was she *that* needy? Did Nathan sense it, too, and was he afraid of it?

No, it couldn't be true. None of it, it was all psychobabble. She'd show 'em! Darci picked up her phone and punched in Keri's number. She answered on the first ring.

"Keri, it's Darci. I need to talk to you."

"Are you all right? You sound shaken."

"I am, a little. But I think my head is clearing, now."

"What's the problem?"

"I think you were right all along, Keri. I didn't need to get involved with someone like Daniel. I need to be involved with someone more like who you said, someone like your friend, Jeremy."

Just as she said it, Darci stopped short, stunned by her own admission. She *needed* to be involved with…?

But, so what? What was wrong with that? Maybe someone like Jeremy needed her, too. No one else seemed to.

"Let's try to work it out again," said Darci.

Chapter 22

"This is my friend, Darci, who needs that toy box I was telling you about," Keri said, stepping into Jeremy's shop, Darci at her side. "It's a Christmas present and she's going to give it, filled with toys, to her son, Nathan."

"What a great idea," said Jeremy. After the introductions, he ushered them further into his workshop. Darci grinned at Keri as Jeremy walked ahead of them to get his scrapbook of photos.

"Nice tush," she mouthed, following close behind.

Keri nodded at the comment, and could think of nothing else to say as a sense of unease swept through her. Should she really be setting up this situation? *Of course she should!*

Darci was dressed down. Jeans, a snug, green button down sweater, her reddish locks pulled up in a ponytail. And her shoes… flat loafers to off-set the obvious height difference between her and Jeremy. Keri watched Darci's eyes closely, and found Darci not even glancing at Jeremy's shoes.

Maybe the girl with the shoe fetish really was changing, but it was what she *was* staring at that made Keri frown.

"I think I remember seeing you at the Fourth of July party," Darci said to Jeremy, "but unfortunately I had to leave early and we didn't get introduced."

"That was quite a night," Jeremy said, pulling the

scrapbook out of a niche above one of his workbenches.

Darci glanced at Jeremy's hand. "I heard about your 'accident' in the fire. It seems to be healing well. Does it hinder your work?"

"Not really, not anymore," Jeremy said. He motioned toward an antique wardrobe in need of repair. "I'm trying to extend myself and get into restoration work, though, and I'm a little concerned about what would happen if I got paint stripper on my hand."

"A good pair of gloves will be important," Darci said.

Keri smiled and piped in. "I didn't know you were getting into furniture repair. When did you decide to do that?"

Jeremy wouldn't look her in the eye. "I've been considering it for a while. It'd be an honor to repair pieces made by master carpenters so many years ago. Maybe I'll learn something."

Keri gazed around Jeremy's quaint, old fashioned shop and studied some of the items he was currently building. An oak desk. An enormous china cabinet. An Arts and Crafts styled buffet. Then Darci said aloud what Keri was thinking.

"A hundred years from now, restorers will be saying the same kinds of things about your work, Jeremy. These pieces are fabulous."

"Thank you," Jeremy said, turning with an awkward smile. Then he glanced at Keri, and quickly lowered his eyes. He turned away from her and flipped open the scrapbook. Darci stood next to him, her hands folded behind her back, and inked at Keri.

"How old is your son, and what kinds of things is he interested in?" Jeremy asked.

"He's seven now," Darci said. "And mostly he seems to be interested in getting his way right now."

Jeremy laughed. "I was like that at that age."

"You were?" Keri asked, surprised. What was this? Darci had been talking to Jeremy for only a few minutes and already had learned things about Jeremy that Keri didn't know after months.

"I was quite the stinker—so my mom says," Jeremy added, still flipping through the book.

"It seems you turned out okay, though," said Darci, flashing her flirty smile. "Gives me hope for my son. Hey, look at that. That's magnificent!"

She pointed at one of the photos in Jeremy's book, stopping the pages from flipping. Her hand brushed against Jeremy's, and she pulled it away as though she was embarrassed.

Keri rolled her eyes.

"Thank you. It was quite a job," Jeremy said, and Keri had to peer between them to see the photo.

"That's the cradle…the cradle with a canopy you were working on when we first met!" she said.

"It's awesome," said Darci.

"It was fun," said Jeremy. "Pretty extreme, though. It's amazing what some people ask for."

"I don't need anything that fancy," said Darci. "Just a toy box, one shaped like a car maybe. Can you do that?"

"What kind of car?"

"Oh—I don't know. Corvette, maybe."

"How about a convertible? The lid to the box can be the roof."

"Hey, I like that idea. It'd have to be a pretty graphic design, though, to actually fit toys in it."

Jeremy began paging through the scrapbook again.

"I know it's in here someplace…" he murmured. "Another toy box, designed like a giant caterpillar. Ah, here it is!"

"Wow," Darci said quietly, and Keri could tell Darci was genuinely impressed. "That is amazing." She paused. “Just amazing.”

Suddenly she turned to Keri.

“I can’t believe the things this guy can make with his two bare hands! I’ve never seen anything like it. I know you’re probably used to seeing the things in this book, Keri, but it’s all new to me.”

Keri said nothing, only nodded. She had never looked through the book herself. Why not, she had no idea. She hoped Jeremy didn’t know.

“Keri talks a lot about you,” Darci said to Jeremy, “but nothing compares to actually meeting you and seeing your work. You’re a talented man, Jeremy Quinn.”

Jeremy smiled a little but said nothing. Keri could tell he was embarrassed.

“Talented but humble. A rare combination,” Darci added.

As Darci and Jeremy continued to talk and look through the book, Keri stepped back, feeling oddly out of place, the proverbial third wheel. She no longer paid attention to what they were talking about, but Jeremy’s soft voice and Darci’s giggles were enough to make her realize it was time to make her exit.

She and Darci had discussed this.

“Leave me alone with him, at least for ten minutes or so,” Darci had said. “Let me work on him.”

But oddly, Keri didn’t want to leave. She studied the couple, trying to imagine them walking through a mall or down the street together.

Ridiculous. Absurd. Darci was three or four inches taller than Jeremy. But Darci sure wasn’t seeming to care! Not anymore.

Keri shook her head, uncomfortable with what she was feeling just now. What was it, anyway? Jeremy was just her good friend, a sidekick, as Darci used to call him.

That was before Darci had truly met him. *Before she was trying to take him over.*

"I'm going into the house, have to use the powder room," Keri announced, backing away further. Neither Jeremy nor Darci seemed to hear her.

She sighed, and left the shop on wobbly legs. She walked beneath the arbor and rubbed her arms, shivering beneath the shrunken brown boughs above her. This place used to seem so magical to her, but now, in early November, things were dead and dry. Barren. Keri looked through the arbor at a cold grey sky threatening rain. She felt just as cold and grey inside.

What was her problem?

She glanced back at Jeremy's shop, and had to suppress an urge to peek in the window to see what Darci and Jeremy were doing. He was being awfully polite to Darci, more than he'd been to Keri these past few weeks since the leaf-pile incident. He wasn't rude to her, she'd never seen him be rude to anyone. But he was distant, and nothing she did seemed to shake him out of it. There were no deep talks, no goofy antics. When she tried to bring up the leaf-pile incident, he'd paled and looked away.

Couldn't she even talk to him anymore?

Keri wondered if she'd really done something that wrong. She'd searched her mind, trying to put herself in Jeremy's position back then, trying to be sensitive to other people's feelings as Kelly warned her to be, but she'd come up with nothing. They hadn't actually kissed!

So, why had Jeremy almost kissed her? Had she been leading him on just enough to make him think she was ready for it? Suddenly she heard Kelly's scornful voice invade her mind.

Y-e-e-s.

Keri almost physically wilted. She'd had so many

thoughts and emotions spiraling in her that day that it was hard to sort them out and analyze her motives, but, one thing stood clearly. She *had* led Jeremy on, then had rejected him at the last second. No wonder he was uncomfortable around her.

Why had it taken this long for her to see that? She remembered Kelly's words… "*You still have to be able to sense what people are feeling before you can figure out if you're hurting them.*"

How could she have been such a dunce wagon?

She wasn't good for Jeremy. He was far too nice for someone like her, too kind. Just as a lot of guys had been in her past. Maybe their kindness wasn't the problem, though, as much as her own fickle nature was to blame. "It's heredity!" Keri said out loud, to no one in particular.

Would she forever be tormented by her own weird nature?

"It's my nature," she said out loud again, only much more softly. Dejected, Keri took a last look at Jeremy's shop, sighed, and walked the rest of the way beneath the arbor to the back door of the house.

She'd go in, relax, and give Darci her ten minutes alone with Jeremy. Heck, she'd even give her twenty minutes alone with him. Maybe they could make each other happy, and that would be a good thing. It dawned on Keri that that was a very selfless thought and she wondered if she really was changing, or if there was still a dab of jealousy behind her good will.

She pushed open the door to the house and stepped in.

Of course she wanted Jeremy happy. Of course she wanted Darci happy.

But happy, together?

As Keri entered the familiar surroundings of Jeremy's little home, she tried to brush the thoughts from her mind. Her head hurt, and she was confused. Nothing seemed right anymore. She tried to shake the disturbing thoughts out of her head as she entered the kitchen.

"Scalawag, Scally! Where are you?" she called. Then, as the silence and stillness of the home settled in around her, she remembered. Scalawag was still very sick, at the vet again. She felt a detached sensation and hung her head. She hadn't been in Jeremy's house since the dog had gotten ill. The emptiness of the home surrounded her, smothered her, just as it must Jeremy day after day. As the almost surreal loneliness of the house pressed in around her, tears pricked her eyes. She wandered through the kitchen, through the dining room, and into the living room where she flopped down on the sofa. She pulled her legs up and wrapped her arms around them, curling into a ball, and gazed vacantly ahead in the gloom. Eventually, she closed her eyes in misery.

This must be the ultimate agony for Jeremy. The ultimate twist of the knife. To lose his wife. His son. And now—even his dog might not make it. *And Keri was lost to him, too,* was probably how he felt.

Just as well. She'd only hurt him more one day. That was her nature, her curse. Keri moaned, feeling more dejected than ever. She sat that way for a few minutes before slowly opening her eyes, letting them wander around Jeremy's humble abode. Then something on the sideboard across the room in the dining area caught her eye. Something…familiar. Curious, Keri gathered her strength and pulled herself to her feet. She walked listlessly to the sideboard, staring at the item until it came into focus.

A card. *Her* card.

She'd sent a sympathy card to Jeremy after hearing about Scalawag, and had forgotten about it, but Jeremy had displayed it. Maybe it actually meant something to him, had helped him in some way. Slightly uplifted, Keri then noticed another card behind it, a card that had tipped over and lay against the wood. Curious, she glanced around, as if afraid to be caught doing something wrong, and picked up the card.

Another sympathy card. But—from whom?

Even more curious now, Keri lifted the card and slowly opened it. She didn't have to read the tasteful note of sympathy type-set on the card; her eyes were instantly drawn to the hand-written note and signature below…

I'm so sorry about Scally, Jeremy. But he's a strong dog. He'll get better. Hope you feel better soon, too.

Keith

"Wow," was all Keri could mutter.

Keith, *her* Keith, had actually spent the time to look for a sympathy card for a sick dog? She hadn't thought him capable of it. But, on the phone he said he was trying to reevaluate himself and become a better person. She hadn't really digested those comments at the time, and hadn't talked to him since. *Although he had said she could call.*

A familiar glow began to fill her. She'd thought there were loose ends with Keith, unfinished business, but had been trying not to dwell on it. After all, he'd dumped her. An unheard of event. Still…

Keri lifted her head and gazed into a mirror above Jeremy's buffet. She studied the face looking back at her. No sign of a droopy mouth anymore, but if you looked hard, you could barely—*barely* still see that her left eye wasn't quite as open as the right one. But she looked normal again, thank goodness. Her hair had grown out to shoulder length, she'd gained a few pounds and her face had filled in and didn't look as sharp and bony as it once had. She even had more color in her cheeks and lips.

She'd grown up. Kind of. Keith would be pleased.

Keri glanced down at the card in her hands—then something else on the buffet caught her eye. An envelope.

Was it from her card—or Keith's?

Keri's heart beat a little faster. She put Keith's card back in place and picked up the envelope, sizing it up as she did. It was smaller than the envelope would have been for her card, it *must* be Keith's. Biting her lip, Keri turned the envelope over…

…and there it was.

Keith's return address in Los Angeles.

Keri had lived in L.A., had covered much of the city selling real estate, but hadn't heard of this address. Not surprising. Los Angeles was enormous. It could belong to any subdivision. Maybe it was a duplex, or an apartment house. Maybe even a real home of his own. She tried to picture what it might look like, but could not. Keith was so vague about his life in L.A., but now the mystery was unraveling. She'd thought of calling him again, but something had stopped her. Part of her hadn't actually wanted to speak to him, maybe because she was afraid of what he'd say.

Afraid he'd get mean and blow her off again.

But now, *now* she could surprise him. The workings of a plan began to form in Keri's mind. She set the envelope back down, and memorized the address. She backed away, still staring at it, mulling over the implications.

But... but... but! Squeaked a little voice in her mind, a

voice trying to shove her plan aside…

...But what would Kelly think? What would Andy think? And, maybe most of all, what would Jeremy think? What would he do without her? For reasons she couldn't understand, Keri hurried back through the house. She'd given Darci her twenty minutes, and suddenly needed to see Jeremy. Why, she was unsure.

She stepped out the door, and cold rain drizzled across her face. Crummy weather! Keri scurried beneath the arbor to the door to Jeremy's shop and found it slightly ajar. She must not have closed it completely. Suddenly, something made her stop, and instead of barging in she cautiously open the door. Ignoring the rain pelting her head, turning her hair into a stringy glob, Keri peeked in.

There stood Darci, working on Jeremy, flapping her big doe-eyelashes at him. And there was Jeremy, leaning on the workbench in front of her, entranced.

A stab of jealousy shot through Keri. She found her hands had drawn into fists.

What was this, anyway? Jeremy deserved to be happy—and so did Darci. Maybe this would actually work. Maybe this was meant to be. Stuffing her emotions back down, Keri took a deep breath, trying to relax and clear her mind.

175 E. Bentwood Street. Maybe it was a sign. The *last* sign she'd need. Something that would clear up all this troublesome confusion once and for all.

Keri forced a smile on her face, smoothed down her wet hair, and flapped out her shirt. Then she stepped back into Jeremy's world.

Chapter 23

I'm disgusted, diary. Keri is leaving for Los Angeles tomorrow, and it's not to catch up with old real-estate buddies. It's to see Keith.

Why do I worry about my sister so much, anyway? It must be my nature to be the worrier of the family. Mom certainly encourages Keri to keep Keith in her life, even though he dumped her, and mom's still reeling with shock that he broke up with her precious daughter.

Do I ever sound like the proverbial jealous sibling. When I read this page ten years from now, maybe I'll have matured enough to laugh at it. Hopefully, we'll all be doing well. In ten years, Katie will be a teenager. Quentin will be in fifth grade. Maybe I'll have another kid by then. Maybe I'll have four or five kids by then... maybe even six. We could try for nine and have a coed baseball team...

"Whoa!" Andy said from behind her, and Kelly smirked. "You want *nine* kids? You didn't tell me this before we got married."

Kelly turned around and looked at him. His face was colorless. "Yes, nine would be great. We could fill the basement with a bunch of bedrooms, buy an old school bus to travel in. It'll be a gas!"

Andy stood back, numb, as Kelly smiled angelically at him. Finally, his eyes narrowed. "You knew I was reading behind your back again."

Kelly tipped up her chin. "And your point is…"

"You wrote that to teach me a lesson."

"Maybe."

"You nearly gave me a heart attack instead."

"Then I'd get a lot of insurance money to play around with."

"Ooh, you're bad."

"You were the one snooping."

"You always said I could read what you wrote."

"But you're not actually *supposed* to do it."

Andy looked honestly surprised. "Oh." There was a hanging silence.

"So…" Andy finally said, "Keri is going to try to reunite with Keith?"

Kelly's playful tone became more somber. "I think so." She sighed and tossed her pen and diary on the desk. "She had no other reason to go to L.A. She told me once she has no real friends out there, and I know it's where Keith lives."

Andy sat down in a side chair near Kelly and rested his chin in his hand. "You know, I think Keith is a jerk, but maybe it's for the best that Keri goes out there. Maybe then Jeremy will get a clue and quit worshipping the ground she walks on."

"I think he's already gotten the hint," Kelly said.

"You do?"

"He hasn't been around for a while. Haven't you noticed?"

Andy paused. "Not really. I'm not always home when you guys are. I don't know what goes on."

"We have wild parties and drug bashes."

"Really? Maybe I ought to quit work and cash in on all that."

"Maybe you should."

Andy laughed, then grew more serious. "So, you don't think Keri is leading Jeremy around on a leash anymore?"

Kelly shook her head. “No.”

“And it’s because of Keith?”

“That’s my guess.”

“Well… maybe it wouldn’t be so bad to get a movie star in the family.”

“Some star. Commercials and an old sci-fi show that didn’t last.”

“Things could change. Especially if Keri is helping him out. Maybe Keri will end up in the movies herself.”

Kelly chuckled. “Now *that* would give new meaning to the nickname ‘Hollyweird.’”

“Yeah, but maybe she could get us free tickets to all her ‘Scary Keri’ movies. Like, ‘Scary Keri Meets King Kong.’”

“And dumps him, too.”

“Dumps the great ape?”

“Yup. Dumps Godzilla, too. And Rodan. Then, in the final ‘Scary Keri’ series, Keri gets dumped by ‘Quinn the Conqueror.’”

“That’s low.”

“Yeah, I know,” Kelly sighed. “I do kind of hope Keith dumps her again, though. He’s not right for her. You know that, don’t you?”

Andy nodded. “And we both know who is.”

“Yes, but Keri will probably never figure it out herself.”

“If she does one day, it may be too late.”

“That day may already be here,” Kelly said. “It may have already come and gone.”

Chapter 24

As soon as Keri stepped off of the plane, she felt good, full of hope and springy inside. She rented a car and driven through the Hollywood Hills for old time's sake, enjoying the views on a refreshingly clear morning. On one lookout, the clouds rose above the skyline like the tops of glowing, peach-colored ice cream cones. She felt more alive than she had in days, especially since it was now getting so cold and dreary in the Midwest.

She speculated on what it'd be like to live out here again, and none of the dark, sinking feelings that had once plagued her returned.

It was a sign, it had to be. She and Keith were meant to be together, and were meant to be together *here*. With Keith at her side, she could bear it here again. Maybe even be happy again. Keri took a deep breath and took a last look at the map she'd printed off the Internet. It would be quite a drive to Keith's area of town, but that didn't disturb her. It'd give her time to plan out just what to say after she knocked on the door.

If he was even home. She figured she'd arrive at his house about ten o'clock. Normal nine-to-five workers would never be found home at that hour, but Keith was an actor, and actors were screwy and unpredictable.

Especially out-of-work actors, but maybe his luck had changed.

Keri planned on hanging around until they crossed paths, and they *would* cross paths. She'd make sure of it.

Jeremy sat and stared silently at his right hand. It was completely white beneath the pink and red burn scars. Cold and lifeless. It was so chilly in the shop he could barely hold his chisel. He hated this clumsiness. When Raynaud's Syndrome set in his hands, they could become too cold to work. And when they did warm back up, it could take long, painful minutes for feeling to poke and prick back into the nerves of his fingers. Maybe he should just turn up the heat.

Jeremy glanced around his shop. It'd gotten more weather-worn with each passing winter. What little insulation there was in the walls didn't hold much heat in anymore, and new cracks and splinters were forming in the walls every year. The windows needed to be replaced. The roof would probably hold up for only another winter or two before it also had to be replaced. It would cost a small fortune to renovate the shop enough to hold enough heat in the winters for him to be able to comfortably work.

Not so long ago—he wouldn't have minded putting the money into it. Now, he wasn't so sure. What was left for him here?

"Hello!" came a cheerful voice from the doorway behind him, and his spirits lightened.

Darci and Nathan had arrived.

Butterflies swirled in Keri's stomach as she drove past the small, Spanish-style house with the tiny front lawn and hanging baskets adorning the arched entranceway.

She mentally checked the address with the plaque on the front door… 175. Yes. This was the address from which Keith had sent Jeremy the card.

Somehow, Keri had expected a home more modern, more elaborate. Maybe even a townhouse, but the home was more cute than formal, and very average. It blended right in with other small, well-kept homes in the neighborhood.

Keri let out her breath, realizing she had been holding it, and continued to gather her courage as she scanned the neighborhood. She wasn't sure why she was nervous all of a sudden; the unease had set in within five miles of Keith's address. A young boy bouncing a basketball on the sidewalk eyed her peculiarly, and Keri's eyes drifted down to her speed gauge. Fifteen miles an hour. No wonder the kid looked suspicious—crawling by that slowly down the street, she probably looked like some kidnapper.

Keri punched the gas pedal and laughed to herself, continuing down the long, narrow street, looking for a good place to turn around. There was little traffic and she was able to pull into a neighboring driveway, and back up. Two teenagers on rollerblades zipped past her, and one, a nice-looking boy of about sixteen, did a double-take and whistled at her.

She smiled, beaming inside. If a teenager could look at her and whistle—she still *had* it. She finished backing up, put the vehicle in drive, and drove back towards Keith's house with renewed confidence.

"He acts like a born naturalist," Jeremy said, watching Nathan scurry ahead and examine the funny-shaped toadstools growing out of the bottom of an oak tree.

Darci shrugged, looking confused. "I've rarely seen him this amused or interested in anything. It surprises me." Jeremy laughed as he and Darci crunched through the leaves in the woods behind his home. It was a brisk day, and the sun shone brightly and turned the normally somber November day into a crisp, sepia-toned wonderland.

A little farther ahead, Jeremy pointed out a thin,

barely detectable path snaking through the trees and underbrush. "Deer path," he said, and Nathan's eyes grew huge. Ducking through the brush, the three explorers soon came to a clearing filled with waist-high grass and weeds.

"Look!" Nathan said, pointing to an area where the grass had been flattened. "Did the deer sleep there last night?"

"I think so," said Jeremy. "They could be anywhere now." He studied Nathan's bright red jacket, and glanced at his and Darci's oversized orange vests. It was hunting season, and though he'd posted no hunting signs all over his property, safety was still a concern for him. Nathan had been so tantalized by the woods that Jeremy had found everyone bright clothes to wear before setting out for the adventure.

"I'm raising him like a city kid, but maybe he has a country kid's heart," said Darci. "Look at him, Jeremy, he's just glowing."

A moment later, Nathan was lying in the grass, staring up at a cobalt blue sky, pretending he was a deer.

"Do deer make sounds?" he asked.

"Sure. All animals make sounds," said Jeremy. "Even some turtles can hiss."

"What about fish? Or worms? Or larvae?"

"Larvae!" Darci said. "Where did you ever hear of larvae?"

"On TV," Nathan said unassumingly.

"Maybe those kinds of animals just make sounds each other can hear," Jeremy offered.

"Like dolphins, when they mind-read each other?"

Jeremy and Darci just stared at each other, baffled. "Maybe, honey," said Darci. She turned and whispered to Jeremy. "I don't know where he's coming up with this stuff! I mean, I know he likes animals; he rode Keri's sister's pony once and was thrilled. When he saw your workshop on the outside, he was bouncing all over, hoping there was a pony inside. But I've never suspected he was this interested in nature!"

"That's not exactly a bad thing for a little boy to be interested in," said Jeremy.

"I know," Darci said, following Nathan's movements with a mother's adoring eye, "but I don't know how to give that to him. I've always been a city-slicker myself."

"You don't seem too out of place here," Jeremy comforted. "You didn't even scream when that spider crawled across my workbench."

"I screamed inside, believe me."

"But you didn't scream on the outside, and that's what Nathan sees."

"What did I see?" Nathan asked, perking up.

"The spider in the barn," Darci said.

"Oh. He was big. Are there any out here?"

"I think most of the bugs out here have gone for the winter," said Jeremy.

"Oh," said Nathan, his smile faltering. "Oh well." He lay back in the grass, then closed his eyes. "It smells so good out here! I didn't know grass and weeds smelled like this."

"Earthy," said Darci.

Suddenly Nathan sat bolt upright.

"We should live here. Move into the woods with a big tent and make campfires. Wouldn't that be fun?"

"Ah, I think you can join the Boy Scouts to do that," Darci laughed. "I don't think Jeremy's woods are for sale."

"Darn. I sure like it here."

Jeremy stared at the little boy, deep in thought, before they moved on.

Keri wheeled into the driveway, shut off the

ignition, and took a deep breath. This was it. Butterflies still swirled inside, but she pushed them back. A tiny part of her wondered why she was doing this. She attributed it to leftover humiliation over having been 'dumped' by him.

But he said he'd changed. She'd changed.

That deserved another try… didn't it?

Mouth dry, nerves prickling, Keri stepped out of her rental car. It was only when her feet hit the pavement that she realized how rubbery her legs were. Just from driving…must be, she thought, but her heart was thumping hard, and her hands tingled.

No time to hyperventilate… this was a *good* thing she was doing! Reuniting was always a good thing. *Wasn't it?* Keri shook her head and brushed her nerves aside. What was wrong with her, anyway? The uneasy tick in the back of her mind warning that she was doing something foolish intensified and tried to tug her back to her car. She sighed, lifted her chin to the sky for a fresh breath, and was dismayed to discover the sky was no longer unusually clear and invigorating but had become a grungy yellow.

Then, from the corner of her eye, she saw a curtain move.

She froze. Keith had seen her. There was no turning back now.

Forcing herself to once more become the bold, self-assured woman Keith knew her to be, Keri shook off her nervousness, held her head high, and strode to the front door. She pushed the doorbell and stood as straight and elegant as possible, trying to picture what Keith would look like now. Would he be blonde again, more tan? Would his hair be short or long? Would he have grown a beard or moustache for a part in some show or commercial. It'd been months since he'd left, and anything could have changed about him.

Heck, less than a few months ago she'd awoken to see a face in her own mirror that looked like it'd melted on one side. The memory made her shudder.

Suddenly the door handle turned... and the door clicked open. Keri's eyes rounded. A petite, plain-featured woman stood in the doorway. "May I help you?" the woman asked in a pleasant voice.

Keri stumbled over her words. "I'm here to see Keith Quinn."

The woman's brown eyes brightened. "Oh—are you one of the realtors?"

"I am a realtor," Keri managed to say, but the woman interrupted in excitement.

"I'm so glad you came! By the way...I'm Jamie Quinn, Keith's wife. It's about time we sold this place!" She opened the door invitingly, and held out her hand.

Keri stared at Jamie's outstretched hand like it was an alien claw. A buzzing sounded in her ears. *Keith's wife?* Keith's *wife?* Keith's *wife?*

"Is something wrong?" Jamie asked, lowering her hand.

Keri took a step back. And suddenly, the scene was etched in her mind, every image frozen with jewel-like clarity. *Keith's little family, standing there, staring at her*. Words at last blubbered out of her mouth. "This isn't what I expected!"

Jamie's former smile vanished. Keri heard her words, but they seemed unreal and far away. "You probably expected to be selling a mansion," Jamie was saying. "My husband *does* tend to exaggerate, but this is a respectable home, and it's in a nice neighborhood. That should count for something."

When Keri only stood blank-faced and stared, Jamie's brow knitted together. "You are a realtor, aren't you?"

Keri struggled to remain lucid as a roaring flooded

her ears. “Yes,” she squeaked.

“Mommy—who’s here?” asked a childish voice, and a big-eyed little girl appeared and hung on Jamie’s leg.

“Who is it?” another voice asked, and a second later the spitting image of a little Keith manifested on the other side of Jamie. Both kids stared at Keri. Jamie stared at Keri.

A nerve began to quiver in the corner of her jaw, and she put her hand against her face and lowered her eyes, gazing at nothing, trying in vain to remain in control of herself. Her chest constricted and it became hard to breathe. A sudden image of an old Bugs Bunny cartoon flooded her mind, one in which Daffy Duck went crazy and bounced around on his head through a swamp. She felt like that. Like bouncing on her head even though she was standing still.

“Are you all right?” Jamie asked.

“Mommy—what’s wrong with the lady?” asked the little girl.

“Is she sick? Like when you broke your leg?” asked the little Keith look-alike.

Suddenly Keri lifted her hands, dragged in a breath. “I can’t do this,” she stammered, backing away, watching Jamie’s face twist in confusion.

“Oh, well I’m sorry if this place is too small for you,” said Jamie, “but I’m certain we can find a realtor who’ll appreciate it. Goodbye.” She shut the door in gentle disgust.

Keri continued to back away, putting her face in her hands. A high-pitched moaning surrounded her, hurt her ears, and it wasn’t until she bumped into the front end of her car that she realized it was coming out of her own mouth. Suddenly the numbness lifted. Keri gasped for air, and stumbled to the car door. Somehow she managed to get inside, fumble for the keys and start the engine. Her body was shaking and she was unable to calm the thunderstorm inside. Tears burned in her eyes, poured down her face and trickled onto her once flattering emerald green shirt.

She had to get out of here, out of this nightmare! She threw the car in reverse and backed out, somehow still having the sense to watch for neighboring kids and pets before squealing off down the road. It took an iron will to force herself to steady her foot on the gas pedal and use some semblance of care when driving while every cell in her body screamed to evacuate the hostile environment like a rocket.

Bone-white hands gripped the steering wheel in front of her, unfamiliar hands, stiff, ugly hands, as the once inviting neighborhood rolled by. It became difficult to see through the graying windshield. Keri swiped the tears from her eyes, muttering awful things, curses amidst her groans, but it became even harder to see. Now why was that?

Then it dawned on her. Of course! Of all things, it was raining! The whole sky had opened up to dump its absurd form of mourning on her.

Passing cars were a blur… and suddenly one stood out. A green SUV with a handsome dark-haired driver at the wheel. Keri saw his eye bulge out at her between swipes of windshield blades, and, just like that, Keith's horrified face was pasted forever in her mind.

Keri lifted her arm and threw Keith the ugly hand signal she'd always detested and thought only fit for losers and rednecks, then she stomped on the gas pedal. A glance in her rearview mirror showed Keith's vehicle spinning in the road, turning to come after her like some maniac on a movie set.

"You're one actor that's not going to catch his victim this time!" Keri yelled through sobs, and drove faster. Her windshield wipers slapped before her like crazed alien arms as she sped on, wheeling through an intersection just as the light changed.

That should stop Keith. This was real life, not a movie set. Keith wouldn't risk his or anyone else's life in a dangerous car chase. But, he did. Keri's jaw dropped as one glance in the mirror showed him dodging around a yellow Mustang, then a white minivan. Another van screeched to a stop as Keith's vehicle sped through and closed in on Keri's rental car.

"You idiot!" Keri wailed.

Keith motioned for her to pull over.

"No!" Keri screamed, shaking her head.

His vehicle came closer, and his frantic face seemed as big as the moon behind the glass. "Pull over!" she read on his lips.

Keri faced a dilemma. She didn't want to see, hear, or think about Keith Quinn ever again—yet if she didn't pull over, especially in this pouring rain, someone was going to get hurt.

"Oh crap!" she cried, and lurched the car to the right, bumped over a curb, and wheeled into an empty parking lot. She skidded next to an overflowing dumpster, banged the rear of her car into it, and came to a stop just as a pile of trash splattered over her trunk and dribbled to the ground.

She turned off the car and buried her head in her arms. A moment later her car door was shaking.

"Keri! Open up! We need to talk!" Keith yelled at her through the glass. "Please!" he added, pounding on the window, his wet hair plastered over his face.

Keri had had it. Every muscle in her body was tightened and roaring to let loose. With a wail she sprung from the car and tore into Keith, arms flailing, feet kicking. Keith first backed at the onslaught, then stood still, letting Keri pulverize him in the rain, screaming and ranting until she was exhausted. At last she dropped to a quivering mess on the water-soaked black pavement.

"Why didn't you tell me?" Keri sobbed, "Why didn't you tell me?"

"Oh, Keri," Keith said, lowering next to her. He tried to put his hands on her shoulders, but Keri shook him off.

"Here we sit, like two drowned rats in the rain," Keith said. "And it's all my fault."

"It sure is! You're a liar… a liar and just a… a horrid person! How could I not have sensed it? All the signs seemed right, seemed like we were meant for each other! Why did you do this to me? To your family! Keith," Keri blubbered, looking back in the direction they'd come from and pointing, "You have kids! You're a father!"

"I know, I know!" Keith said, pushing hair out of his face. "It's hard to explain, Keri. But my wife and I were separated. I had left her, I left my family. I thought I was unhappy with them. I actually thought I hated my life here, but I didn't. What I finally learned, after Jamie got hurt, was that it wasn't my life I hated, or my family. It was my lifestyle!"

Keith rose to his feet, and even with the rain streaming in his eyes, Keri could see he was crying. "I hated this place! It wasn't for me, not anymore. Maybe it never was. Jamie knew it all along, but it took her being in a nasty accident for me to even start to realize it."

"Separated or not, you were still married!" Keri sobbed, gazing up at him, rain stabbing at her eyes. "I had a right to know!"

"Yes—you did," Keith admitted. "I was waiting for just the right time to tell you. Jeremy wanted me to tell you, too. But I just couldn't. The right time never came."

"Never came?" Keri asked. "Never came? The right time was every minute of every day since the first time we met! There was no *wrong* time!"

"I know. I screwed up. Big time. I never wanted to hurt you—I never wanted to hurt anyone!"

"Oh, but you said you *changed*," said Keri. "Some c-h-a-n-g-e. You've now hurt everyone!"

Keith lowered his head. "I don't expect you to forgive me. Not for a long time, if ever. I can't even expect my wife or kids to forgive me now. I've been a royal screw-up for years, and I'm finally getting what I deserve."

Keri wiped more rain from her eyes, then slowly, shakily, rose to her feet on spongy legs. She took a deep breath, trying to collect herself, hating to look at Keith's miserable form, but finding herself staring at him anyway. "For your information," she sputtered, watching Keith lift his red-rimmed eyes, "Jamie thinks I'm just some snobby realtor who thinks your house is too puny to make a buck over. So, you're spared on that end. If I were a nastier person, I'd go back and tell her who I really was. But all I really want," she added, her voice breaking and becoming softer, "is to go home!"

"Keri…" Keith said, reaching for her.

"Go away!" Keri sputtered, spinning out of his grasp. "Get in your car and leave me alone. I need to be alone."

Keith nodded slowly, then began to back away. "I really am sorry," he said. "I really, really am." He lowered his rain-soaked head and got into his vehicle, started the engine, took one long last look at her through the gloom, and pulled away, his tires hissing in a mist of water.

A moment later, he was gone.

Keri shuddered, suddenly chilled in her soaked clothes. She looked around her. Everything was silent and deserted; the only sound was the pelting of the still falling rain, splashing into puddles at her feet, soaking the garbage strewn over the back of her car.

She'd never felt so alone. She stared at the garbage, at gooey paper cartons, vegetable peelings, coffee grinds and nameless unmentionable slop, and felt just as strung out as the trash. She leaned against her car door, turned her face up into the rain, and let it pour over her as if it could wash away the pain.

As she stared up at the soggy grey sky and sobbed, her heart breaking, a strange quiver, and then an all-to familiar heaviness came over the right side of her face.

On top of everything, her Bell's Palsy returned with a vengeance.

Chapter 25

"So, what do you want to talk to me about so desperately that you called three times?" Keri asked, flopping down on Jeremy's couch.

Jeremy sat down quietly on the arm of the couch next to Keri. He folded his hands in concern as he studied her face.

"Yes—it's back," Keri said, forming her words slowly so she wouldn't sputter. Part of her just didn't care if she did sputter, as black and angry as she felt inside. She wanted to sputter and scream at the whole, rotten world.

"What happened?" Jeremy asked.

Keri looked hard at her cute Irish friend, the one who had jumped into a fire and gotten burned for her, the one who she'd wanted to leap on and kiss in a leaf pile not too many weeks ago. But as she stared at him, all she felt was a bitterness she just couldn't get past.

"Keith is still married," she said flatly. "He has two kids."

Jeremy tilted his head back and closed his eyes. He said nothing as he got to his feet and turned away from her. Keri watched his shoulders heave in a weary sigh.

"I wish you would have told me."

"I'm glad Keith finally did," Jeremy said.

"He didn't. I flew out to L.A. to see him. I drove to his house for a surprise visit. Guess who was the surprised one."

Jeremy said nothing for a few moments, then, "I'm sorry you found out that way."

"Why couldn't you have told me?" Keri cried. "Why did I have to go through all of that?"

"I thought Keith was a thing of the past for you."

"He is, now! But I was never totally sure. Besides, you should have told me long ago. Back when we first met."

Jeremy turned to face her. "It wasn't my business."

"Whose business was it then?"

"Keith's." Jeremy sighed. "I begged him to tell you, and he said he would. In his own time."

"He never did. All this time. And you knew it."

Jeremy remained silent.

"You *knew* it," Keri said louder, accusingly.

"It wasn't my place."

"You were my friend."

Jeremy lifted his head. "Were?"

Keri shrugged off the implication.

"Things could have been different if you'd told me, you know. *Would* have been different."

A confused look came over Jeremy's face.

"In what way?"

Keri stood. "Between you and me. If I'd known Keith was such a jerk it might have... I don't know...might have opened up a different world between us."

Jeremy said nothing, but the hurt and confusion in his eyes said it all.

She got to her feet. "I don't know what to think now, or what to feel. I know I'm spoiled, Jeremy, I've never gone through something like this and maybe I'm taking it out on you. But I really, *really* wish you'd have told me."

Jeremy nodded, and she could tell there were things spinning around in his head that he longed to say, whether it was in his own defense or what, she didn't know. Part of her wanted to hear it, a larger part of her didn't. Not now, not yet. Not while she still simmered, her face looked like a drooping jack-o-lantern on one side. It was cold and grey and dreary every time she glanced out the window.

She sighed miserably and flopped back on the couch. I'm a mess…I know I am," she said, putting her face in her hands.

"And what I did, or didn't do, helped make you that way," said Jeremy. "I'm sorry."

"Whatever," Keri said, the word coming out of her mouth so fast and cruel she couldn't stop it. But it felt good to say it, nonetheless. Felt good to blow off an apology.

There was an awkward silence between them.

"So—what did you call me for, anyway?" Keri finally asked, leaning back against the couch, her eyes dull with lack of concern.

Jeremy didn't answer for a few moments. He slipped his hands in his pockets and gazed slowly around his home with saddened eyes. Finally he turned to her.

"I wondered if you'd do a market analysis of this house."

Keri sat up straighter. "A market analysis?"

"Yes."

"But why?"

Jeremy sighed. "I've been kicking around the idea of selling this place for a while, and now I think it's time."

"But the family ties…your shop," Keri said. "The woods. Won't you miss that? Or do you need someplace bigger? I know of a beautiful new home with a big pole barn that'd work great for the woodshop, but it's only on half an acre and…"

Jeremy interrupted. "I won't be needing anything

else."

Keri looked baffled.

"I'll be moving South. To Georgia. Closer to my parents, and my sister."

Keri went limp. "Georgia?"

Jeremy nodded. "There's not much left for me here. And the winters are so cold. It's hard on me physically. It's difficult to work. It won't be easy to leave. There are so many memories of my family here. It's just lonely now."

"I suppose," Keri muttered, unbelieving what she was hearing, "with Scalawag and Keith gone, it would be…"

"Not just them," said Jeremy, eyeing her, and Keri knew exactly who he meant. In many ways, she was gone for him, too. A kind of sorrow, of defeat set in her bones.

"Are you sure?" she asked weakly.

"I think so."

Think so? Maybe he wasn't *positively* sure. Maybe she could talk him out of it yet. Maybe he was hoping, somehow, that she would. Hoping she'd beg him to stay—for friendship's sake.

But then something else tugged at her, the bitterness, hurt and humiliation that had infested her since she found out about Keith's family. She stared at Jeremy, looking so dejected and alone, and knew she could probably do or say something that would make him stay, or at least feel better. But the stubbornness in her own nature refused to give Jeremy a break for not telling her about Keith.

He *should* have told her! It would have saved her all this anguish, this heartbreak, this return of Bell's Palsy.

"If that's what you want, I guess I could do that for you," Keri quipped. "I could have it on the market in a few days."

"Good. I need a few days to clean and straighten up."

Keri nodded. A sudden thought struck her. "Does Darci know you're thinking of selling?"

Jeremy shook his head. "No, but Nathan's love of the woods is what reinforced the idea. Maybe Darci would be interested in buying it."

"But I thought you and Darci were getting to be good… friends," Keri said.

A strange flicker crossed Jeremy's eyes, as though he was caught thinking of something he ought not to. Keri searched his face, but nothing revealed his thoughts. "Jeremy?" she asked.

He changed the topic. "Do you think I ought to get the carpets cleaned? Update anything?"

Aren't you and Darci more than friends? Keri wanted to shout, but all she did was look away.

Funny, the thought of Jeremy and Darci as a couple had at one time actually made her jealous. Especially when her thoughts of Keith had become dim. A little of that lingered, but it was so tinged with bitterness she couldn't separate it from the anger. Such an onslaught of emotions had spun and circled inside of her these past few days that she didn't know what to think anymore. She was unable to keep one sensible thought in her head.

"I'm not sure Darci could afford a home with ten acres."

"If she's interested, I'd make it so that she could," Jeremy replied.

"Oh," was all she could manage to say. Then, "She's such a city girl, I'd still be surprised if she'd consider a country home."

"She loves her son; I think she'd do anything that would benefit him." He looked at her, vaguely surprised that Keri wouldn't know that about a supposedly good friend.

Keri sank into the couch. Should she have known such a thing about Darci? She'd known the girl for many years. She knew Darci loved Nathan, but the thought of being selfless enough to give up a lifestyle for a child was an alien thought to her.

But maybe not to someone with a kid.

Keri thought back to when Kelly chastised her for not sensing other people's feelings. This was a prime example. A muscle in her jaw jumped as a blush of shame crossed her face.

Shame. Another emotion to add to the festering brew of emotions churning inside her.

Suddenly she rose to her feet, feeling panicky. "I won't be taking up any more of your time. I'll get to work on that market analysis."

"Are you all right?" Jeremy asked.

"Why do you ask?"

"You seem anxious all of a sudden, and you're pale."

"Oh. I didn't realize that," she lied. *Wow.* Jeremy had picked up on her feelings in an instant. Could she have done that for someone? Or even acknowledged it if she had? How insensitive was she, even after she thought she'd changed?

Keith had said he was changing, too. "Maybe for his own family," Keri mumbled under her breath.

Jeremy drew closer. "Excuse me?"

"I'm just thinking out loud," Keri said, backing away. She raised her hand to her face and turned, as if suddenly over-conscious of the drooping side. How long would it last this time? How long would she spend most of her time shut up in the basement *feeling sorry for herself.*

So what if she was feeling sorry for herself! No one else seemed to, and after all she'd gone through.

Jeremy has gone through much more.

She shook her head, unable to fully acknowledge the thought. After all, after everything that had happened, he was now leaving her, too.

She could stop him.

Maybe it'd be good if he left, though. Then she'd be free. Free of the Quinn cousins at last. Free of the miserable pair who'd kept such important information to themselves.

Miserable pair?

Keri wasn't sure where the hostile thoughts were coming from, but they puffed up inside her life a toxic gas and burned through to the outer skin. She looked back at Jeremy, sweet, lovable Jeremy, and yet part of her wanted to scream at him that he was nothing but a miserable little creep, whose lies… or lack of sharing important information… had made such a fool out of her. A fool!

That was it! That was what was distressing her even more than the hurt or the pain of Keith's betrayal. *She'd never been made such a fool.* Keri bit her lip, managing to stop ugly words from spilling out, ugly words she knew she could never take back and that Jeremy might never recover from.

"I really have to go now," she sputtered, hurrying away, making her escape before she lost control of her tongue. "I'll talk to you later."

She saw Jeremy nod, and then gaze listlessly at the floor. Past his shoulder she caught sight of the door, the door that led to the other door, the secret door in the wall that entombed so much of Jeremy's anguish. And suddenly, she realized it. *She* was the only one being the jerk, but it was too late to remedy it, for her feet were scurrying her along as though controlled by some inner, evil twin. She bolted through the kitchen and out the back door into a day as cold and horrid and grey as her soul had become.

Chapter 26

"We came close to kissing once, but then we both drew back and kind of laughed," said Darci. "We're just not each other's type, although I really wish we were. Nathan thinks Jeremy is so cool."

Keri took a sip of coffee, careful not to let the hot fluid dribble down across her chin. She no longer cared if Darci was shocked over her appearance, but her friend seemed more mellow and at ease than Keri had seen her in months, maybe even years, and she hadn't freaked out at all over her handicap as she had the first time.

Keri set the cup down on Darci's kitchen table and sighed. Then suddenly, it struck her. She'd made a mental observation of Darci's emotions, and those emotions hadn't been obvious or flamboyant emotions, either.

"You seem quite peaceful about it all," Keri said. "Not having a man in your life used to upset you a lot more than this."

"Think so?" Darci asked, looking past Keri into the air. "Maybe I'm finally maturing. I don't need a guy, do I? I never did."

"No, you don't," said Keri.

"But, sometimes I think I'd *like* one," Darci added playfully, and Keri laughed.

"Besides, you and Jeremy are so close," said Darci. "I'd always feel weird about that if we became more than friends." She then made a wry face. "Nope. It'd never have worked out."

"I don't know how close we are," Keri said. "I felt so awful about him not telling me about Keith that it's pulled us apart. I'm not sure it can be fixed again."

"Oh, come on. Keith was the creep, Jeremy was just stuck in the middle."

"Maybe. But it was still wrong."

"I guess so."

Keri looked into Darci's eyes. "Would *you* have told me about Keith, I mean, if you'd found out he was married?"

"Sure."

"See!"

"But I'm not related to Keith, or living with him, or had a past with him. I'd just be a nosy bystander eager to put some nasty guy in his place."

"You thought Keith was fantastic once."

"Well—so did you."

"I guess we were both wrong."

"Fancy that."

Both girls chuckled.

Darci toyed with her cup. "Keri. You've got to give Jeremy another chance. Friendships like that can't just be tossed away. Maybe he should have told you, maybe not. But it's not like it didn't torment him. He wasn't being thoughtless or mean on purpose."

"There's no point in it," said Keri, pushing her cup away and resting her face in her hands.

"Oh, come on. Don't be so stubborn."

"No. I'm serious," said Keri. "There'd be no point in it. It'd only make matters worse."

Darci gasped. "How can you say such a ridiculous thing?"

Keri turned in her chair. Her lower lip trembled and her throat grew tight.

"Keri?" Darci asked.

“He’s moving. To Georgia.” With her face still in her hands, Keri couldn’t see Darci’s mouth drop open, couldn’t read the shock on her face. But the slight gasp of shock rang in her ears.

“Georgia?”

“His parents and sister live there.”

There was a lingering period of silence.

“But his home is here, and so is his shop. *You* are here.”

“Me?” Keri half sneered. “I’m not much.”

“That’s a weird thing to say.”

Keri got to her feet and fingered the tabletop, head still lowered, wondering how she could feel so hollow inside. If she were a paper sack, she’d fold in on herself and blow away. “It’s really for the best,” she said. She looked up at Darci. “There’s such a big part of me that’s still mad at him, Darci, I just can’t get over it.”

“Do you want him to go?”

“I don’t know. Sort of. And I don’t want him to leave at the same time. I’m just so mixed up about it all. Besides, winter is here and it’s hard on him.”

“I know. He has Raynaud’s Syndrome. It’s hard to do intricate work when you can’t feel your hands.”

“He told you about that?”

“Yes… in general conversation.”

“You’re a good listener.”

Darci drew back, obviously surprised, yet pleased by the statement. “I am?”

“Well—yeah,” said Keri. “For all your worries, and your vanity, you have always been there for me. On top of that, I’ve come to realize, you’re also a great mommy. Nathan may have troubles, but he’s still lucky to have you.”

Darci looked away, her face flushed by the compliments. “I never knew you thought that,” she said. “I guess I was so concerned with keeping up with you, that I didn't know how you really felt."

"Keeping up with me!" Keri exclaimed. "I was always the one looking at the kind of shoes guys wore, just because you did."

Darci's jaw dropped. "You mean, all this time, we judged men by their shoes just because we thought the other one expected us to?"

"I guess so!"

"How stupid!"

"It is! If I'd only judged Jeremy by his beat-up old boots with rusty buckles, we'd never have become friends."

"I didn't even notice what shoes he wore the last time I saw him," said Darci.

Keri leaned on the tabletop. "Darci, maybe there's hope for the both of us yet."

"Now that would be something new and different."

Keri slid back in her seat. "There's something else I have to mention to you, Darci," she said quietly.

Darci leaned forward.

"Jeremy wants me to sell his house."

Darci gasped. "How do you feel about that?"

Keri tried to brush it off. "I don't know… I think I can deal with it."

"You can?"

"Sure," Keri said, wondering how certain she actually sounded. "Anyway, it's in pretty good shape, and all the mechanicals are updated. It's also on ten acres."

"I know," said Darci. "Nathan loves those woods. I've never seen him fit in somewhere like he did there. I never would have guessed." Suddenly, Darci sat up straighter. Her words came out softly, almost too low to be heard, but the excitement in her eyes was unmistakable. "How much is it worth?"

Keri told her.

Darci whistled under her breath, then kind of smiled to herself. "What was I thinking," she said. "I know who I am. I could never afford that."

Keri's shoulders slumped. So, Jeremy had been right. Darci, because of her love for her son… really was interested in moving to the country. She mentioned another figure.

"What house is that?" Darci asked.

"Jeremy's," said Keri. "The price he'd sell it for if you and Nathan were interested in it. He doesn't owe anything on it, and all he wants is for someone to love it."

Darci sat still, obviously stunned.

"You should see all the plants and flowers in the spring," said Keri. "It's a paradise. And you wouldn't be too isolated, it's on a good road and there are other homes nearby. I even saw a kid Nathan's age playing with a Golden Retriever about a half-mile down the street. It's in a good school district, too."

Darci looked at Keri in wonder. Tears formed in the corners of her eyes. She wiped at her nose, then glanced at her sleeping boy's bedroom door.

"It could completely turn him around," she whispered. "I *saw* it, Keri! I saw how Nathan acted out there, away from the city. Maybe it's all he needs, maybe it's all he's ever needed."

"Well, that—and you," said Keri.

Darci nodded, struggling to remain in control.

"Something good for me might happen out of something bad for you," she said.

Keri raised her hand as though to swipe the words away.

"Don't look at it like that. I'll be moving on one day, too. Like I always do. I'm the perpetual gypsy and that's just the way it is."

"It doesn't have to be that way."

"I think maybe it does."

"That's absurd. Your mom lives here, your sister, brother-in-law and niece and nephew live here. I live here. Isn't that enough?"

When Keri didn't immediately reply, Darci sank in her chair. "Would it have been enough if Jeremy decided to stay?" she finally asked.

Keri looked away. "I don't know." She paused, then, "There's always been something restless in me. Something unsettled. If I stay in one place too long, I don't take roots, I just dry up and wither away."

"How do you know that for sure?" Darci said. "When have you ever stayed in one place for more than a few years? Never!"

"But I feel it creeping in, no matter where I am. I'm afraid that if… if I don't move on, it'll take hold."

"What will take hold?"

Keri looked up at the ceiling. "I don't know!"

"Keri, yes you do. *What* will take hold?"

Keri grimaced, struggling for an answer that would make sense. "Well, maybe finally being a responsible adult. A good neighbor. A good mentor for little nieces and nephews, a good daughter, a good sister, a good friend; you name it. Darci, I've never been good at any of it!"

"And as I've said, you haven't stayed in one place long enough to be sure, or to even learn how to."

"But what if I can't? What if there's some creepy little side to my nature that can't be reformed, or tamed. Then what?"

"I think it's time you took that chance."

Keri buried her head in her arms. "I don't know," she mumbled, "I just can't figure myself out. Maybe Kelly is right when she calls me 'Scary Keri.' Especially with my face looking like melted wax again."

"That will go away. It did before, it will again."

Darci paused, then added more carefully, "Maybe it's happening to you for a reason."

Keri's head popped up. "A reason?"

Darci looked a little embarrassed at what she'd said, and shook her head. "No—forget what I said. I didn't mean it."

Keri knitted her eyebrows. "I think you did mean it. What do you mean by it?"

Darci sighed. "Well, just that—if you keep having problems like this with your face, you may be forced to stay in one place for a while, where people are, well, are used to it. It'll force you to find out who you really are and learn maybe what, or whom, you really want."

Keri leaned in closer to Darci. "Did Daniel the child psychologist teach you this kind of stuff?"

"Some things don't have to be taught. They just kind of *are*."

"So you think I should stick around for a while longer?"

"I definitely think you should at least stop running away from everything."

Keri made as much of a chuckle as she could with her twisted mouth. "That's deep, Darci, but, maybe I'll think about it. Maybe I can learn to finally get something straight in my head."

Chapter 27

Snow streaked sideways past Keri's windshield as she steadied her hands on the steering wheel, feeling panicky. Not panicky for herself, but for Jeremy. He was moving today. In this blizzard.

It was happening too fast!

Time had whirled by as fast as the snow, and Keri had no sense of where it had come from or where it was headed. It'd been as sudden, as fleeting, and as ungraspable as the wind. A few weeks ago, she, Jeremy, Darci, and Darci's lender were all sitting together in a ten by twelve office and went through the paper-signing ritual for Jeremy's house. Keri had done this a hundred times, and even this time she'd been very professional, very business-like, (or robot-like, said the little voice in Keri's mind) and had gotten it completed in record time.

Afterwards, Keri stood as straight as a board as a teary-eyed Darci hugged her. She remembered smiling and nodding slightly during the embrace, but it hadn't seemed real. Some remote-control button had been pressed and she'd done her job. She'd barely managed to look Jeremy straight in the eye that day, but out of the corner of her eye caught him with a kind of resigned expression on his face.

He'd seen her looking at him, and she'd turned away…

Afraid of what might be showing on her own face.

And now, two weeks later, she was turning into

Jeremy's driveway for the last time as a visitor to the home he once called his.

The snow cleared slightly, and Keri parked next to Jeremy's pick-up truck, noting that he'd put a cap over the back. Through its windows she could see the truck bed jammed with boxes and miscellaneous items. He'd sold much of his furniture several days ago, and had only kept things truly needed or sentimental to him. Earlier that day, a moving truck had come and packed up much of the equipment in Jeremy's shop and was currently on its way to a temporary home in Jeremy's sister's garage down South.

Things were wrapping up way too fast for her to fathom, but, she'd told Jeremy she'd come to say goodbye, and she was going to keep that promise.

Keri stepped out of her car, tightened her coat against the blinding snow, and hurried to the front door. When there was no reply to her knock, she tried the door, found it unlocked, and stepped inside, softly calling Jeremy's name.

It was a shock to hear her voice sounding so hollow in a disturbingly barren room. Shivers crawled across her skin as she turned in circles, gazing at what was once a warm, comfortable and slightly cluttered living room, now turned into an empty box. She noted a lighter area in the carpet where Jeremy's old sofa had been, and she was struck by the memory of the two of them slopped contentedly back in it together, with old Scalawag resting at their feet after their first trip to see the children at the hospital.

A stab of nostalgia swept through her, so wrenching that Keri shuddered, and shook her head, trying to shove the memory aside. She forced on her most durable, professional face, straightened her shoulders, stifled an ambush sob, and walked toward the front of the house to the kitchen.

"Jeremy?" she called, her voice sounding more quivery than she intended. "It's me. I'm here."

There was no reply. "Jeremy?"

Still nothing. She walked slowly through the rest of the house, her footsteps making lonely, creaking sounds on the floorboards, and found the rest of the home just as empty. And it was cold, too. Jeremy had obviously turned the heat down in his departure.

Suddenly Keri stopped. Panic gripped her.

Departure? Could he have left already—not wishing to say goodbye to her? No. His truck was still outside, collecting layers of snow. He had to be here... somewhere.

And then, she knew.

He'd be in the place where he'd spent most of his time, where he'd designed all of his creations, where he'd fulfilled client's dreams...in his workshop.

Keri pushed open the back door, again stepping into a whirling cloud of white. She jump-trotted through the snow beneath the arbor to the barn. It was too numbingly cold to stop and knock; instead, she gently pushed open the door and stepped in.

It was dim inside, and frosty cold, but her eyes immediately found the lone figure of Jeremy Quinn standing in the center of the emptied room. If he'd seen or heard her enter, he made no sign of it. He stood as if in a trance. Keri recognized his grandfather's bandana wrapped around his head, pulling his hair out of his face as he gazed ahead into space, his hands cradled in his pockets.

Something again sank in Keri's chest, and her throat grew tight. "Jeremy?" she said.

Slowly, he turned toward her, and Keri caught a gleam of wetness below his eyes as subdued light from the window fell across his face. She stepped toward him on rubbery legs, and then she saw it: the heart-breaking look of apathy behind those sad, damp eyes. For the first time she was glad that her drooping face was unable to totally portray what she felt within.

Jeremy was leaving.

Her steps became more sluggish. It was nearly as impossible to lift her feet as it'd been when she'd gotten her foot stuck in the swamp the day she'd met Jeremy and Scalawag here at the house. The memory made her heart sink even further. Any more, and she'd become nothing but a pile of sludge creeping across the floor.

"You've come," said Jeremy.

She coughed slightly. "Of course."

Keri came to within a few feet of him, then froze, suddenly too nervous and emotional to move or to speak. Instead, she glanced about the old barn, taking in the smell of old wood and sawdust and emptied-out dreams.

"I think I'm ready to go," Jeremy finally said.

"This all happened so fast," Keri managed to say through a choke-tightened throat. Then, realizing how emotional she sounded, she took a deep breath and pulled her mind elsewhere, allowing her sagging mouth to speak for her as though it was being used by the disembodied spirit of her once ultra-professional self.

Her voice became remote. "But I think things worked out for the best," she heard herself say.

Jeremy turned full-face to her. His huge blue eyes were moist, but not without the strength behind them Keri knew existed.

"I think you're right," he said.

"I see you're wearing your grandfather's bandana," Keri said, smiling thinly. "That's sweet. And sentimental."

"It was a sweet and sentimental night that I showed it to you in your sister's barn," Jeremy said.

Keri gulped, and nodded, her eyes drifting to the floor.

"We had a lot of good times, Keri. Great times. I'll never forget them."

She looked up. "Never forget them?" she asked. "That sounds so final."

"It is," said Jeremy.

Keri's voice began to tremble. "What do you mean by that? We can still call one another, write…"

"Stop," Jeremy said softly, raising his hand. "Keri, look at me. Really, really look at me."

It took every ounce of Keri's remaining strength to pull her eyes straight to Jeremy's.

"Maybe you've known, maybe you haven't," he said, then paused, as if searching for words. But he never took his gaze from her face. "But I have known, Keri," and his next words were almost unbearable, "I could never be just friends with you."

Keri's lip wobbled, and her heart thumped in her ears, but no words came out. No words could come.

"This is it," Jeremy said, then something broke in his voice and he had to turn away.

Keri's mechanical, disembodied-spirit voice finally came through.

"I guess that's for the best, too, then."

Numbly, Jeremy nodded, still looking away. Keri watched a tear slip down his cheek. She stiffened inside, reminding herself to be calm, reminding herself she should probably still be mad at him, forcing herself to take herself out of the moment. It was the only way she'd survive this.

Jeremy turned back toward her. "It's time for me to go."

"I'll lock up—if it's okay with you," Keri was mortified to hear her other-self say.

"That will be fine," Jeremy replied. Then, suddenly, he was close to her, immense, really, and he wrapped his arms about her. She remained stiff in his embrace, his wonderful, curly hair tickling her cheek, his scent filling her nostrils.

He turned slightly; his breath warm in her ear. “I’ll miss you.” Then he pulled away, and Keri screamed inside and tumbled over herself at such hideous emptiness.

He smiled limply at her, then turned, and without a backward glance walked across the workshop and out the door. The door blew open, then shut, in the wind. Open, and shut. Darkness; then Jeremy’s receding figure a blur in the blizzard. Darkness; then his figure a smaller blur; darkness, then just a dot.

Moments later, she was still frozen as the sound of his truck’s engine came to her, sounding so near yet so many light-years away.

It dawned on Keri that she could run to him. That she *should* run to him. That she might still, *still* change the outcome of this.

But nothing in her body worked. She couldn’t remember how to move her mouth to shout, let alone will her feet to move. It was someone else’s body. That zombie. That robot that some called Scary Keri or Keri Ferrita, the ‘Man-Eat-a’ that controlled her now.

A sudden shriek of wind buffeted the nearest window of the barn and startled her to her senses. And suddenly, she could move. She raced out the barn and kicked her way through the snow toward where Jeremy’s truck had been, but where there was now only an oblong area of shallow snow, and tire tracks that lead toward the street.

“Jeremy!” she screamed, glancing wildly down the street for a sign of the retreating vehicle. “Don’t leave me!”

She caught a distant blur of color in the snow, the retreating color of green. Then the breath caught in her throat as the shape of a shaggy, misshapen head revealed itself in the front seat through the snow. The head turned, and a canine eye stared at her for a moment; a sad, yet somehow accusing eye, before that eye was extinguished by a blast of snow so thick she could see nothing else. The same freezing whiteout burned against her face and neck and took the remaining breath from her lungs.

"Jeremy!" she finally gasped, "how can you just leave me like this?"

And then, she knew. He hadn't really left her. She had left him. Weeks before, in the leaf pile. The knowledge weakened her legs, and she dropped to her knees. Tears blurred her eyes as the gut-wrenching realization settled into her very core. She'd never really thought all of this out. Analyzed it. Why had she held such a wall up against Jeremy, the one man who'd treated her the best of any man ever, the one man who could, when she allowed, bring out the very best in her?

Keri sobbed and hunched over, bringing raw, stinging hands to her face. Freezing wind and snow thrashed down her neck. Had she built the wall because of the stupid diversion of Keith? Was it really…as her mind tried to tell her now? Or, was it something else…something a little more frightening?

"He can't get to know me, the *real* me," Keri heard herself sob. "It'd only be a matter of time before he learned how I really am. That I don't really know who I am!"

Those words wrenched out of her mouth as a final purging, and Keri dropped all the way into the snow. Jeremy was good at helping hurt, broken, and wounded things, be they sick children, disfigured dogs, or, maybe even sick and disfigured people, like her. But what had she to offer in return? A *flaky, insensitive carcass of a woman who couldn't even help herself*. That was what.

She wasn't good enough for him.

She felt like a stranger in her own shoes, and that she was feeling all of this through that wicked stranger. A strangled groan spilled out of her. Soon the groan became a wail. She sobbed and rocked in the stinging snow, unable to feel the cold any longer, unable to care what became of her. Time seemed to melt away; it grew darker. When at last the darkness of night settled in, so did a silence so viscous that she could no longer hear her own moaning.

Eventually, however, she did hear something. Another form of moaning. If it wasn't coming from her own lips, where was it coming from? Had she passed into the land of the dead? Funny, the thought did not frighten her. Then she felt a weight press against her arm, and something cold and soft pushed up against her cheek and tried to lift her face.

"What the—" Keri muttered, at last opening snow-caked eyes.

Before her, a face slowly came into focus. A brown and white, pointy face with icicles hanging from fur and clots of snow caked over its eyelids.

Keri bolted upright, her eyes wide open. She shook her head and found a small, terrier-mix dog sitting beside her, staring straight at her. Thin, probably starving, probably half frozen. But that wasn't the oddest thing….

Just as Scalawag suffered from a mangled front leg, this dog was missing most of a back one. Whether it was from a birth defect or accident, Keri couldn't tell. All that was registering in her now was that this suffering little animal had appeared, like magic, and rescued her. He'd actually come to rescue her.

And in return, she must rescue it.

The dog watched her as she arose. He still whimpered slightly, but was able to wag his tail. "You poor beastie," Keri said, "poor, poor beastie." Then she bent to lift the animal in her arms to take home.

Chapter 28

I write about Keri's life so much in this diary that I'm going to wrap it up and give it to her as a present when we're in the old folks home. But she does keep it interesting around here, and gives me so much to write about.

It's been a little bewildering these past few months. I was sure that Keri would flip and become even more unstable and strange than ever after Jeremy left, but just the opposite seems to be happening. Andy and I don't get it.

Since she adopted Tripod, she's spent more time with him up at the children's hospital than she ever did, even when Jeremy was here. She seems calmer than I've ever seen her. I wonder what's going on in her head. Andy wonders if she's seeing a shrink who's prescribing fun drugs, but I've found no sign of that, and, believe me, I've looked.

Yes, Keri, if you ever read this, I searched your bedroom. I had to know why you seem to be so much more relaxed in your own skin these days. If it's because of medication, then fine, but why won't you talk to me about it?

Just this morning you got up, made us all breakfast, and took Katie and Quentin for a walk. It's close to spring now and I can sometimes hear the birds chirping outside the window, and that's a happy sound. Do you hear them, too? What makes you so content that you can muck out the barn, fix a broken fence, and vacuum the whole house without the slightest hint of payback besides living here? Are you going to kidnap little Quentin and run off with him and pretend he's yours?

No—that wouldn't work. His name doesn't start with a K. But you seem off that kick, too. You've even convinced mom it was time to break that tradition, which couldn't have been easy to do.

So, what is it, Keri? What makes you so whole these days? Jeremy seemed good for you, but you've improved since he left. It just doesn't make sense.

At any rate, I guess we'll just accept the change and be happy for you as long as it lasts. I sure hope it lasts. Fifty years from now, when we're in the home, we'll know.

Kelly had just finished diapering the baby and picked him up when she heard sounds coming from her office. She headed toward the hallway in curiosity just as Katie broke through her office door.

"Look what Aunt Keri gave me, mommy!" Katie squealed, and brought forth a big pair of wax lips and stuffed them over hers.

Kelly raised her eyebrows. "I see! Doesn't she want them anymore?"

Katie shook her head. "No. She gave me a big stuffed snake, too, and a little teddy bear. She said they were lonely and needed a little girl to play with them."

"Oh," was all Kelly could manage to say as she walked into her office, prepared for anything.

She found Keri still pulling things out of her 'closet from the past,' and a pile had collected on the floor. Tripod wagged his tail and sniffed the items as Kelly approached.

"Keri, what are you doing?"

Keri turned to face her. Over time, her features had

once again become more normal, except her left eyelid, which still drooped slightly but wasn't obvious unless you knew what to look for.

Keri sighed, then smiled. "It's about time I cleared out this junk once and for all." She paused. "Do you want any of it? What's left is going to Goodwill or the shelter."

"Oh, I couldn't," Kelly said, stunned. Then she thought about it. "Well—maybe!"

She came over to Keri and placed Quentin in her sister's arms. "How about the necklace Andy gave you instead of me when we were teenagers?"

"Take anything you want," said Keri, bouncing the baby in her arms. "It's all going."

"Well, if you insist."

Soon Katie was standing beside her, rummaging through the pile. "Look mommy! Pretty earrings. Do you like them?" She held up a small box with pearl earrings inside.

"They're nice, honey."

"Take them," said Keri. "I can't even remember who gave them to me. I probably never wore them."

"Probably not. Probably dumped the poor guy and forgot about it."

Kelly took the box, then began to fish through the pile of gifts, some outlandish, as the wax lips were, and some obviously more elaborate, as the diamond necklace she just pulled from a red velvet box.

"Is this real?"

"I don't know," said Keri. "It's yours if you like it, either way."

Suddenly Katie pulled out a ceramic plate with a two inch tall mouse molded onto the edge. "I like this!" she said. "Why does it have a mouse on it?"

"It's a cheese plate," said Keri, as Tripod sniffed at the object. "I think someone gave that to me in tenth grade. At least he knew what I liked."

"Why are you doing this?" Kelly asked, suddenly straightening as she pulled a gold necklace out of its box. "Is this the one Andy gave you?"

Keri peered closer. "Yup. It's not real gold, but it's kind of pretty."

"It's ghastly!" Kelly laughed, "It's half an inch thick. No wonder you never wore it."

"No one ever accused Andy of having good taste… except, of course, picking you over me," Keri said.

At that, Kelly felt her eyes sting. "Thank you."

"Well, it's true. It was always true."

Kelly gazed at her sister, and Keri turned away. Suddenly she could hold her questions no longer. "What's going on with you, Keri? You seem more relaxed nowadays. Are you seeing a shrink?"

"What's a shrink?" Katie asked. "Is it like a little man, like Jeremy was?"

Kelly held her breath, wondering how Keri would react at the mention of Jeremy's name. She and Andy had decided not to talk about either of the Quinn cousins, actually, unless Keri brought up the subject. And so far, she hadn't. Kelly supposed Keri talked to their mother, or Darci, about Jeremy and Keith, but she didn't even know that for certain.

"No, I'm not seeing a psychiatrist, Katie," Keri said, rocking Quentin and making faces at him. "That means a special kind of doctor. Not like the one for my face, but doctors for the mind."

"Oh," was all Katie said, no longer interested. Then she went about her business scouring through the pile again, Tripod wagging his tail happily at her side.

"It's hard to believe Quentin will be a year old in a few months," Keri said, "He's getting so heavy! He'll be walking before you know it. Time sure is flying by."

"It is," Kelly agreed, wondering how to bring up the

topic of Keri's transformation again.

"What makes you want to give all of this away after so many years?" she asked. "It's like you've had a complete mindset change. I'm confused."

Keri let Quentin down, held him by the arms, and let him take a few wobbly steps before he collapsed on his rear and giggled. She seemed not to hear the question, like she was in a different world. Kelly held the ugly gold necklace loosely at her side, and studied her sister, befuddled.

"Did you know," Keri suddenly began, not looking up at Kelly but continuing to play with Quentin, "that Darci never had any real concern about what kind of shoes the guys she dated wore? She only talked about it because she thought I was the one who was concerned about it. I only talked about it because I thought it was important to her."

Kelly said nothing, feeling certain that this little revelation had a deeper meaning, but she was unable to fathom it. She remained quiet, waiting for more of an explanation. "I tried so hard to live up to what people's expectations of me were, and then they became my own expectations. I'm not even sure where the two crossed. And I really don't care anymore. It's not worth the stress."

"Really?" was all Kelly could say.

Keri sat on the floor next to Quentin and let him poke at some of the items in the stack.

"Really."

"That's pretty deep, sis," said Kelly. "How did you come to that, uh—realization?"

Keri shrugged. "It just came gradually. I've been trying to see myself through other people's eyes, and a lot of the time I just saw a fidgety wreck, like you once called me. And you were right, I was never really happy."

Kelly felt guarded excitement. "And now you are?"

Keri looked up and locked eyes with Kelly. "No. But I'm getting there. I have to."

Kelly found herself grinning, unsure why. The explanation didn't make a lot of sense, but it made *some* sense. She had a hundred other questions she could ask, but bit her lip. Uppermost in her mind was how much longer Keri planned to live in the basement, and if she was going to pursue buying her own home in the area, as she had once talked about. If she did, it'd have to have a nice yard for a quirky, three-legged dog. The little terror adored Keri, and never left her side.

Maybe that was it… the little dog. He needed her, and Keri had to be more stable than she'd ever been in her life to take care of such a pitiful little creature.

Keri and the dog had a lot in common.

Still, that couldn't be the whole reason for Keri's personality change. Kelly couldn't quite banish the notion that it somehow had something to do with Jeremy Quinn. Even if he now lived hundreds of miles away apparently having no contact at all with Keri.

Chapter 29

"I'm so glad you like riding in the car," Keri said, turning to look at Tripod. "This has been a long, long drive. Even for me."

Tripod lay on the seat next to Keri, his head resting on his paws while he gazed adoringly at his master. His tail thumped against the upholstery.

"We're almost there," Keri said, to no one in particular this time. "Hopefully, this little jaunt will turn out better than it did the last time I tried to sneak up on someone."

Her stomach soured as the unpleasant memory of Keith's wife answering the door reappeared in her mind. She quickly pushed it aside, but took a deep breath, realizing that she was taking a big chance again and it was entirely possible it could work out badly.

It had been six months since she'd seen or had any correspondence with Jeremy. And now she was going to show up unannounced, at his home in Georgia. Well, his parents' house, anyway. It was the only forwarding address he'd given for any extra business needs following the sale of his home. She was close now, driving through the small, quaint town of Greenwood. The warm sunshine poured in through the windows and the scent of flowers hung thick in the air.

She'd hoped for a positive reaction upon arrival, but was nevertheless braced for a negative one. She deserved a negative reaction, after all the head games she'd played with poor Jeremy. And they had been games. Deep inside, she'd known that all along.

But she hoped, truly prayed, that she was a stronger person now, possibly even a better person. Rather than the stumbling phony she'd been becoming in the recent past, Keri hoped she was truly becoming a more compassionate and less selfish individual.

This was the only way she'd ever be able to confront Jeremy again, and be worthy of him.

Keri knew that one doesn't just stop and think to oneself, "Hey, I did something nice today for someone. I'm a good person." One shouldn't have to think about it much at all. If it's not built into a person before, and you're trying to change, then, at some point, the change should become natural rather than a thing one has to confront and analyze and wrestle over. Which, she'd done. And done… and done. It wasn't until after she'd given up, assuming she was hopeless that people began to comment how she seemed so much more relaxed.

Surprise, surprise.

She might never be a Mother Theresa, but she hoped that one day, some day, she'd have something to offer someone like Jeremy that would make him proud. If Jeremy did reject her, she would fight for him. And if he still rejected her, if it became clear he'd moved on and her chances with him were long past, it'd be no one's fault but her own and she'd have to live with that.

Keri turned down a street, *the* street, a lovely boulevard with tall trees arching over the road and Spanish moss drooping from the limbs. She passed older, well-maintained homes painted cheery colors—pale blue, sunny yellow, tasteful greens and peaches. She marveled at them. Each yard was like a serene painting; some even had picket fences.

She wondered what it'd be like to live here. She'd never been to the South before. She reached over and stroked Tripod's head. "We're almost there," she said, steeling her nerves. "The last time I saw Jeremy, he said, "This is it." But that wasn't *it. This* will be it."

She then wondered what Jeremy's parents would be like and if they'd heard of her. If they had heard of her, just *what* had they heard? Jeremy wasn't one to say a bad word about anyone, yet if he talked about her at all, it wouldn't be too hard to piece together the fact that she'd broken his heart. What parent could tolerate looking kindly upon the face of the person who'd broken their son's heart?

She knew she'd never take the place of Hannah or Seth, and she didn't want to. Keri could only hope that Jeremy still had enough space left in his tortured heart for her to slip back into it one day.

Hannah. Seth.

Keri wondered if Jeremy had a home of his own now, and if that new home included a hidden shrine to his beloved family. Keri remembered walking through Jeremy's house with Darci, showing her its finer details, then freezing as she'd entered Jeremy's office. Should she tell Darci about the hidden room? It didn't seem right to talk about it. It was a private place, a sacred place. A place Keri had shared a few precious hours with Jeremy after that bittersweet Fourth of July evening.

But by the time Keri had nerve enough to glance to the back of the room, she'd found Jeremy had answered that question for her.

There'd been a real door put in place of the hidden one. The shrine had reverted back into a normal, everyday closet. Keri hadn't mentioned the transformation to Darci, and she never would. That room was Nathan's bedroom now, and that was a good thing.

Keri found herself smiling, buoyed by the thought of Darci and Nathan doing so well. Nathan had made friends with the little boy down the street and his golden retriever, and the kids planned many tree-forts and adventures together for the summer. Darci was making pies and meals for an elderly widow nearby, and was reveling in the woman's wisdom and companionship. Who would have thought.

Even if things didn't quite work out for herself, Keri was still at peace with the knowledge that at least they worked out well for others she cared about. People who truly deserved happiness.

With that thought in her mind to steady her, Keri reached Jeremy's parents' house. She pulled the car into a long driveway leading to a cream-colored Craftsman-style home surrounded in foliage. The quantity and colors of flowers were a pleasant shock to the eyes. It was a warm, welcoming home. A place Jeremy would love. As she stared at the front door, her heart thumped against her chest. It was all she could do to fight off the feeling of déjà vu—she *had* done something like this before and it had gone badly. So badly.

Keri brought her hand to her face, absently fingering the area which had given her so much trouble. She knew she looked normal now, but she'd deliberately underdressed for the occasion. A crisp white shirt, skirt, and a light coat of mascara were about as elaborate as she got nowadays. Today she wore a green blouse, jeans, and a brush of lip gloss. Her hair, longer now, was pulled back in a high ponytail. It was quite comfortable for a long ride in a small car with a three legged companion. She turned to Tripod. "Wish me luck, boy. I've got to do this or forever wonder." With that, she thrust herself out of the car and walked boldly toward the door.

Anyone could answer that door. Anyone. It could be Jeremy himself.

It could be Jeremy's new wife or girlfriend.

She had to know. She rapped on the door—and held

her breath, her heart hammering. A moment later, the door clicked and began to open.

"Give me strength," she whispered, having no idea what she'd say to whomever appeared in the doorway.

A second later, a small, grey-haired man with a thick beard and tiny glasses stood before her. Smiling eyes peered out at her behind the rims of his spectacles.

"Girl Scout cookie time?" he asked.

Taken aback, Keri glanced behind her to see if a little girl with a box of cookies was anywhere near.

"Just kidding," the man chuckled. "You look a little more grown up than that."

"If the Girl Scouts sold pickles or cheese, I might still join them," Keri found herself saying.

The man rubbed his bearded chin and gazed at her, seemingly surprised by her retort. Suddenly a wide grin came across his face.

"I'm not used to someone giving it back to me," he said. "Not lately, anyway. How can I help you?"

"Is this…the Joshua Quinn residence?" Keri asked.

"Depends on who's asking. If you're selling vacuum cleaners, it's not. If you're selling hats, then come right in. Got a huge collection. Could always add more."

Keri smiled. She could have shown up in her clown outfit, and wouldn't be out of place here.

Suddenly a large shape lumbered around the corner and stood by the man's legs, cocking its head in a curious manner. It was a dog…an incredibly misshapen dog with a crooked front leg, torn ear and one large, curious eye which was now gazing at her.

"Scalawag!" Keri cried, "You got better!" She reached down to hug the animal, and Scalawag gave her one of his best doggie smiles. "Oh I'm so glad he made it, I was never quite sure what became of him," Keri murmured, her throat tight with emotion. Tears pricked her eyes as she straightened. "Jeremy must be thrilled. Is he here?"

At the mention of Jeremy's name, the man's face drained of color. He seemed barely able to speak. "You don't know what happened, do you?" he asked softly. An awful pall settled over the room as he paused, then added, "Who exactly are you?"

Keri took an involuntary step backward. Her lip trembled. "I'm Keri Ferrita." She paused, looked into his eyes, then added, "From up North." She grimaced, almost expecting Mr. Quinn to scream, "Who? Keri Ferrita…the Man-Eat-a?"

But he did no such thing. "So *you're* Keri," he said, gazing at her.

Keri nodded. It was all she could do. The silence stretched on for a minute, then two, as his demeanor became solemn, almost sympathetic. He looked away.

Keri's voice sounded husky and foreign to her. "What's wrong—what happened?"

"I think you'd better come in," Mr. Quinn said, motioning her inside. "We need to talk."

Keri's legs wouldn't move. They were rag legs. All she could do was stand and stare, her heart a lead ball in her chest.

"Please," he said. "It's all right. Jeremy is a fighter."

A fighter? What could have happened? How could she not have known something happened? She turned slightly toward her car. She may need Tripod, as well as Scalawag, close by for this.

"Can my dog come in?" she stammered.

"You have a dog too? Most of my best friends are canines." He petted Scalawag, then added, " Bring him in."

Keri nodded, and forced her legs to move, but walking was surreal; slow, as though an invisible gelatinous mass smothered her body. At last she reached the car, opened the door, and let Tripod hop out. She led him toward the door on spongy legs, her mind reeling. "Come on, Tripod. It's okay," she said, not at all certain everything really was okay.

Mr. Quinn smiled at the sight of the spunky little animal. "Fitting name," he said.

"My brother-in-law came up with it," Keri said. "He's good at things like that."

"I like people with a sense of fun," Jeremy's dad said. "More grown-ups should grow-down a little. And I don't just mean height."

Keri allowed herself a lean smile as he led her and Tripod into his home. The two dogs sniffed curiously at each other for a few moments, their tails curled into question marks, then seemed to decide each was acceptable to the other and relaxed. Inside the décor was cluttered, yet tasteful, the colors cheery. It helped give Keri some hope that Jeremy's situation wasn't as bleak as what she imagined. Her Jeremy wasn't a quitter. Mr. Quinn led her past a kitchen warmed by honey-colored cabinets, and Keri realized that he probably designed and made them himself. He gestured for her to take a seat in a round breakfast nook surrounded by windows. Sunlight streamed through lacy curtains and dappled a creamy linen tablecloth. A centerpiece of freshly cut dahlias gave the area a sweet smell. It was quaint, comfortable, and much too dreamlike. Too surreal.

Maybe she *was* dreaming this. Maybe she was pulled over at a rest stop somewhere snoozing off her fatigue. This was all a dream. It was unbearable to think otherwise.

"Would you like something to drink?" Mr. Quinn asked.

Keri shook her head. "I'm fine, but do you have something Tripod could take a sip from?"

"Certainly."

After filling a plastic bowl with water for the dog, Mr. Quinn took a seat across from Keri. He sighed, folded his hands together, and lowered his eyes.

Keri's throat tightened.

"There was a car accident..." she heard him begin, and it was like a fist in the gut. The words that followed echoed and faded in her head...

"... head trauma... been in a coma for five weeks now... just like Seth had been...don't know the prognosis, only time will tell. Much prayer..." were the fragments of speech which threaded through Keri's ears.

An accident.

Keri had been so worried about Jeremy's driving down South in a blizzard, only to find that now, months later, that he'd gotten into a terrible collision on a clear spring morning. Apparently a teenage driver had been startled when a deer leaped into the road in front of his truck. He'd lost control of the vehicle and hit Jeremy head-on.

The teenager was doing fine now...

...Jeremy was not.

"We almost lost him that night," Mr. Quinn was saying. "They told us he had a lot of brain swelling, and they were forced to put him into a drug-induced coma to help it subside. He's been like that ever since. His brain waves are now normal, but he just doesn't come around. Wherever he's gone, Keri, he's gone deep."

Keri slumped into her chair and put her face in her hands. Her chest tightened and it became hard to breathe. Tears leaked down her face, and she began to shiver as though it was only thirty degrees in the room instead of near eighty.

"I'm sure he'll be okay—in time," Mr. Quinn said. He leaned forward, patted Keri on the hand.

She looked up at him.

"Maybe you'll help make a difference. S*omething* has to. Even Scalawag can't seem to bring him around." At that, he started to tremble. His composure gone, his face reddened and he began to wrench up and down with the force of his sobs.

Instead of releasing the all-out wail brimming in her throat, Keri drew in a great breath of air, then another, and somehow steadied herself. She clutched Mr. Quinn's hand. "He will be all right. He will!" she said. "You wait and see. He's good at fixing furniture, and dogs, and people—and he *will* fix himself, too. He just needs a little more time. Hang in there, Mr. Quinn!"

Mr. Quinn nodded, and let go of Keri's hand to wipe his tears. It took some time for him to collect himself.

"I'm sorry," he said, "I'm not usually like this. It's been a rough month. Jeremy's gone through so much in the past that I'm not sure how much more he can take. Don't get me wrong, Keri. I believe in heaven—and that's where he'd go. Heaven is no more of a miracle than the fact that we all exist in the first place. I'm just not ready to let him go yet. And neither is his mother. She's at the hospital right now, standing watch over him."

"I'm not ready to let him go, either." Keri said. Suddenly she stood up. "I have to see him."

"Go, maybe it will help," said Mr. Quinn. "No one knows what he can hear—or see. Sometimes his eyes will open, sometimes he will react to voices or touch. But it doesn't last. We don't know if he understands where he is, or even who he is. But we don't know that he doesn't, either." He took a quivery breath. "But he'll snap out of it. He will. He has to."

Mr. Quinn teared up again, but there was a determined look on his face. "He's my son," he added.

"How far is the hospital?" Keri asked.

"Not far. I just came from there a while ago."

He gave Keri the directions, and before long they were heading back outside to her car. The lazy hot sun and bright flowers made the reality of what Keri now knew seem more bearable…but only slightly so.

"Do you think you can find it all right?" Mr. Quinn asked as Keri let Tripod hop into the front seat.

She nodded. "I'm good at finding things. Thank you."

"Now you come back here later, don't even think of staying in a hotel," Mr. Quinn said, a sad twinkle in his eyes. "Wouldn't want that little pup of yours tossed out on his ear.

Or on one of his last legs."

Keri smiled. "I'll do that." Then she reached over and hugged Jeremy's dad. It dawned on her that he was about the same size as Jeremy. Then she released him and got into the car. She started the engine, waved and began to back out. Suddenly, she stopped.

Mr. Quinn hurried to her window. "Do you need me to write down the directions to the hospital?" he asked.

"Well, no," Keri said, watching as Scalawag stared curiously at her in the driveway. Then she added with a tinge of embarrassment, as Scalawag began to wag his tail as if he knew what she was thinking, "but could you tell me if there is a costume shop nearby?

She was just about to push through the hospital's door, when her jaw fell.

"It can't be," Keri muttered, backing against a low brick wall in shock. She sat down hard on the masonry, and Tripod rested against her leg.

"Keri?" the man asked as the door closed shut behind him. "Is that you under there?"

She half-grinned. "It's me, Keith. Just like the first time you met me."

"I remember. The clown suit, balloons…the floating arm trick. Seems like ages ago."

"In a way, it was ages ago." She was shocked to see Keith again. But the shock wasn't from feeling a sense of loss, or even of humiliation or revenge.

She was shocked that she had forgotten about him. Shocked, but incredibly pleased.

He looked good, as usual, but more casual than she'd ever seen him. A faded gray T-shirt and baggy jeans. Shaggy hair, a touch of a beard. He didn't look like a person putting on airs or building an image, but rather, just a normal, slightly haggard individual leaving a hospital where a loved one lay in unnatural sleep.

Keith stood before her, and smiled sadly as Tripod sniffed at his shoes.

"Reminds me of Scalawag," he said.

"He does," Keri said. "I found him at Jeremy's house the day he moved. Jeremy never mentioned him, so I figured he hadn't been around before." She reached down and pulled the little terrier to her side. "Yes, Tripod is my knight in shining armor. Or, in a shining ruffle, anyway."

Keith laughed. "Tripod. I like that." Then he sighed, and his demeanor grew more somber. "Keri…you have every reason to hate me. So I'll get on my way. But Jeremy needs you now. He always did. I'm so glad you came."

Keri eyed him peculiarly. "Keith, I don't hate you. In fact, I hope everything is going well for you. Los Angeles will never be for me again, but if it's for you, then make the best of it, and be happy."

Keith's eyes rounded, and a half-smile came over his face. "I haven't lived in L.A. in months," he said. "I moved—with my family—to Wisconsin, not long after your uh, your visit. My wife's parents and sisters live there." He paused, then, "It's been good to relocate.

Great, really. I'm even working in landscape design, just like I wanted to as a teenager."

"Well, what do you know," said Keri.

Keith nodded. "Yeah, what do you know."

"I'm glad," said Keri, straightening. "I really am glad things worked out for you. It's a good thing when one finally finds oneself."

"It is," he agreed.

Keith turned and looked up at the hospital behind him."But why doesn't it ever work out for Jeremy?" He shook his head. "Some people get all the worst breaks. I don't get it."

A strange look came over his face, then Keith slowly turned and gazed at Keri. His eyes grew damp. "I know one thing," he said, voice quivering, "one reason why something didn't work out for Jeremy. And that something was you."

Keri looked at him, puzzled. "What?"

"It was because of me. I sabotaged his whole relationship with you. Back then, I didn't care."

Keri's brows furrowed. "What are you talking about? It was all a mistake, a stupid judgment. It's over now, and that's it."

"No," Keith said. He paused a long time, and Keri watched in astonishment as tormented emotions shifted across his face. This was no acting.

"It wasn't just bad judgment," he said all at once, more firmly now. He looked Keri straight in the eyes, pinning her to her seat. "I knew Jeremy was falling in love with you. I knew it from the start. I didn't care. I just wanted something he didn't have—even when I had it myself. I don't know why. Especially after all he'd lost."

Keri's mouth dropped. "You *knew*?"

"Everyone knew."

"Everyone?"

"Everyone but you."

Keri looked down, then sideways, then at Tripod, everywhere but at Keith. She started trembling again.

"I'm sorry," said Keith.

"So, you think Jeremy really—*really* was in love with me? Especially after losing someone as wonderful as Hannah?"

"He was," Keith said. He gently tipped her chin up with his hand and looked into her eyes. "And I have no doubt he still is."

"He can't be! He shouldn't be."

"But he is."

"But I haven't heard from him in months!"

"Has he heard from *you*?"

"He didn't want to."

"Didn't want to?" Keith asked, surprised. "Why?"

Keri's mouth quivered. "Because… because he said he couldn't just be friends with me."

Keith nodded. "Oh."

"And I can't just be friends with him, either," said Keri. "I don't know why it took me so long to realize that, or to accept it."

"Then go to him."

Keri nodded, wiping her eyes. "I didn't know he was injured. I just came down to see where I stood with him. This has all been a shock. I had no idea any of this had happened! It's not fair." Keri took a deep breath and stood up. She rearranged her pink and white polka-dotted clown outfit and checked some of the balloons safety-pinned to her collar. They batted lightly against her bright clown nose in the breeze. She wiped at her tears once more.

"You're messing up your makeup," said Keith.

"How can ya tell?" Keri asked, trying to grin.

"Oh—I can. Wasn't there an old song called 'Tears of a Clown?'"

"I think so. It fits me. Even when I'm not dressed like one. What a fool I've been."

"I was, too," Keith said.

They smiled sadly at each other for a few moments, ignoring the passing stares or quickly lowering eyes of passersby.

"I guess I'd better get up there," Keri finally said. "Room 304, right?"

"Right."

Keri stared up at the hospital windows. A sheet of white clouds swept over the roof of the tall brick building and a flutter of wings drew her attention to a pair of nesting pigeons. It seemed too quiet and still outside. Lonely. Lonely because people came and went here with such hushed voices and solemn steps.

"He can't die," Keri whispered.

Keith stared up at the opaque windows with her. "No. He can't."

"He mustn't."

They looked at each other again. Keith reached down, gave Keri a light hug, and patted Tripod on the head. Then, without another word, he turned and walked away.

He did not look back.

After explaining who she was to Jeremy's mother and sister, Leah, Keri and Tripod left the waiting room. She walked down the hallway toward room 304, her baggy outfit swishing against her legs and her clown shoes flopping against the floor.

"What a great family," Keri murmured to Tripod.

Tripod wagged his tail, more at amused passersby than at Keri.

It'd been a little rough getting permission to bring a dog to Jeremy's room, but after convincing officials Tripod was a therapy dog and showing her credentials from the hospital up North, they'd relented. Keri had seen Leah in the waiting room right away and had recognized her from photos in Jeremy's father's house. Leah was sweet and somewhat reserved, but who wouldn't be when a stranger dressed up like a clown barged in with a three-legged dog?

But it was Jeremy's mother who'd surprised Keri the most. "That lady has to be five or six inches taller than Jeremy's dad," Keri whispered to herself as she walked down the hall. And what a lovely, kind woman she seemed to be. Slim and elegant, with a steadfast look in her eye. She'd known who Keri was, and hadn't seemed upset Keri had come. Or even surprised. In fact, she'd seemed relieved to see Keri there.

Leah had seemed a touch more wary, although friendly enough. Apparently she and Jeremy were very close. She was a person Keri hoped to get to know well in time.

The Quinn family, Keri mused. And not one of their names started with a stupid K.

Those kinds of thoughts were distracting enough that Keri was able to walk down the corridor to Jeremy's room without sinking in dread. After all, she'd done this kind of thing dozens of times before, visiting and entertaining sick children, and she loved it. Ultimately, she probably got more out of these visits than the kids. But, this was different. Way different. The strength she'd summoned slipped away and $terror stirred inside her. She put her hand to her forehead, feeling perspiration. "How can I do this?" she muttered, tears stinging her eyes.

A wretched feeling lurking inside of her came to the surface: What if knowing she was in the room actually made Jeremy worse? What if she'd hurt him so badly that even the faintest sense of her being nearby made him sink deeper into the coma? Keri frantically turned and looked down the hallway to the waiting room to see Mrs. Quinn and Leah nervously flipping through magazines to pass time.

Keri straightened her shoulders with resolve. *She couldn't freeze up.* She had to tell Jeremy how she felt, whether he understood or not. And she had to do it now. Reaching his room at last, Keri closed her eyes, let out the breath she'd been unconsciously holding, and pushed open the door.

A figure lay in a bed close to the window. Still. Silent. An oxygen tube ran into his nostrils. Keri's heart did a lazy flip-flop as she noticed Jeremy's grandfather's bandana wrapped around his forehead, covering a bandage. He seemed so small and innocent. Childlike almost, with the exception of a few days growth of beard. As she neared, Keri noticed his eyes were open to slits, but she'd been warned he did not see. His was a strange, impassive face.

"Oh, Jeremy," she moaned, choking down a sob. Her heart swelled as she stood over him and gazed down at a face entombed in a slumber she could never comprehend. The faint rising and falling of his chest was the only sign any part of his physical body was still attached to this reality at all. Keri's legs threatened to give out, and it was all she could do not to crumble to the floor and crawl out of the room.

Then Tripod brushed against her leg.

Keri gave her dog a small smile, and found the strength to reach down to pick him up. She smoothed the ruffle around his neck and cuddled him, facing Jeremy.

"Look, Jeremy," she said, weakly waving Tripod's paw. "Look who I found at your house the day you left. He was new to the neighborhood, and half starving. He only has three legs. I adopted him."

Keri stifled a sob and rocked Tripod back and forth like a baby. "I was so worried when you left me in that blizzard," she began again. "I called after you, but it was too late. I never should have…" and the air seemed to stop in her lungs, "I never should have let you go! You could have gotten in a terrible accident in that storm, and instead, you got in a terrible accident here." Keri was unable to prevent the tears from spilling.

"Oh, Jeremy," she said, reaching out to grasp his hand. She recoiled as she noticed the worm-like burn scars criss-crossing his skin. Gasping, she let Tripod down on the floor, then slumped into a chair near the bedside. After a few moments, she was again able to take Jeremy's cool, limp hand in her own, and traced the scars with her finger.

"These scars are my fault," she said. "How can you forgive me for all that's happened? So much of this is because of me. We should have been together from day one—and I was too stupid to realize it."

Keri lowered her head and turned away, hot sticky tears clinging to her cheeks. When she could stand it no more, she reached into her smock and pulled out something to wipe her face. She brought the object to her eyes, then froze.

It was the remnant of her coat…the one Jeremy had burned himself in the fire to rescue.

She'd forgotten she'd put it in her pocket. Lately, she'd been keeping it in just about every pocket of everything she wore, just as Jeremy kept his grandfather's bandana near. It hadn't been a conscious act to do it, but more of a routine, much like automatically brushing her teeth in the morning. Her hand trembled as she stared at the ragged piece of cloth with the singed edges. Suddenly, unable to hold onto the now offensive piece of material, she pushed it onto a small table by Jeremy's bedside and refused to look at it. Again, she found herself leaning over the bed, her head resting against Jeremy's side and her hand clutching his.

"No one has ever been such a friend to me as you have," she groaned, shaking her head. "And I took it for granted! I knew you thought of me as more than a friend, but I led you on. I'm not sure why, but it wasn't because of Keith. It was because…because…" Keri tried to look into Jeremy's face, but as she lifted her head one of the balloons flopping about her neck got pinched against her shoulder, and burst, shattering the silence. She leaped in her chair, heart pounding, and glanced around, half expecting a gaggle of panicked doctors and nurses to swarm through the door looking for a maniac with a gun.

But as moments passed and silence once more settled in, her heart steadied back to its normal rhythm. She sighed with relief.

"Weird things always happen around me," she said, trying to regain her composure as she turned back to him. "You know that. You first saw me after falling in a swamp." She paused, thinking of the sandal Jeremy had cleaned and brought back to her. That sweet, thoughtful gesture. In retrospect, that had meant more to her than any piece of jewelry or gift she'd ever received from suitors in the past.

"You know," she said, clenching his hand and looking tenderly at his expressionless face, "I think…" and her words tumbled out in sobs, "I think I've been in love with you ever since you brought my shoe back in that paper bag."

The disclosure gutted her. She leaned into Jeremy's side, unable to stop the sobs wrenching out of her throat. In the far recesses of her mind was the hope that the disclosure might magically awaken Jeremy. She could *almost* feel him raise his other arm and caress her hair as she cried, *almost* heard a faint whisper escape his lips.

But no such magic occurred. He remained silent and lost to her. "Please pull out of this," she pleaded. "I don't know what I'm going to do without you! I waited this long to see you so that I'd be stronger and more whole when I got here—but I'll never be whole without you." Keri continued to sob, turning her head back and forth, feeling the sheets rub against her face. Suddenly, her clown nose caught on the bed, flipped off, and clattered across the floor. Keri looked down, stunned, as Tripod dashed after the ball-like object and snatched it in his mouth. Then he looked at her, wagging his tail.

"This could only happen to me," Keri moaned, putting her face in her hands. "Tripod—come!" she finally said.

Tripod trotted to her and deposited the object in her outstretched hand. Keri stared at it, wiping her eyes. What had she been thinking, coming here dressed up like this? Jeremy was in a coma. And even if he wasn't in a coma, he wasn't a child. He probably wouldn't be amused at her attire, at least not in such dire circumstances.

"I'm such a fool," Keri said, trembling uncontrollably as she plopped the clown nose on the table next to the fabric. Both were repulsive to her now.

"I'm sorry, Jeremy," she moaned, looking at him once again. "I can't seem to do anything right!" She dragged herself to her feet. "I have to go now. It's better that way." Then she found herself staring hard at Jeremy, willing him to move, to open his eyes, to yell at her. Something. Anything!

But, nothing.

Then, on impulse, Keri bent over and kissed him softly on lips which felt much too cold and dry. She hated herself for rejecting him in the past, when this kiss could have been warm and reciprocated, as in her long-ago dream. But it was all she could do now. It might be all she could ever do.

Jeremy still lay deathlike and pale.

Keri picked up Tripod and staggered out of the room.

Chapter 30

At times faces hovered overhead or lingered in the corners of his vision. Voices murmured unintelligible words; at least he thought they were words. Sometimes it was annoying, like the buzzing of a thousand bees beyond a door he could not see. Then everything would fade.

His world was fragments, images and sounds. And a paralyzing heaviness. Often he was cold, then the coldness would drain away and he'd become too warm. But, always, he was helpless to alter his circumstances, whatever they were.

Mostly, he didn't care.

Drifting wasn't so bad—if that was what he was doing. Drifting, not as on air, but from one muddled sense to another before blackness swallowed him again.

Lately, though, his senses were becoming a little sharper. He wasn't certain he liked these changes. The darkness was not fearsome but comforting, a numbing bliss he could linger in and escape whatever lay beyond. But there were new things now. Maddening, unintelligible words, and sometimes even faces. Round, glowing faces blurred and scarred by shadow.

Was he dead? Was this some shifting purgatory, a place to reside for a time, until whatever sins he had committed were atoned for?

He preferred the darkness. Somehow, he sensed there were things on the outside of that darkness too dreadful to bear.

Then came a face stranger than the rest. The nose was a blur of red, the hair a swash of yellow. The face muddled together and pulled apart like a fun-house vision. He tried to retreat from this new threat, but instead of being pulled back into soothing darkness, the face grew larger. Pressing in toward him.

Retreat… he wanted to fade back! There was a voice too, a familiar voice from what seemed a thousand years ago. It pained and encouraged him at the same time. Was this an angel…or a demon? Was he being strained from this purgatory into some new place of existence?

He wasn't ready! Straining, he pulled back. Back. There.

Yes.

The darkness closed in again. The face ebbed. The voice faded…

Crack! A sharp noise suddenly scattered the darkness into zigzagging particles. What kind of horror was this? The particles continued to zigzag like dust motes, scattering, then pulling together, then scattering again. Each time they scattered they seemed to be less in number however, less dense when they drew back together. There was also a brightness beyond them he hadn't noticed before. A light he couldn't quite comprehend. All he sensed was that eventually the threatening face was gone, and the particles were disappearing, too. Melting away, like fog in the sunlight.

Yet soon other things began to appear. Blurred shapes came into focus, and he slowly began to comprehend them. A ceiling light. Ceiling tiles. From the corner of his eyes he detected cream-colored walls…a chair. A lamp. A small table.

On the table was, curiously, a shiny red object. Much like a ball, yet not a ball. Next to it was a swash of brown. A lump of fabric of some sort. Familiar fabric. Fabric that had once meant something to him, but had meant so much more to another.

And then, he remembered. He forced opened his mouth. "Keri!"

Keri's stomach churned as she knocked on Joshua Quinn's door once again. She had to tell him she couldn't stay, that it'd been a mistake to come here. She'd screw everything up even more than it was. She was the proverbial turd in the punchbowl of life. She'd driven in circles for hours before coming to this conclusion. A crazed clown and her deformed dog cruising the quaint streets of Greenwood like a neurotic goat infiltrating a flock of innocent sheep. She didn't fit in. Even after ditching the clown outfit and cleaning up at a fast-food joint, she was an outsider. What had she been thinking?

She owed Mr. Quinn an explanation, that much she could do. There was nothing else she could do for his son. Her throat constricted as she raised her hand to knock once again. Yet before she could complete a second round of knocking the door burst open.

Mr. Quinn's eyes looked wild. "Keri! We've been looking all over for you!"

Keri's heart dropped.

"Jeremy is awake!"

Mr. Quinn held Tripod as Keri took the hospital stairs two at a time, too excited to wait for the elevator. She burst through the doors of the third floor and rushed past the stunned nurses as if they were in slow motion before catapulting through Jeremy's door. She staggered forward, eyes wide, unsure of what to expect, but no longer afraid.

Mrs. Quinn and Leah stood in front of Jeremy's

bed, blocking him from sight. When they heard her enter, they turned and nodded knowingly to each other.

"You have more company, honey," Mrs. Quinn said to her son, then she and Leah parted and walked around both sides of Keri, leaving Jeremy open to view.

Keri stared at Jeremy, heart racing, as his mother and sister left the room. He was sitting up in bed, an unusual glow in his eyes. Never had her heart felt so full, never had she experienced such gratitude, relief…and love.

Jeremy smiled a simple, neutral smile as Keri moved toward him with knees that once again became rubbery. She half expected her legs to melt as she approached him, causing her to grow smaller and smaller as she neared, enabling her to sink to the floor in a humbled form of repentance, begging him for his forgiveness. When she at last reached his bedside, her eyes never once leaving his, she lost all strength and sank against the mattress.

"I'm so glad you're back with us," was all she could murmur as she gazed at him, trying to read his face for any sign of bitterness or annoyance that she was in the room.

His expression remained oddly vague.

Keri lowered her head as the words tumbled out. "I want to make everything up to you. All the times I toyed with your feelings. Jeremy, I was wrong, and I'm ashamed. I hope you can one day forgive me. I'd do anything to make you happy."

Jeremy's eyes turned toward the bedside table. His voice was hoarse, but steady, "Can you put that clown nose on for me?"

Keri looked at the table, and her eyes widened as she saw the remnant of her former outfit still in the room. The fabric from her old coat remained too. She picked up the nose and put it over her own. "Sorry," she